in the day

Kevin Marman

Longmarsh Press
Totnes

Published by Longmarsh Press 2013.

Longmarsh Press, 5 Brook View, Follaton, Totnes, Devon TQ9 5FH

www.longmarshpress.co.uk

A CIP catalogue record for this book is available from the British Library.

ISBN 978-0-9561705-3-8

Printed and bound by the Brightsea Print Group, Exeter.

Cover designed by Kevin Marman.

for mum and dad

"Tom?"

"Yes, Shirley."

"Tom... do... do you think that n-nuns miss out by... by never being allowed to *m-marry*?"

I glance in the rear-view mirror and see Shirley's face framed between Lizzie's and Mark's in the back. It's a serious face and she wants a serious answer - just like any inquisitive girl of 9 or 10 would. Shirley, though, is 56.

"It depends on what you mean by 'miss out', Shirley. You know the old saying - what you never had, you never miss."

"Is that *true*, Tom?"

"I think so. If you've never had something... then how can you miss it? You'd never miss cream cakes if you'd never eaten them, would you."

"Yes," she says, though to herself. She looks out of the window at the passing street. Her expression, with her wide eyes and deep wrinkles, is a wonderful contradiction of knowing innocence. Apparently, when she first came to the home, she didn't speak for weeks on end. Now you can't stop her.

"And... And Tom?"

"Yes, Shirley."

"Tom... do... do you think... do you think that... *I've* missed out by... by never getting married, Tom?"

I shake my head. "I really can't answer that, can I, Shirley."

"Why?"

"Because I'm not you, Shirley."

"N-no," she says, and chuckles.

Then she leans forwards, eyes wide, as if she's had a *eureka* moment.

"Are *you* married, Tom?"

"No, Shirley. Not any more."

We're approaching a pelican crossing, and the lights change from green to amber. I realise too late that I've said more than I should.

"Didn't it... didn't it work out for you?"

I glance up at the mirror again - at her expectant face.

"That's a personal question, Shirley. You know about asking those."

"S-sorry," she says.

"That's alright."

I pull up at the crossing and look around to check everyone. They've all been remarkably quiet, despite the buzz of the day. Shirley puts her hand over her mouth and begins to cackle in her own strange, mischievous way. Ralph peers at me over the top of his glasses, then pokes out his tongue. It curls down his chin like a plump, pink fish. I wink at him.

"Watch it, sunshine!"

"*Zunzhine!*" Mark echoes from the back, pointing out of the window and up at the sky.

Ralph laughs. I turn back as a woman is crossing in front of us. I can't see her face, but something about her catches me off-guard. *Lucy*, I think... though it isn't, of course. It's the hair that does it. The wavy bob. The coppery flicker of it in the sunlight. She has a similar way of walking, too: shoulders set, head down, as if she knows precisely where she's going and intends to get there. She has a small child strapped to her back in one of those papoose things. The child looks at me and smiles, pointing a finger. I pull a face and point my finger in return. I feel a sudden kick against the bottom of my seat.

"What's your problem now, Ralph?"

"*Mun finger mun thumb*
mun arm mun leg
mun nodda ma head..."

"Keep moo-ving!" I finish the line for him, and he laughs again.

As if on cue, the lights change again. The woman reaches the other side and turns away. The child, though, swings its head and continues to look at me. I release the handbrake and pull forward.

"And... And T-Tom?"

"Yes, Shirley."

"Tom... are there... are there some people who... who... aren't cut out for it, Tom?"

I can't help smiling.

"Yes, Shirley," I say.

"Why?"

I catch sight of the woman and child in the mirror as they reach the corner. Then they're gone.

"I don't know, Shirley. There just are, that's all."

I turn onto the beach road and suddenly the whole thing is stretching out before us.

"I can see the *sea!*" Shirley cries, starting forwards again in her seat. Her eyes look like they're about to burst.

"*Zea!*" Mark repeats, rocking excitedly. There's a large gob of dribble in his beard. He's a big lad, and the bus shakes with the movement.

"Calm down, Mark."

"*Calm,*" he says. Then he stops.

I drive slowly along the busy part of the beach. The jetty. The arcades. The ice cream parlours and fast-food joints. Pizza. Pie and Mash. Fish and Chips. People everywhere, out in the sun.

We pass my flat and I point up to it.

"That's where I live," I say.

They all look up there.

"Is th-th-that where you *live*, Tom?" says Shirley.

"That's what I said, Shirley."

I can just make out the things on my window sill. The tea-light lantern. The binoculars. An empty wine bottle. Below the window, steam trickles from the vents of the ground-floor café.

"How... How long have you lived there, Tom?"

"Not long, Shirley. Just a couple of weeks."

"Is it... *nice*?"

"It's alright. It has a nice view, anyway."

We pass the clock tower and the promenade gardens. A line of B & Bs. *The Viking* is open and a couple of old gents are sitting out front with their pints and cigarettes. The same ones I

7

always see. Beyond them, through the doors, the place looks busy. People perched at tables, their drinks back-lit - amber, nutbrown, ruby, silver. The lunchtime crowd. Drink and a meal. Maybe just drink. It looks comfortable. It's there in my head.

The sun's always over the yardarm somewhere in the world, boy, dad used to say.

I keep going until we get to the quieter stretch, up near the sailing club. We pass a line of paint-peeling beach huts - several of them in use. Older folk slumped in deck chairs. Kids playing in the sand around the steps. *Just like little houses*, I always think - numbers on the doors, tiny windows with pastel curtains, stoops. One even has a fake chimney. You could live in one of those, at a pinch - if there was nothing else. Dad did, once. Squatted it, anyway. I glimpse a face at a window in passing - a woman reaching a cup down from a cupboard. *Like people playing at houses*. A child's laughter trills through the air suddenly. I close my window and turn up the radio.

At the end of the Promenade, jutting out onto the beach, is The Blackjack Café.

"Tea for me, please," Lizzie pipes up. "Two sugars. You buy it for me, please. Lunch we having. When?"

It's just after half-eleven. It's a bit earlier than they'd normally have it back at the home, but I pull up anyway. It's a treat, after all.

"How about now, Lizzie?"

Beaming, she grabs at her seat belt clip. She only has about six teeth left in her head, and she can't have false ones. Not the way she is. She's bad enough with her glasses, without sticking a set of dentures in her mouth.

"Now, yes please. Like sandwiches. What sandwiches? Wait and see. White bread, please. You get it for me. Don't like brown bread. *Yeuck!*"

I switch off and turn to look at them again - four strange, wonderful faces, gaping at me expectantly. I sign to Mark that we are going to eat and drink. He grins, *ahhh*-ing his approval, and starts rocking again.

I sign to him to calm down, and he stops. Ralph puts his face up right next to mine.

"*Mun finger mun thumb*
mun arm..."

"And who pulled your chain, mate?"

He cackles again. Shirley wide-eyes me, raising her hand.

"Are we... are we just having a *l-laugh*, Tom?"

"I think so, Shirley. Yeah... we're just having a laugh."

"Why?"

I open the door, then glance back at her as she covers her mouth with her hand.

"Because it's better than crying, love."

The café is busy and there's only one large table free, near the window on the other side. As I lead them over to it, eyes move in our direction and the hubbub of conversation shifts to a lower register - or so it seems to me. Maybe I'm just too sensitive to such things. There are the usual smiles, the usual averted gazes, the usual gawking kids and fidgets. The looks that say either *ah, bless!* or *not next to me, please*. As always, I wonder if they ever notice these things. If they ever pick up the signals.

What about those who move among us looking perfectly normal on the outside, but...?

Those among us who are not among us.

I get them all seated and go over to join the queue at the counter. While I'm waiting, I keep my eye on the table. They're all sitting quietly, and I'm suddenly struck myself by how vulnerable they seem. More so than children, really. Mark is staring fixedly at the table top, rocking again. Lizzie is fiddling with her handbag, picking it up and looking inside and putting it down and picking it up again. Shirley eyes me and lifts her hand to her mouth to cover a laugh. Ralph sees me, too. He puts up a finger, then a thumb, then an arm, then he sticks out his leg. I pull a face at him and he grins. They're well-behaved, but anyone coming in off the street would still notice them before noticing anything else. It's what makes me feel that these efforts to treat them as 'normal', however well-intentioned, are misguided. It's like we're doing it to make ourselves feel better about it. Whichever way you look at it, they're different. For me, it's their difference that makes them special.   Their difference is what I like about them.   No bullshit.   No conditions. What you see is what you get. It's the whole reason I started doing the job in the first place - after years of working with the 'normal.'

Lucy was amazed when I took it on. The irony of it. Me, who never wanted the responsibility of a family. It wasn't quite as simple as that. But by that time I was all out of trying to explain.

"Tom?"

"Yes, Shirley."

"Tom. Do some... some people b-behave according to the... the wrong *motives*?"

I sip my coffee. Through the serving hatch behind the counter, I can see people moving about in the kitchen.   I recognise one of them from AA. Emma, I think her name is. Still in her 20s, but looking older. That's what it does. Had a tough ride. Holding it together now. Doing her best. Keeping it in the day.

"Some people do, Shirley."

"Why?"

I put my cup down again. I honestly don't know where she gets some of this stuff. Perhaps it's from the church she goes to.

"Because...   I don't know, Shirley.   Because they do. Maybe they just get their motives confused or something."

Lizzie picks up her bag.

"Where sandwiches?"

I glance at the kitchen hatch again. The woman I know, Emma, is handing some plates through to a waitress. She sees me and raises her hand. I do the same. Ralph copies me. Maybe he's seen it, too.

"They're just coming, Lizzie. Keep your teeth in."

Shirley coughs. "And Tom... Tom, is there... there a lot... lot of *i-ignorance* in the world?"

"I think there is, Shirley, yes."

"Why?"

I look her squarely in the eyes.

"Because some people are just afraid to ask questions. Unlike you, love."

I help the waitress to dish out the sandwiches. Cheese and tomato for everyone except Ralph, who'll only eat ham and pickle. As usual, he inspects inside each sandwich first to make sure. Lizzie eats hers a layer at a time: top slice, filling, bottom slice (efforts to change her habits never work, so I don't bother - it keeps her happy). Shirley takes genteel little nibbles, mumbling to herself the whole time, mentally framing her next set of questions. Mark just eats. Food is food to him, and he takes it in without the least indication of interest or satisfaction. His approach to eating is purely functional - like going to the toilet. Lizzie belches, says 'Pardon', then carries on unabashed. They eat without any sense of self-consciousness or inhibition, as with just about everything else they do. In some ways, I envy them.

While they're occupied with their food, I sip my coffee and look out of the window. It's my favourite kind of day, with the worst of the heat over and a freshness in the air that isn't quite autumnal. Warm enough, though. There are even a few hardy souls in swimming, their heads bobbing like buoys above the waves. Seagulls wheel and scream overhead, like bits of cloud blown apart by the wind. Far out there, alone and abandoned, the pier head sits like a fairytale castle - a mirage, shimmering in the haze. It's the first thing I see in the morning, when I draw the curtains, and its winking red light is the last thing I look for at night. Thirty years since anyone walked there - since storms destroyed its connection with the land. Just the birds out there now. And ghosts. A no-place place. A part - but apart...

"Tom?"

I see a chap standing on the tide-line, waving out to sea. Someone out there, shoulder deep, waves back. *Not drowning*, I think. *You can't wave if you're drowning.*

"Yes, Shirley."

"T-Tom... Are there... are there some th-things that are... are b-best left unsaid?"

It's uncanny how she can do that: ask a question that seems to cut right into your thoughts. It's like she's developed a special insight to compensate for what's been lost.

"Probably, Shirley. Sometimes." And then, to pre-empt her usual rejoinder: "Sometimes it can be a way of avoiding hurting someone's feelings."

Do I really believe that?

She widens her eyes.

"You mean... You mean like kee... k-keeping a secret?"

"Yes, Shirley. You could call it that."

Mark stands up suddenly and points at his crotch.

"Go on then, mate," I say.

He wanders over to the toilets, immediately going for the door to the ladies. The doors don't have the symbols he usually recognises.

"Not that one, Mark," I call out, and he turns to the other one as automatically as if I'd aimed a remote control at him and pressed a button. Through the window, I see the kitchen side door open and Emma steps out - a cigarette between her lips. She closes the door and lights the cigarette, then leans back against the wall and blows a long stream of smoke into the air. I'll bet that feels better.

"And Tom."

"Shirley."

"Do you... do you have any... any *s-secrets*, Tom?"

I look at her. There are things I should say - things I'm supposed to say. But she knows them anyway. So what's the point?

"No, Shirley, I don't," I say. "And if I did, I wouldn't tell them to you. Then they wouldn't be secrets any more, would they."

And she cackles.

~

Secrets.

I'd heard it said over and over, in AA meetings:

Your secrets make you sick.

Depends what they are, I'd always thought. Everyone has them, after all.

Everyone.

Keith Richards. The woman on the checkout at Lidl's. The Archbishop of Canterbury. The chap who reads the gas meter. Emma, standing outside the café that day, smoking her cigarette. Even Shirley, who just about understood the concept.

We all need something we can keep to ourselves, that no one else can ever know - as long as it doesn't harm anyone. Other people already know too much, and what they *don't* know they make up. They put two and two together... make seven. They do with people like me, anyway. And people like Mark and Shirley and Lizzie and Ralph. Special needs. *Intellectually disabled*, they think. *Incapable*, they think. *Stunted*, they think. *Mental*, they think. They make assumptions. They judge.

And yet, people like them - Mark, Shirley, Lizzie, Ralph - are some of the best people I've ever known. The respect they showed me was unconditional. The affection, too. I'd never experienced it before - outside of family, leastways (and not always there, either). It was something new. It made me feel special for the first time. I understood them. It was like an instinct. You can't be trained for jobs like that. You click or you don't. And I clicked. Perhaps because I'm a bit like it myself.

They have their own ways of seeing the world and understanding it - finding order in it. Just as we all do. The questions. The signs on the doors. The signals. Ralph could spend all day placing dominoes end to end in a certain pattern and never get bored. Take one away, though, or reverse it, and the order is broken. His world is disrupted. He becomes anxious, then angry - violent even, if it's not restored. That's how his world is.

I understand that. It makes sense to me. Why wouldn't it?
Like I said, I'm like it myself, in certain ways.

One of my secrets, you could say.

One I didn't even know I had.

Until it made me sick.

~

My name is Tom Seagrave. I'm 49. I live alone now, but I was married once - to Lucy. Nearly four years we were together. That's all. I've lived alone since we parted, though: 2 months in my campervan, then 4 years in a bedsit, then 14 months here - in my rooms, overlooking the sea. I'm better off alone, and I don't feel lonely. There are people I see - at meetings and therapy groups. My elderly mother lives nearby, too. She's 86 in a couple of weeks. Dad died 7 years ago. I have a younger sister - Karen - who lives in Hackbury with her husband, Rod. I don't see a great deal of them, but we keep in touch. We had a bust-up a few years ago and didn't speak for ages, but we've made our peace now. They have a grown-up family: twins, Adam and Chris, and a daughter, Natalie, who's a 6th former. Rod's a businessman, and they're quite well off. My older brother, Michael, was killed on duty in Northern Ireland when he was just 23. He'd have been 60 next year. He was his own man. We didn't see much of him once he'd joined up. He'd always wanted to get away. I can't remember too much about him now, but I suppose that's what happens. We don't forget. We just don't remember so well.

Certain things, anyway.

I not in paid employment just now. A year it's been. When I became sick, I had to give up work - that job that I loved, with those special people. It became part of the problem, though, in the end. I saw things going on. Bullying. Abuse. I couldn't deal with it. I didn't know what to do.

It reminded me too much.

And then one of them died, and it didn't surprise me. But it finished me. My machine shut down.

It's my first time like this. I've always worked, right back since I left school. I've had loads of jobs. I've never stayed anywhere long (the last job was the longest - 5 years). I get bored easily and need to move on. It's just part of the way I am. I've worked on farms, and in shops and offices and breweries and care homes. I've sold washing machines and microwaves, sat on checkouts, dug trenches, bottled wine, driven vans. I've changed tyres, done payroll, pumped diesel, ploughed fields, kept books, answered phones. I've changed incontinence pads on grown men. I've picked apples, stacked shelves, heaved bales, dollied barrels, mucked out pig-sties, cooked meals, groomed horses, ushered courtrooms, typed letters, input data. I once taught a young man with Down's to knit. I currently do just 3 hours voluntary work a week in a library. *Baby steps*, my key worker, Carly, calls it.

I have a Mensa-tested IQ of 157, but no formal academic qualifications. I was hopeless at school. I was bullied right through it, by teachers as well, so it wasn't somewhere I enjoyed being. I don't like to think about it now. Last March, I was diagnosed with a condition called Borderline Personality Disorder. Apparently, I'd had it for years. It had been at the heart of so many of my problems... things I'd always put down to shyness, depression, anxiety. Inadequacy.

From schooldays on, I've never felt like I fitted in anywhere - like I'm always on the *outside* of things. Like the world's a party, and I've not been invited. I try to avoid social situations anyway, and I've always been awkward with friendships. To be honest, I find it hard to understand why anyone would want to be friends with me. My relationships with women, too, have always been difficult and unstable. My emotions go haywire. I want the person, and then I don't. They're everything to me, and then nothing. I try to finish things. And then, when it's over, I go to pieces and want them back. There never seems to be a middle ground. Yes... I *am* better off alone. And they're better off without me, probably. It doesn't stop me wanting something, though. I'm still human. We all need love.

I never feel really very... *certain* about myself. How can I explain that? It's more than just lack of self-esteem. It's like sometimes I'm sure I know who I am and what I'm doing - and then it collapses, and I feel like someone else has taken me over. When it's like that, I become unsure of my role in life - in any sense - or what I represent to other people. I feel like I'm nothing - like a ghost, haunting myself.

My moods can change drastically. Some days I feel confident - almost invincible. Other days, I simply need to hide from everything and everyone. I can switch from calmness to anger in an instant, and often over trivial things: someone talking too loudly on a mobile, someone forgetting to signal at a turning, someone saying something silly that I'll interpret as a threat. Anxiety is a constant problem for me. It doesn't need to have a physical source, like being in crowds. It can just be there. Likewise, I'll often feel... *empty*. Numb. Again, there may be no clear reason. It's just like there's nothing inside. A vacant space. Like everything's been sucked out of me.

Structure and routine are important to me. If my routine gets too upset, so do I. I've had panic attacks because of it. I'm obsessive-compulsive, though I'm working on that, with Carly's help. I still check and re-check little things: light switches, taps. I used to count the steps when I went out walking, but not so much now. The same with buying things. It could only ever be even numbers: 6 apples - not 5 or 7. Now, I'll try not to count. Or I'll buy a bag already made up, so I don't have a choice. Or I may buy 2 bags as a compromise. I get depressions that can be incapacitating. Even medication doesn't stop them.

I can be impulsive - especially in ways that are harmful to me. I'll hurt myself in some physical way. Cutting, usually. And alcohol, of course. That's the main thing. I'm an alcoholic - as was my dad, and his dad before him. Maybe they had the condition too, and didn't know - as I didn't. It's not the cause of things. It makes them worse, but it's not the cause. It's the symptom. A psychiatrist once tried to convince me otherwise. 'Drinking is your problem,' she said. 'Stop drinking, and you'll get better.'

She was wrong. Because, 10 months ago, I *did* stop drinking. And that's how it's been since. And although things have improved in many ways, in other ways they've become harder. At 49, I'm having to learn a new strategy to cope with my life - especially my emotions. It's a daily struggle.

But I'm also not cutting now. 10 months since the last time with that, too. I stopped it all at once - the drinking, the harming. The New Year, I decided. A fresh start, maybe.

I never expected to be like this. I thought I'd just get better, like that psychiatrist said. But as Carly says... it's taken me years to get sick, so I won't get well again quickly. It will take time.

I'm giving it time. I'm learning. I'm starting to fit things together. And within those parameters, I try to live a normal life. I take it a day at a time.

I keep it in the day.

~

Tuesday. The first day of a new month.

It was a good day today. I drew the curtains this morning and saw a clear sky, and the pier head out there - like a ship that had sailed too close in the night and got marooned on the rocks. My flat faces north, so I couldn't see the sun - but I could see the shadows it cast: the lamp posts, and the roof-tops along the front. I could see it shining on the surface of the sea, and semaphoring off cars as they passed. I could see it, too, in the bright feathers of the gulls in the car park by the jetty. They sleep there at night, and in the morning they're there - ranged across the tarmac on their long thin legs, like tiny feathered ear-studs pinned to a tray.

The wind was up and the turbines were turning, way out there at the edge - like cogs wired up to the cosmos, working the day forwards. There were other things out there, too. Container ships. Ferries. Trawlers. Barely moving, like ornaments on a shelf.

After my fix on the day outside, I put on running kit, sweat shirt, track bottoms, then went to the kitchen to make a coffee. I ate a banana while I drank it. I switched on the *Today* programme for the news, but I wasn't really listening. I was thinking about the day ahead. Not my work day today. That's Monday. My voluntary job. 3 hours at the main library in Hackbury, showing people how to use the computers. That's all, for now. Just those 3 hours, until I feel ready for more. Build it up slowly. My baby steps. After Christmas, I may increase it. I'll worry about it then. For now, it's 3 hours on one day, and it's Monday, and today's Tuesday. So I'll concentrate on that.

When I'd finished my coffee, I packed my gym bag: fresh clothes, towels, shower gel, under-arm, moisturiser, bottle of water. Then I put on my trainers and went to the gym.

I joined in January, when I began my recovery. I'd always tried to keep physically fit anyway - but I needed the extra incentive this time. It's a ritual now - like breakfast, or going to bed. Even on the work day, I go there.

I had a good workout. I did my warm-up first, as usual, to get my body ready. Many people don't bother with the warm-up. They just jump straight in, then wonder why they get injured. It always makes me smile in films, where some ancient cop hero - a Clint Eastwood character, say, or an Al Pacino - legs it after an Olympic-trained crook, running for miles, up flights of stairs and across rooftops, right off the bat. It doesn't work like that. You have to warm-up first - especially if you're their age and usually inactive. But I suppose they can't shout *'Hey, can you wait just a motherfuckin' minute while I do some calf extensions here? I can't go pullin' no goddamn muscles today. It's my retirement party later, an' I wanna try my luck on the rookie broad with the massive hooters.'* Apart from anything else, it would spoil the dramatic tension. It would spoil the pace.

I went on the rowing machine first. A nice limber up. I rowed 2,000 metres in 8 minutes 7 seconds on maximum resistance, which is pretty good, I think. Then I did 5k on the treadmill in 24 minutes. I like to push these things as far as I can. I like to push my body to the limit. I can't do things by halves. I can't jog. Carly said I should try taking it easier, just now and then. Relaxing more with it. But I can't. It just isn't me. I do something up at the edge, or I don't do it at all.

It was the same with the drink.

But that's in the past. This is what I do now.

After the treadmill, I rubbed myself down with my towel. Then I went downstairs, changed into my trunks and finished off in the pool. I started doing a lot of swimming over the summer. Sea-swimming then, of course. Every day, I'd go down and swim out to the buoy line, then back again, using the pier head as my guide. Something to head for - though it never really seemed to get any closer. The harder and faster I swam, the more out of reach it got - like it was moving, too. Teasing me. Letting me get a little nearer, then shifting farther out. Distances at sea are misleading like that. When you get to the buoy-line and turn, the shore looks like such a great distance away, and it takes a long time to reach. But when you're back and you look out to where you were, it hardly seems any distance at all. Almost a paddle. Maybe it's refraction - like when on some days the turbines look so close, even though they're eight miles out.

I love the sea, though. I love being in the sea - floating there in it, feeling it wrap itself around my body, like in the womb. Lying weightless on the surface, looking up at the sky. Adrift in the sea. Adrift in the day, without a care.

Free.

Too cold for the sea now, though. So I went in the pool, and did 16 lengths front crawl, which is a quarter of a mile. And then I was done. I got out and went to the changing area, where I did some final stretching to warm down. Another thing that many neglect. Just as you prepare your muscles for exertion, so you must allow them to settle again. You have to respect your body. I've learned that. As the poster in the gym says, '...*it's the only one you've got.*'

That's what so much of it is about. Carly's always saying it. '*Respect yourself, Tom.*'

I must respect myself. Yes.

I showered and changed, then went home. I emptied my bag and put my things in the washing machine. Then I did one final exercise I've been taught. I sat in the armchair, quietly, and closed my eyes. I concentrated on my breathing. I let thoughts flow through my head naturally - good ones and bad ones. I held each thought for the space of a few breaths. Then I let it go. Another thought - another few breaths - let it go. Allow the thoughts in, acknowledge them, let them out again. Every day. Just a few minutes. Quiet time with my thoughts. Preparing my head.

After that, I had breakfast. Muesli and chopped banana, with honey. Honey's better than sugar. Nothing at all would be best, but I still find I need the sweetness. I'm taking sugar in my drinks again, too, after years of not. Just for now. It takes time for the body to adjust.

I put the washing on. I made the bed and cleared away. I rang mum to make sure she was okay (she was). I made a coffee and sat by the window to drink it.   I went on the computer and looked at some forums I use, but I didn't have anything I wanted to say.

At 1, I made some lunch - a pouting fillet, with carrots and peas. Afterwards, I wanted to nap, but I fought it off. Daytime napping upsets my sleep at night. I went out instead - just for a walk. I looked in the shops. I rented a DVD and came home to watch it - *The Wrestler*, starring Mickey Rourke. I don't like wrestling, but I was engrossed with it - with the character. His coping with age, with loss, with illness, with being alone, with the last days of his career. I was lost in it. For those 109 minutes, nothing else mattered. When it was finished, I watched it again.

Then I sat at the computer and wrote these few things in my journal.

And now it's time turn in.

So. Another day done.

~

2nd November

I had a shock this morning. I was late up - though not as late as I first thought. My watch alarm went off, as usual, at 7:00. I pressed the button to stop it. Then I did something I never usually do: I rolled over and went back to sleep. When I woke again, my watch showed 9:05. I couldn't believe it. I jumped out of bed and ran to the kitchen naked to put on the kettle. There were so many things I wanted to do today. What had happened? I'd overslept by 2 full hours. Why? I could feel a panic edging up.

The kitchen clock said 8:06.

I looked at my watch again. It has a function that shows the time in another country, and I'd set it for France - an hour ahead. I must have accidentally pushed the button when I turned off the alarm. So I'd gained an hour - even though I was still an hour late. *Look at it positively*, Carly would say. *Glass half full, not half empty.* Not the best metaphor for me, really. But that's what I tried to do. I'd gained an hour, not lost one - even though I'd lost one, anyway. The day was an hour longer than I'd thought it would be, just a couple of minutes before. I could feel the panic subsiding straight away. I went back to the bedroom and pulled on my track bottoms and hoodie. Then I made my coffee and sat down to drink it while I ate a banana.

I had some bad dreams in the night. I get them now and then, like most people - but last night I had two in succession. Anxiety dreams. In the first one, I was standing at a roadside with a middle-aged man who was dressed in a suit and tie. It wasn't someone I recognised. We were both watching another man park a furniture wagon. Because the road was narrow, he had to drive the wagon up over the pavement, making it tilt over. As the driver jumped down from the cab, it tilted over further. The older man left me and joined the driver, and they both walked along the side where it was tilting, towards the back. I knew I should be going with them, but I was afraid. As they walked along, something moved violently in the back of the wagon - something huge, like an elephant. The sudden shift of weight was enough to topple the wagon over completely. It fell on the two men, crushing them. I could hear their bones snapping - their legs and spines breaking. I ran to a house door and knocked frantically. A woman appeared and I shouted to her to call an ambulance. Then I ran back to the wagon just as the driver's head popped out from under the edge. He was still alive, but there was blood running out around his eyes, like tears. I said to him *'Don't worry... an ambulance is coming.'* But then his eyes closed, and he died.

I woke up from that one. I lay there thinking about it for a few minutes. The images were so vivid in my head – the driver's face, the blood in his eyes. I gradually drifted back to sleep. And then I had the second dream. I was living in some kind of guest house - but it was also like a care home. It was like I had a choice about living there, but at the same time I *had* to live there because there was nowhere else for me to go. The other thing is that it was owned by a woman who used to be an employer of mine. A bully, she was. She made my life difficult for a time. In the dream, everyone who worked for her lived in this house. I left my room to go to the toilet, and on my way back someone told me she was looking for me. I was scared. What did she want with me? What had I done wrong now? I spotted her searching one of the other rooms. I managed to get back to my room without her seeing me - but when I got there I found that all the drawers and cupboards had been emptied, and all my belongings were packed up on the bed ready for me to leave. I was being thrown out. I sat down on the bed and cried. I had nowhere to go.

And then I woke up from that one. It was a few moments, though, before the feeling passed: the sense that she was after me, and that I was going to be homeless. It was like having a drinking dream. I've had several of those since I stopped drinking. It's a common thing for alcoholics. I'll dream that I'm drinking - and then I'll wake up believing it, and feeling guilty for giving in. And then I'll realise.

When I woke from the second dream, my bedroom walls were grey with the light through the curtains. It was 6:35, and the alarm would soon be going. I dozed until it woke me. And then I rolled over and slept for another hour and thought it was two.

I did my usual at the gym today: stretching, rowing machine, treadmill, swim. I sweat so much when I'm on the treadmill that when I finish it's everywhere: over the machine, on the floor, pouring down my face and body. Liquid calories, burnt from my body. My banana and coffee, plus last night's supper.

Walking back through the park, I noticed the leaves falling faster than they had been up until now. There's a small round sandpit in the park, by the children's playground. Its concrete rim makes it look like a giant's breakfast bowl. It was full of leaves - like bran flakes, waiting for a cascade of milk to pour down from the Great Jug in the Sky. I bought some raisin bran on the way home and had a bowl of that for a change, with soya milk cold from the fridge.

After breakfast, and my meditation, I tried to read for a while. It was a travel book, about a man who, after losing his job and his marriage, packed up a truck and travelled the backroads of America in it. He took just the basics: a sack of clothes, a sleeping bag, a jug and bucket, the few hundred dollars he had left in savings. It was an adventure. Something different every day. He was taking life by the horns, and grappling with it by just *going*. I envy anyone who can do that. I wish I could. Life should be lived that way, I think. You don't get another try at it. You only live through each day once - and even that's not guaranteed. Anything could happen. A truck could fall on you. You might lose your home.

I didn't read much of it. Just a few pages. I've read it before, anyway, so I know the story. I've re-read most of my books over the years. Someone once told me that the only *true* reading is re-reading. The first time is like your first visit to a foreign land: it's all new, with so much to take in and assimilate. With each subsequent visit, though, you know where you are, so you notice the things that you'd missed before, when your eyes were dazzled by all the newness. This time, you notice the shape of a leaf, the sound a bird makes when it sings, the scent of a flower, the colour of the sky over mountains at dawn or at sunset. The small details - where the beauty of life really lies. The things the poets signpost for us.

I have a great number of books. Book shelves and cases take up a lot of the space in my flat. I have books stored away, too, in my kitchen cupboards, because there's plenty of space in them (I only keep the crockery and food I need). I read a statistic somewhere recently that said over half of Britons have read less than a third of the books on their shelves, and 1 in 10 have read none of them. I've read *all* the books on my shelves (and in my kitchen cupboards). Even the Bible, which I haven't re-read. Having books and not reading them is like having rails of clothes and never going out (which I'm sure some people must do). Or having a wine cellar and never opening any. It's not like being an alcoholic and not drinking, though.

So... I read that book for a while. Then I put it aside and decided to write today's journal. I don't do it everyday. Just as I feel like it. I've always written, since I was a kid. Nothing serious - though I've had some things published here and there. Short stories and poems. It's just something I've always done and enjoyed. It stopped when I became sick, like everything else. So the journal's good exercise for me. I just write a few things. Thoughts, feelings, observations. My little diary. My little secret.

I was about to switch on the computer when my copy of *The Complete Works of Shakespeare* caught my eye. I wondered what Shakespeare might have achieved if he'd had a word-processor, too. How many more masterpieces might we have if he'd been able to type at 70 words-per-minute, as I can. On the other hand - what he was doing was the *real* thing. Paper, quills, ink. The basic tools.

That thought made me decide to *write* today - not type. I sat at my desk and took out a pad of paper. Then I emptied my pen pot out and went through it. I had 11 ballpoints, but only 5 of them worked any longer, so I threw the others away. There was also a Rollerpoint, which worked, but not well. Then there were 2 fountain pens - a cheap Parker (which I got as a Secret Santa present in one of my jobs) and an expensive Cross, which I won in a competition. The competition was to invent a word. My word was '*willness*', which describes an illness you can will yourself into on a morning when you don't want to go to work. The symptoms worsen when you pick up the phone to call in. It makes your voice croaky, your nose bunged up, your head full of migraine, your stomach churn, you sphincter twitch. I've used it myself several times in my life, I admit - though more often for genuine illness. Days when I couldn't face it. Days when it crowded in on me and I couldn't get up. Days when it was more than my will at work. The thing is, though - I coined a word, and it won me a pen. Which makes it the best reward I've ever had for writing. A £50 pen for a single word.

Next to the pens, I had 7 pencils. I only ever use them to mark sections and underline sentences in books (I like to remember the good bits, and it's better than folding down corners in dog-ears). They were all quite blunt, so I found a pencil sharpener and sharpened them up. There was something quite satisfying about doing it - like an artist preparing his brushes, or a mechanic cleaning his wrenches and spanners and slotting them back in their places. The sound of the blade cutting into the wood, and the shaving emerging like a little brown ticket. 3 standard hexagonal-edged wooden HBs, plus one that was just a stub and a bit. A blue RSPCA one, made from a recycled drinks cup. Another one with a pink rubber on the end (the only one where that end hadn't been chewed). And a round-edged wooden one - a Christmas tree gift one year from Lucy. She loved anything made of wood. We had wooden plates, wooden knives and forks and spoons. Wooden pegs for our washing, or to seal bags of sugar or rice. She loved writing, too, and had lots of pencils. She only ever used pencils. I remember seeing her hand-written notes and poems, in writing so small, but so neat you could easily read it. She used to doodle branches twisting around the page. Leaves. Runes. Celtic symbols. Stars and moons, and winking cats with long whiskers and fluffy ears.   In a box in one of my kitchen cupboards, along with my books, I still have cards, envelopes, notes that she gave me, decorated in that way.   Decorated with kisses, too, and words like '*love*'.   She always used pencils.   She gave one to me, one Christmas, a few long years ago.

I finished sharpening the pencils and brushed the shavings into the bin.   Then I sat in the armchair, crossed my legs, and put the pad on my knee.

And using Lucy's pencil, I began to write.

~

3rd November

I was up on time this morning. But after I got back from the gym and had breakfast, I decided to lie on the sofa to do my meditation. Just for a few minutes. I went out like a match in a gale, though. I slept for an hour and a half.

I don't like sleeping during the day because it disturbs my sleep pattern at night. It's a habit I thought I'd gotten out of. I don't understand it. I slept really well last night. A full eight hours. And then - another hour and a half. I lost an hour yesterday, too (even though I gained one in another respect). If I did that every day, it would add up to two-fifths of my life. Almost a half. A huge part of my life - *out* of my life. Not awake. Not conscious. Not doing things. Not seeing the sky and the sea, and hearing the birds, and my blood pumping through my body. Not aware of anything, except my dreams. Out of the world. In it, but not.

I used to use sleep as an escape. My way of avoiding the world. I used drink for the same reasons. A way of being able to bear the waking hours. I've done enough of that sort of thing now. I want to put all that behind me. I want to live in the day, and enjoy it. I don't want to lose it any more.

To wake myself up, I went out for a walk - just to the end of the breakwater wall by the jetty. Poseidon's Arm they call it - reaching out around the boats and hugging them close to the shore for safety. There's a bench at the end of it, and I sat there for a few minutes and breathed in the livening sea air. Way out across the wintry chop, the pier head stood sentinel, as always. I could see tiny rows of gulls, strung out on its railings like frozen handkerchiefs on a line. Through binoculars, the pavilion is a caved-in ruin - like a broken skull. I prefer to see it at the distance, though - the outline of its former glory still there, with the silver cupola resting on top like a ceremonial helmet, as if to protect it from further onslaught.

Further out still, the turbines were turning - their arms like the limbs of gymnasts doing cartwheels and back walkovers. Beyond them a container ship headed for Norway or somewhere. I could make out derricks and cargo bulks, and the bridge tower, like a block of flats rising above the decks. With the distance, it hardly seemed to be moving. I held up my thumb and finger, pincer-like, to measure the gap between it and the fixed point of a turbine. I watched it slowly disappear behind my thumb. I wondered if there was someone up there, on the bridge, with a pair of high-powered binoculars, checking our coastline.

What might they be seeing?

The seafront buildings, cluttered together like ornaments on a shelf. The Christmas tree lights of the arcades. The odd shapes and lines and corners and edges. The clock tower. The steeple-points of the churches. The water tower up on the hill, like a huge concrete mushroom. A broken jaw-full of teeth and fillings. They might even see me, sitting there on the end of the arm. They might be wondering who I am.

Where, in the six-billion piece jigsaw puzzle of human life, did I fit in? Am I an edge piece? Am I a corner? Am I a part of the sky, or the trees, or the grass, or the earth? Am I one of those blank colours that could fit in any one of a dozen different places? Am I the missing piece, under the sofa? Or am I part of a different puzzle altogether - not quite fitting in anywhere, but getting pushed into place, after a bit of snipping at the edges? Am I a bit with wording on it? Am I a bit with a face?

The tower clock knelled the twelve, breaking my reverie. Another morning gone. Passed forever. Another day over the yardarm. I got up and took the short walk home for lunch.

At the gym today, I saw one of the young women I used to work with. A *service user* or *client* as they used to say, whereas I always thought *person*. I was feeling low for some reason - one of those mornings when I couldn't get motivated - but seeing her cheered me up. Lorraine was always one of my favourites (though we weren't supposed to have them). She has Mosaic Down Syndrome. She needs support, but she's very capable and can do many things independently. Have a wash. Get dressed. Prepare her own food. She can hold a good conversation, too, and has a great sense of humour. You couldn't leave her alone anywhere, though. She could wander into the road. Turn on the gas. Let strangers in.

Her face comes alight when she walks in and sees me.

"*THOMAS!*"

She says it loudly, and several people turn around to look. One chap stumbles on his treadmill. Luckily, he's not going fast. He looks like someone who's walked up a stair that isn't there.

"How are you, Lorraine?" I say.

"What you doing, Thomas?" she says, in her big voice. She's such a pretty lass. A big smiley face and ginger hair - the gold of her dangly earrings glinting through it. There's nothing about her physically to suggest she's any different to anyone else. You'd know, though.

"I'm working out, Lorraine. Like you should be."

She chuckles in her inimitable way. I know the question before it comes.

"Did you have bangers for breakfast, Thomas?"

"No, mate. Not today."

"I did. I love bangers."

"So do I, Lorraine."

Her carer - who's playing with her damn phone - leads her over to a cycling machine. As she goes, Lorraine starts to take off her coat, letting it drag on the floor behind her. I go over to the mats to do some stretching, and try my hardest to ignore the fact that Lorraine's on the cycling machine, while her carer's still playing with her bloody phone. *Put it away, you stupid bitch, and do your fucking job.*

I used to love working with Lorraine. It was always fun. Laughter was such a big part of the day, anyway. How many jobs do you get like that? How bad can life be when you spend your day laughing, and making a difference in people's lives? I'm not trying to make a special case for myself or my abilities. It was a reciprocal thing. They made just as much difference to me. After the divorce, they were there. It was like finding a family. Care work isn't something you train for. A lot of the training was crap, anyway. It's an attitude of mind. It's something inside you. It's about empathy and understanding, and seeing a need that you have yourself.

It's about helping someone out of their coat and encouraging them with their work, instead of checking your fucking texts.

I used to clown around a lot with them. They brought it out of me. Lorraine would lock me in the store room when I went in there, and I would holler and pretend to be trapped. When I finally let myself out, she'd be in hysterics - her face like a tiny red balloon, her eyes streaming.

"*Gotcha, Thomas!*" she'd cry. Then I'd go back in there, and she'd shut the door again, and off we'd go once more.

She always called me by my full name. Thomas. Most people call me Tom. My mother does, and so does my sister. Carly, my key worker. The people at the groups and meetings. I don't mind either way, really. With Lorraine, though, it was always Thomas.

Just before I leave, I walk past Lorraine - ignoring her carer - to say goodbye.

"I'm off home now, Lorraine."

She looks at me with a blank face. It's like she's confused.

"Why did you leave us, Thomas?"

Uh. That catches me out. Why indeed? How can I tell her?

"I wanted to do something else, mate."

Her brow furrows.

"What else did you want to do?"

She doesn't mean it as anything else but a normal question. But it fills me with guilt for some reason. I pull a huge grin, though, and her smile comes back.

"I wanted to have a rest. You wore me out!"

She chuckles then, and starts cycling faster.

"Just like you're going to wear that machine out, too. Look at you... peddling like the clappers and getting nowhere."

"See you later, Thomas," she says through a grin.

"If I don't see you before," I say.

Then I go. And the carer doesn't look up from her phone once.

I wonder how things are at the home now. Not good, if the evidence of Lorraine's carer is anything to go by. In a couple of weeks, they're having the inquest into the 'client' who died there. I wasn't on duty that day, but I had to give a statement about what I knew of him, and about the place, and what was going on. I poured it all out. For the first time, I said what I should have said long before. It's a bad memory now. A horrible end to a wonderful time. I don't want to think about it. I'll worry about it when it happens. But it's there, looming up. I have my chance to say my piece - maybe to help set things straight.

It's the least I can do.

I used the word-processor to write my journal today. The handwriting went okay yesterday, but took too long. My handwriting is difficult to read as well. It always caused trouble for me at school - like everything else. It's inconsistent in its style. It starts off okay, but soon turns to scrawl, with letters that loop off all over the place and lose their shape and become unreadable. The exercise was good, though. *Proper* writing.

I try to say the relevant things, but my thoughts meander. I sit down and open a fresh page, and wait for the big bang to happen: nothing at first... and then the explosion, and thousands of stars and planets are born. Solar systems of letters and words, galaxies of sentences and paragraphs. A burst of writing, expanding across the page, filling up space, stopping only when everything in my head's been said.

I find writing so difficult, too. It's hard work. Harder than digging a hole, or flying a jumbo jet. You can learn those things. You have all the manuals and instructors and tools to help you. With writing, all you have is an empty page. No teachers or books can tell you what to put on it - though plenty might try. You're on your own with it. Your success or failure is entirely down to what comes out of your head. If nothing comes out, then nothing is written. Your pick and shovel are taken away. Your flight instruments are turned off. You can't do the thing you have to do. You are useless. That's how I felt before, when it stopped.

I write quicker with the word-processor. I can type fast enough to keep up with my thoughts, which seem to flow at roughly 70 words-per-minute. That means I don't have to think about them for too long. The longer I think about them, the harder it is to write them. In writing, I get the words out of my head. I get the thoughts out of my head, where they'd otherwise fester and rot.

So the word-processor is a boon for me. I bought my first ever one in 1990 - a second-hand Amstrad. Before that, I had a Smith-Corona manual typewriter, bought from Woolworth's with money I'd saved from my first job. I used it so much I wore it out. At the end, the roller looked like a charcoaled corn-cob husk.

And before *that?* My very first typewriter. A Petite children's model. A Christmas present from my brother Michael when I was 10 and he was 20. I wanted to write even then. It was my sanctuary. I liked reading stories and making up my own. While the other kids in the flats played football in the car park or chucked stones at each other, I sat indoors and read stories. Sherlock Holmes was my hero. That started me off. The other kids had posters of pop stars and footballers on their bedroom walls. I had a picture of a middle-aged man with a grey moustache, in a tweed jacket and cloth cap. Sir Arthur Conan Doyle. He wrote Sherlock Holmes. A wonderful thing. That's what I wanted to do, too. Write stories. Like Sir Arthur Conan Doyle, in a tweed jacket and cloth cap.

10 years old. 39 years ago.

When dad was my age, he had a grown up family. I'd already left school and was working, saving up for that first Smith-Corona. Karen was starting her CSEs. And Michael, who bought me my first typewriter, had already been dead for 3 years.

49. It's just a number. That's what people say. It's more than that, though. It means my body is a certain biological age, and presumably that it shows in certain ways. Yet the strange thing is, I look in the mirror every day and see the same face staring back at me - the face that's always been there.

Is it different somehow? Are there more lines and sags? It doesn't seem so. And yet...

...my passport expired last year. I only realised a few months ago. I'd only used it once, and don't think I'd even looked inside it in all that time. But I found it one day, in the back of the drawer. And there was the photograph of me, taken when I was 38. And then I realised. My skin was smooth. My hair - longer then - still held some of its natural colour. I looked fresh-faced and... yes, *youthful*. I could have been in my late 20s. It was still me, there was no doubt of that - but not as I look now. Slowly, stealthily, invisibly, the years had done their work.

I don't feel any older - though I suppose I should. I'm still a good runner. I don't carry any extra weight, and my body's in pretty good shape (considering what I've put it through and done to it since that photo was taken). I hadn't even met Lucy then. I hadn't known I had an illness. All of that was still to come.

No... I don't feel any different. But I must be. I must be changing. I must be running down. Because no one escapes it.

No one.

Even though I've tried. A few times, I've tried. But not any more.

I hope.

~

Friday

Friday is housework day. After gym, I had some breakfast, then got the vacuum out. I emptied the dust canister before I started. I only have a small flat, and there's only me in it, but by the time I'd finished it was almost a third full again. Enough to fill a coffee jar. Mostly it was fluff - like a grey wodge of the most boring candy floss in the world. But there was a lot of grittier stuff, too - curving up the side of the canister in layers of varying shades, like one of those seaside ornaments full of different coloured sands. The instruction manual that came with the cleaner says that nearly 1,000 dust particles per square centimetre settle on domestic surfaces every hour. So maybe it shouldn't surprise me.

Where does it all come from, though?

What is this quintessence of dust? as the good prince asked.

According to a science website I looked at, it's estimated that humans shed the entire outer layer of skin every day or two, at a rate of about 7 million flakes per minute. 7 million flakes weighs about 20 milligrams. Multiply that by the minutes in a day and you have roughly 28 grams of skin a day. That's about 2 pounds a month - which explains why my vacuum canister fills up so quickly. I don't shed it all here, of course. A fair bit of it will be at the gym. Some will be in the shops I go to. Some will be in the group room at the alcohol centre, and some in AA meeting rooms. There'll be a flurry at the library where I do my voluntary work. Another at my mother's. An occasional scattering - just a few flakes, not settling - at Karen's. Most of it will be here, though. Right here in these four small rooms. My dust settles around me, in drifts. I see it blizzarding in the light through my windows and from the lamps. I will end up as dust, and am turning to dust as I go.

I stripped the bed and put the things on to wash. I vacuumed the mattress, as I do every week. It might have been my imagination, but the level in the canister seemed to be very much higher after that. I put the vacuum away, took the rubbish sacks down, then tidied up. It astonishes me how out of order everything gets during the week, without my even noticing it. It's only when I come to clean up that I realise. Little islands of things everywhere. My laptop, plus its separate keyboard and mouse, on a board in the middle of the living room floor, where I left it after I last used it on Tuesday. A pile of books beside - not on - the coffee table. Trainers and boots strewn across the hallway, like roadkill. My camcorder, on its mini tripod, on the cistern in the loo. What did I take it in there for? I have no idea. I don't even remember putting it there.

I find this happening more and more. Absent-mindedness runs in the family, on mum's side, and I know it's coming out in me (just as the other stuff comes down dad's side). I have two pairs of glasses - one for reading, one for distance work. I keep telling myself to put them in one place when I take them off, so I know where they are. But I keep losing them. I'll search the flat high and low (which doesn't take long in these small rooms), but still not be able to find them. Then they'll turn up somewhere unexpected: under the desk, or in a food cupboard, or beside the loo. I try to figure out the sequence of events that have led up to my leaving them in such places, but I rarely can. One day, after searching for 20 minutes or so, I was despairing and starting to panic. Then I remembered something I read in a Poe story years ago: that the best place to hide something is the most obvious place to look for it - like hiding money in a safe. I looked in my glasses case, and there they were (Q.E.D.) - glaring out at me, blank-eyed and haughty at my stupidity (Q.E.D. that, too). Keys are the same. I have a key rack in the kitchen. My keys go on it every time I come in and am finished with them. They're never there when I want to go out again, though. Perhaps my brain, not my skin, is turning to dust. Perhaps that's what a lot of the grey matter is in my vacuum canister. Brain dust.

After I'd done all the cleaning and tidying, I made a coffee and sat for a while with my book. The man and his van, travelling America. I found a passage I especially liked and I underlined it with a pencil:

Other than to amuse himself, why should a man pretend to know where he's going, or to understand what he sees?

Why indeed? Do I pretend to understand where I'm going? Do I understand everything I see? Does all of it - *any* of it - need to have purpose and meaning?

I've always struggled to figure out what my life is about. Why I've never felt like I 'belonged'. Why I've never felt truly happy. I find it hard to understand that concept: happiness. My diagnosis makes me think it's a part of my condition - the way I'm wired. My feelings, emotions, thoughts, urges, instincts, habits - all of those things are bound up in it. So much has happened to me, and so many things go on in my head, that every experience I have is liable to tip the scales one way or the other. Carly says I can learn to control this. I can stop and analyse my thoughts and responses in situations that cause me anxiety or otherwise affect my mood. Are those thoughts and responses realistic? Are they rational? *Ask yourself what's the worst that could happen,* she says. I do. I try, anyway. Sober for 10 months, no cutting for 10 months - it shows that I'm learning. The other stuff is still there, though. It won't go away. I can't make *un*happen things that have happened. I just have to try to accept them, and move on.

But it's hard, and there are no certainties. Which I suppose goes for everyone, really. None of us knows what might happen next week, tomorrow, in 12 minutes time, or 20 seconds. The only certainty is: we have this day once, and when it's gone we can't have it back.

It's what we choose to do with it that matters.

With that thought in mind, I made a very definite decision about where I was going, and what I was going to do. I put my laptop in my bag and went for a walk to the library. I thought I'd try doing some writing in there, in a different environment. In public, not private - so a challenge. Get out for a while instead of spending all day cooped up in here. Scatter my dust around a bit. Distract. I could keep warm in there, too, and save myself some money, which is something I really need to do. I could look at the books, and maybe find something new to read.

I found a quiet table near the back, and took out my stuff. I opened a can of Pepsi I'd bought. I ate an apple. My fingers picked randomly at the keys, like hens pecking through gravel for seeds. I'd had an idea for a story I wanted to write - about a couple in a failing marriage. Some phrases fluttered moth-like through my head, and I tried to pin them.

But the noise kept distracting me. An irregular clicking, like *avant-garde* music filtering out of someone's earphones, or a clock mechanism with arrhythmia. I looked around for the culprit. It was a fluorescent tube, in a bank high up on the ceiling. I could probably reach it if I stood on my chair - though they'd never allow it.

But then my ulterior motive suggested something. There's a woman who works in the library. I don't know what it is about her exactly. At first sight, a few weeks ago, my eyes lingered a split second longer than normal before shifting. Her clothes were odd - on the verges of being fashionable, but not quite there... but also not fuddy-duddy or plain. I thought about John Lennon's Rolls-Royce for some reason: the old, classical lines and shape, but tricked out in psychedelia, with the overall effect not being *quite* right, but pleasing anyway. She was difficult to age - not that I'm good with ages - but I guessed late 20s or early 30s. Maybe it was the hair and the clothing again: young, but at the same time not so. I wanted to talk to her, though I didn't know what I was going to say, as usual. I've never been good at that kind of thing, and I'm out of practice, anyway. Out of practice at something I'm not good at - like a sky-diver who's terrified of heights, or a swimmer with hydrophobia.

Maybe, I thought, if she comes around now - to put some books back on the shelves, or to sneak a peep at this older man who comes in sometimes and looks quite nice, and is maybe not as old as he looks - then I could say something like

"If you wouldn't mind holding my chair, I could reach up and change that flickering tube for you."

Or maybe I'd say *faulty* tube, in case she misheard me and thought I was swearing in the presumptuous way lots of people have nowadays. That would break the ice. She would see how helpful I am. What a practical person I am, too. Fearless, even... if such qualities were what she took to. And while she held the chair and looked up at me - unhitching the old tube with practised ease and lowering it into her hands (which isn't a euphemism, but sounds like a good one) - I could ask a few questions. *What's it like working here?* Or *What are you reading at the moment?* Or *Have you ever thought that it might be fun with an older man?* Or she could politely refuse my offer, citing *insurance* or *health and safety* or *unions*, which would mean finding another gambit. Maybe I could keep getting books out and going to her to check them out, until one day she says '*That's a really good one. Have you read any of his others?*' - which might be a problem if it's *Mein Kampf*, but at least then I'd know. I could see if the *Kama Sutra* might raise an eyebrow, though.

But she wasn't working there today. She was off. Probably spending some *Kama Sutra* time with her boyfriend. Or maybe her girlfriend. Or sitting at home writing poetry, or designing posters for a far-right rally. Or thinking of me. And the flickering tube, plus the sniffing of the schoolgirl sitting nearby, hunched over Peter André's autobiography, finally drove me out again.

I wouldn't have spoken to her anyway, probably. And what would have come of it if I had?

Back at the flat, I made some dinner. Then I sat down to try writing again. But the words wouldn't come. A whole load of leaves were tumbling in my head, but as soon as I grabbed at them, they blew out of reach. I could feel the anxiety rising inside me.

Was it gone? Had it stopped again? Was there nothing left to say?

Then Carly's words came to mind. Challenge it. *Was it rational to think this way?* No. It hadn't stopped. There was plenty to say. I just needed to find the right way to say it.

I made a coffee and sat for a while by the window, watching as the day gave way to evening. Ship lights were twinkling, far out where the sea met the sky. A man and woman were standing by the railings on the jetty, arms around each others' waists, watching it too.

I thought about that story again. The couple in the failing marriage. I didn't need to do any research. It was something I knew about - even if I didn't fully understand what had happened.

Did I?

Maybe the answers were all there - locked up inside, like so many coins in a money box. All I had to do was break it open and pour them out. Then I could count them to see what I had.

Something occurred to me then - a thing I'd once read in an interview with a famous writer. She'd been asked where it came from - the things she wrote. 'The heart,' she said. 'It all comes from the heart. Not the brain. You don't think... you *write*. The thinking comes with the second draft. The first draft comes from opening your heart and pouring it out.'

Yes.

The light was almost gone. The couple on the jetty were walking back - him slightly ahead, his arm hanging back, his hand in hers. Just like he was leading her along.

I finished my coffee and drew the curtains.

Then I sat down at the computer, and opened a new page, and opened my heart, and began to write with it.

~

November 5th

Bonfire Night. The night we British remember the Gunpowder Plot. In 1605, a group of Catholic conspirators - led by a man named Robert Catesby - plotted to kill King James I (of Bible fame) and the lords and members of the House of Commons by exploding 36 barrels of gunpowder, smuggled into the cellars of Parliament through a tunnel dug under the wall. Their plan was to overthrow the government and the Protestant church and replace them with a Catholic dynasty. The plot was uncovered just in time, and one of the conspirators - Guido Fawkes - was caught literally with the matches in his hand. Over 400 years later, we still burn him in effigy. And people still do the same: try to blow up others whose beliefs they don't share. Many times, they succeed. The methods have changed a bit. Long-range missiles. Roadside bombs. Flying jets into buildings. It makes no sense to me. Life is so precious.

I've learned that. Life is so precious. All life.

My life.

As a child, I always loved Bonfire Night. I looked forward to it almost as much as Christmas. It was part of the magic that slips away later, as childhood does: imperceptibly, but relentlessly. The summers grow shorter. The days flick by like the riffled pages of a book.

There's one Bonfire Night I'll always remember. I was about 6. Dad came home from work that night with a huge box under his arm. If I saw it now, I'd probably be surprised at how small it seemed. But then, it looked as big as a suitcase. Michael lifted the lid and there they were, nestling in a bed of blue tissue paper, like lucky dip prizes. I wanted to touch them, but Michael wouldn't let me. All I could do was gaze at them - the fantastic colours, and the magical names: *Crackling Cauldron, Golden Orion, Mine of Serpents, Shimmering Cascade, Chrysanthemum Fountain, Silver Tree, Roman Candle, Whirligig.* Such promise they seemed to hold, lying there in their mysterious chemical smell. I can still see it all. It was in our back room in the house in Wandsworth. Mum was in the scullery getting dinner ready. Dad sat in the chair by the paraffin heater. He spread his newspaper on the lino before him, then took off his boots and tipped out the grit. And Michael and Karen and I sat there, at the table, looking into this box of treasures. And the night was outside the window, waiting for us.

Later, in the back yard, we huddled together in our coats and gloves, watching rockets rip across the black velvet night. And when it was done, and the box lay empty, and the genies of duff squibs had vanished in puffs of pink and green smoke, the five of us trooped down to the river, where a huge bonfire roared on the shore by the slipway. For a time that seemed long, but may have been minutes, we stood staring into the orange-white flames - the heat stinging our faces - while around us elastic human shapes danced and lurched in shadow-play, and faces faded in and out of the night like lanterns, or phantoms glimpsed in a dream. Christmas was next. Life was exciting. And we were together that night: mum, dad, Michael, Karen and me.

We were there. We were together. All of us.

And nothing had happened.

And everything was good.

Which is more than I can say for today. I slept badly, and finally gave up as dawn was approaching. I stood by the window, in my track bottoms and yesterday's t-shirt, watching the line coalesce from the darkness as what had been night became sea and sky. It was raining. It seemed to have rained all night. The street cleaner trundled his cart along - hooded up like a monk in a day-glo habit - and began to tip out the litter bins. The gulls barely stirred as he moved through them - the odd flick of a wing and turn of a head. Yesterday, the first thing I'd seen was a rainbow - or, at least, the bottom end of one, hovering over the sea right there. I'd not seen one so close before... drifting, as it seemed, just yards from the shoreline, with the pier head shimmering through it. An omen, I'd thought.

It augured well. Not that I'm in the least superstitious, or a believer that life is foreplanned, or directed by a Chess Grandmaster in the Sky. But here was a rainbow, anyway - a ribbon of light and colour in the day, and possibly hope. A signpost to treasure.

And yesterday was alright, as I've said. I did what I needed to do - and I *didn't* do what I need to avoid, which was good. Before bed, I took the Honda out for a run - up along the A road to the next town in the star-riddled night, overhung with a thumbnail of moon. I bought the bike for my birthday this year, using up the last of my divorce settlement. I'd been saving it for something... some time like now, when it might be useful to tide me over. But then after everything, when I started recovery, and things were stabilising again, I woke up one morning and it was there in my head. I wanted a bike.

I'd last had one 30 years ago, at the end of my teens. A blue Suzuki. I bought it when I started work. £5 a week on hire purchase. In the two years I had it, I used it up. I loved the speed and the freedom it gave me. Three times it nearly cost me my life - including the closest I've ever come. One winter morning, on my way to work, I was overtaking a milk tanker going up a narrow hill. I was half-way past, near the brow of the hill, when a lorry came over. I couldn't make it, and it was too late to brake and drop back. I pulled into the side of the tanker and waited for the impact. I saw it in flashes. The lorry. The look on the driver's face. The headlong rush of oblivion. The last split-second of daylight I'd ever see. I said *No* to myself as I felt something brush past my elbow... and then I was out the other side. When I arrived at the yard, I got off the bike and almost fell over. I sat on a barrel until the shaking stopped. My left leg was stinging and I looked down. When I'd pulled into the side of the tanker, my leg had gone up against its rear tyre. It had burned through my wellington, my boiler suit, the leg of my jeans and my sock, and sliced a raw curve of skin out of my calf. Another inch and it would have pulled me under the tanker instead. But it didn't happen. For some reason, it didn't happen.

I still come awake crying out at night sometimes when the film of it spools itself into my sleep. One was enough. Michael - five years before that - was enough. Two would have killed them. Two would have been the absolute end.

One was enough. One was too many.

And now, three decades later, I had one again. In all that time, I'd hardly given a bike another thought - until that morning. So I went to a showroom, and there it was. An old one, but sleek and black, with a racing fairing and upswept exhaust. 500cc. The right size and the right price. The salesman brought out the keys and started it. I sat astride it and touched the throttle. It didn't roar or rattle or scream. It quietly rumbled, like a brewing storm. I borrowed a helmet and took it for a test ride. 30 years, and it was like yesterday. The power made me shake. It had been waiting for me. I got back and the salesman came out. I flicked down the side-stand and stepped off. I patted the seat. *'Mine'*, I said.

I've always enjoyed being out on the road at night. Less traffic about, and the beam of the headlights reeling me in. On the bike last night, though, the darkness seemed heavy about me - like ink soaking into the light. I whipped past an artic at 75 and felt myself sucked sideways. The road was clear and dry to the end of my beam. And suddenly I saw it - or rather, I felt it. A wheel coming off, the bike slewing sideways and spinning, the stars disappearing, the moon swallowed up, the earth fading out. The end of it all. 3 short seconds - possibly 2. And then nothing. Not even a memory. It would be so quick. So quick.

And this is what's there today. This feeling. It's on me like a cold. This is how it always comes. So I go through the motions. I make coffee, I dress, I put on my waterproofs. As a change from the gym, I get my pushbike out from under the stairs and set off along the seafront in the wet. Up past the pubs and arcades, and over the hill and along to Coastguard's Point. Early-day people, sexless in cagoules, walk their dogs on extended leads. The bike wheels throb in the ruts along the sea wall, and the day is of greyness and damp. Along the Reach, caravans sit silent and empty, like abandoned shoe boxes. The toy propellers keep turning, way out there on the smoky edge.

I turn back and push hard for the last half-mile. I can see the light winking on the pier head - the little fortress island of it, lying offshore from the rest of things. No use to anyone or anything, except as a resting place for sea birds. A curiosity. A vacant, unused space - echoing with the laughter and Sunday-tryst whispers of its own private ghosts. It might be quite a congenial place to be today, I think.

Back indoors, I shower and dress and make some porridge for breakfast. And still it won't go. I make a coffee. I take my tablet. I try to keep occupied. Distracted.

The phone rings, and it's mum to ask if I want to come to dinner tomorrow. *Yes*, I say. *Alright*, I say. *That will be nice*, I say. *Thanks*, I say. *Yes... that will be nice.*

It *will* be nice, probably. As long as we're careful with what we discuss. I'm used to it now - but it still irks sometimes. The comments. The challenges. She means well. She just doesn't think. Regardless of that, she's still all there is.

Evening, and the sky is erupting. The sounds. Like artillery fire. Like guns going off, out in the night.

The fires are being lit. Things will be turning to charcoal and cinders and ashes and smoke. The fires will burn and consume the night, and faces will dance in the flames like demons.

Like in the final night.

Like a night long ago, when we were together, and Christmas was coming, and childhood was holding on for now.

And life was the next thing.

~

49

Sunday

Grey again.

I draw the curtains at 9:00 this morning on a day of smoke. The horizon is smudged and close, and the sea is stirring to violence. It grabs at the promenade wall, slips its grip, recovers and grabs again and again, over and over. The window is patinated with rain. Seagulls tumble aimlessly, like ashes on the wind. The pier head is invisible - engulfed in it.

Such a day is this.

I went to a meeting after all last night - the Saturday night one I always used to go to, but have been missing lately. I've dropped off the meetings, and the weekday groups, too (whose approach I find more helpful in many ways). Partly it's been about feeling better, feeling stronger, trying to get back to normal living. So I haven't been going. Which might be the problem. I've been missing the input. And last night the feelings were creeping up, as they do, like strangers in the dark. My mood had been dropping throughout the day. It's like a tide going out, exposing rocks, rotting timbers, corpses. So I went to that meeting.

It was raining in the wind, and the camper was out of diesel, so I took the train - something else I've not done for ages. I always used to enjoy train journeys - before earphone music and loud mobile conversations changed them forever. Why must people have music wherever they go, and constant communication with the world? What's wrong with quietly reading a book? Or drowsing to the cradle-rock of the carriage, and the comforting *du-du-du-dum* of the wheels as they pass over the rail joints? It's the only sound I ever need on a rail journey - next to the station announcements and the peep of the conductor's whistle. The sounds that carry back down the years.

The standard rail length is 60 feet, which is 88 *du-du-du-dums* to the mile. You can gauge the speed of the train from that. 88 per minute is 60 miles per hour - faster than the average resting heart rate, but slow enough not to make you breathless.

If you breathe in for 3 and out for 3 - 4 if the train's moving faster, 2 if it's slower - that would be about right for meditation. The rocking would aid that, too. If you closed your eyes and imagined enough, you could be in the womb - and you wouldn't need music or ringtones or voices in there. You'd have the primal sounds. The primal communication.

Distraction is all it is, I feel. Distraction. Why do people seem to need it all the time? The radio in the morning, the CD in the car, the iPod in the supermarket, the TV in the evening. Constant noise. The soundtrack to the daily movie of life.

But what's everyone distracting from? Thinking? I think it is... and I should know. Of all people, I should know (so why do I question it in others?) Thinking. Because of what thinking brings with it. The smiling man with the basket of snakes. The things we don't want to have right now. The niggles and resentments. The regrets. The money owed. The grudges. The jobs to do. The need to keep up with things, constantly keep up with things as they pull ahead of us further and further. Our disillusionment. Our lack of fulfilment. Our inability. Our inadequacy. The gap between what we are and what we think we should be.

The incompleteness.

The emptiness.

We don't need to be thinking about those things. What we need to do is drive all of that stuff out. Engulf it in sound. Drive it out. Drive it out. Drive it out out out out *out*...

I need to do it myself. The places my thinking takes me are not places most people would want to go.

The meeting was good. I was glad I went. It made the difference I needed it to make. It was nice seeing those faces again, having a chat over tea and biscuits, feeling that I was with my own: people who understand what it's like. Before it started, the Secretary lit a pool of tea lights in the centre of the table. Then, after the readings and announcements, the main lights were switched off and we sat for a while in silence, thinking our thoughts. I closed my eyes and thought about dad. Then I thought about mum. I thought about Michael. I even spared a thought for Karen. I tried not to think about me. I let it all drift around in my brain, like leaves - their faces, down through the years. The things we'd done. The things that had happened. The things that were happening now. Was there something I wanted to say about it all? I wasn't sure. I'd see how the meeting went. I had stuff in my head, no doubt - the music and ringtones and voices I live with. The things that had been rising for a couple of days, like a far distant train on its way up the tracks to where I lay tied down and helpless - the steel vibrating cold on my ear *du-du-du-dum... du-du-du-dum... du-du-du-dum...*

And then it began. I kept my eyes closed and listened to the voices - listened to the people speak quietly about their day, and their struggles, their roller-coasters and washing-machine heads and monkey-minds, their triumphs and tragedies. One woman began softly weeping as she told her story. I opened my eyes and saw her face in amongst the others, glowing there in the candlelight, her tears running down her cheeks like melting wax, her eyes in diamonds, sparkling and flashing.

At a suitable pause, I *did* speak. I spoke of my thoughts, and my fears, and how during these last couple of days they'd fused together and become the same. And how fear was really the only thing to fear, and that it was a feeling, and feelings weren't facts, and how - hard though it was - I hadn't picked up. It had crossed my mind, but I'd cut it dead. I'd seen its distorted, bug-eyed face looking in at me through the spyhole, waiting out there, knocking and waiting, and knocking again - the persistent seller with the bag of surprises, the evangelist peddling destructive faith, the stranger with the hidden stiletto. But I hadn't slipped the chain and lifted the latch. I hadn't allowed the foot in the door. I'd pulled the curtain across again. I'd shut my ears. I'd walked away. I'd switched my mind to other things. Other things to do. Too many things. So much to do. So far to go. But I wasn't projecting. I was keeping it manageable. In perspective. I was keeping it in the day, where I could handle it. I was keeping it in the day. And the day was all I had and all I knew and all I needed to know, and yesterday's history and tomorrow's a mystery, and when it comes it comes, and I'll see what it brings with it when it comes, and deal with it when it comes, and worry about it then, when it comes - and until it comes I'll keep it right here, in the day, where it belongs. I'll keep it here. In the day.

And everyone said *'Thank you, Tom'*. And it was silent again, apart from a cough, until the next person started speaking. Then I closed my eyes again, and listened. And then I felt better.

I'd hoped there might be someone there who could give me a lift back, but they all came from other areas. So afterwards, I made my goodbyes and wandered back down to the station in the soaking drizzle, past blaring pubs and knots of smokers, and all-night shops awash with neon, like lighthouses for the lost. It was everywhere. Everywhere. I could have got it, easily. Everywhere. But I kept moving forwards, and got to the platform, and got on the train. The carriage was empty, and I closed my eyes again, gently rocking to the metronome *du-du-du-dum* and let my mind roam where it would - across fields and seas and ancient views - while outside the window the night tunnelled by in tracer fire and rain.

Home again, I sat at the computer. But the words wouldn't attach or cohere. So I left them, and picked up my book and went to bed. There was noise in the street. Cars pulling up at the take-away, people staggering back from the pub - shouting as only drunk people or mobile phone users do. There was still an occasional pop or zip, or a distant boom, like bombing beyond the hill. But I slept. In the night, there were voices, and I roused briefly. Then I slept again, and I didn't dream. Not once.

So... Sunday. Grey November. The fires are dying. The embers are settling. The sea is rolling and the wind is high.

I went to mum's after gym. She doesn't live far away. About a mile, in a small block of flats on the other side of the park. They're all elderly people, so it's quiet. She's on the third floor and has a balcony overlooking the park, so she can sit and watch people playing tennis or bowls, or walking their dogs. She's comfortable there, and she's settled, which is a blessing. She's 85 and lives independently. The flats are warden-assisted, though, and she just has to press her pendant button if she has any problems: a fall, or a hypo. She's lived there alone since they separated, and the council re-housed her, and dad hit the streets. 20 years. She still has his pension, and some savings for the first time in her life. After a lifetime without, she no longer has to worry about money. She can catch a bus to Argos and buy herself a new telly or microwave if she needs one, and not have to think about how it will be paid for. She'll say things like '*Do you know, I've got over seven hundred pounds in my savings account now*', as if it's a lottery fortune. But it is, for her. Often, it was figures like that that were owed, and no guarantee about where it was coming from. And now, there's a reserve. For the very first time. She has that small pension of his, plus her own.

She has his photograph, too - on the dresser. The same one that I have on my wall. He's in his uniform, at the barracks. He looks so young - 18 or 19. It's the photo that's old. I look at it and I see me as I was. Then I look in the mirror and see him as he became. Alike in more ways than one. We understood each other as no one else did - not even mum, with her years of living with it. Not the knowledge that comes from shared circuitry. He was my confidante, at the end. My best mate. My drinking buddy. We understood. He had it and he gave it to me, like a strange gift. A silver chalice. Spiked. He wasn't to know - though I think he did.

I took her a bunch of tulips, which pleased her. She was looking well and seemed sprightly in her step, with not a trace of a limp. Her hip operation in the summer should have been routine, but nothing ever is with her because of everything else that's wrong: arthritis, diabetes, Chron's disease, hypertension.

A 3-night stay had turned into a month, including a few days in an isolation ward. The complications just kept knocking on. We didn't think she'd come out. It forged a truce between Karen and me, which was something positive. The common effort during a war. The breaking down of barriers. If the truth was known, neither of us knew what we would do - even Karen, with all her resources. It was one of those things you always acknowledge, but are never prepared for.

But then, as on so many occasions before, mum rallied - drawing on those superhuman inner resources that had carried her through the years with dad. The years after Michael. And now she was more or less back to normal. Doing shopping. Keeping house. Cooking dinners.

She'd laid the table for two, with tumblers and a bottle of Shloer. That always makes me smile. Shloer. What people do with their speech when they're drunk. She likes to be alone in the kitchen, so I left her to it - listening to the ancient sounds of the pan lids clattering, spoons *rat-tat-tatting* on plates, the radio on low. The sounds of Sunday dinnertime all the way back to the start.

I looked at the photographs on the sideboard. Me, in my running kit, dark-haired, huge smile, hands aloft - trotting home in my first London Marathon. 1986. A triptych with Karen: her and Rod, outside the church, when they got married; her and Rod on their Silver Wedding day a couple of years ago, with the twins Chris and Adam, and Natalie; between those, a school shot of Karen in her final year. Karen. Two years younger than I am, and almost a grandmother. Space for more photos yet. They have a house, and a motorhome, and a Rolls, and a gite. *'They've done so well for themselves,'* as mum always says. *'They're happy.'* I'm never sure what any of that is supposed to mean. Just what it says, probably.

And then there's Michael. The way I remember him - the way he will always be. The last one taken. 23. Another uniform - Princess of Wales's regiment. Just before leaving for his second tour of Northern Ireland. Where the sniper got him.

Sultan Street, Lower Falls. Where he left us for good. Though he was gone many years before that.

Dad's photo is separate from the others, on the dresser. I'm never sure if that means anything, either. Whether it's symbolic. Like she wants him there, but on his own. A part, but apart. Maybe, too, it's the fact that next to it, behind a glass door, are her bottles. Like he's standing guard there - or she's teasing him, putting him with it. Whisky, sherry, port, ginger wine, Bailey's, vodka, a big bottle of Martini she won in a raffle at a jumble sale. It's there from one year's end to the next. She doesn't drink much. She can't, because of all her problems, and all the meds she's on. But she has one occasionally. She gets it out if Karen and Rod visit, or at Christmas. She'll have something to help her sleep sometimes. The door has a catch, and when it closes the bottles rattle against one another. If you do it very slowly, though, it hardly makes a sound - not that she'd hear it, probably, with all the noise out there. But she might come in suddenly to look at the clock. If she goes to the toilet, she wouldn't hear it at all. Her hearing's not good, anyway. When she's got the telly on, it carries out to the landing - like she's got people in. If it's *EastEnders*, it sounds like the old days with dad.

"You can pour the drink if you like," she calls.

I jump, like somebody's pushed me. Or nudged my conscience. I pick up the bottle, take off the top, fill the glasses. The photos have put me in mind of something. For her birthday, I want to do an album. All the best ones, cleaned up on the computer, then put together in one place for her. I need to get hold of them somehow, and this would be the perfect opportunity. I know where she keeps them. The cupboard in the dresser. I'll pick my moment.

It's a huge dinner, as it always is. She cooks everything: carrots, peas, sprouts, runners... and lots of roast potatoes and roast parsnips, because she knows I like them. As usual, though, something's wrong. The gravy's too thin. Or the broccoli is overcooked. She notices. I don't.

"I knew I should have put another teaspoon in," she says.

It's a dull day, and she's lit her candles. They glint off her glasses. She splashes some gravy on her cardigan, curses, then wipes it with her serviette after wetting it with her mouth. Like she used to do with a handkerchief to clean my face when I was a kid. Everything is on the table. Mint sauce. English mustard. Horseradish. Cranberry sauce. Salt and pepper. It's like Christmas.

"It's fine," I say. "I like it like this."

We eat, talking about family trivia. Karen's up-coming holiday in Cuba. Adam's baby-to-be. Her birthday in a couple of weeks (86). Christmas. The motorway smash-up on the news. The horror of it. The speed of it. They can't have known anything. There, then not there - like that. Like a bullet in the heart. I try to keep it neutral, but it rarely stays that way. I'm always on tenterhooks. She usually drops something in. One of her bombs.

"Rod's really busy."

"Is he?"

"They're doing so well. Big foreign orders coming in, Karen says. They're having to take on more workers to handle it."

I wait for it. I know it's coming.

"Perhaps you could speak to him. You never know... he might have something for you."

"I've got work."

"I mean a *proper* job. One where you go out, and get a wage."

"I *earn* a wage."

"Doing what? You never talk about it."

"I've *told* you. I work from home. It's all computer-based. I don't talk about it because it's boring."

"It can't pay you much, either. You never seem to have any money."

"I manage. I don't need much money."

She pulls a runner bean string out of her mouth and puts it on the side of her plate.

"It can't be doing you any good, though... cooped up in that flat all day on your own. You ought to get out more. Be with people."

"I've got the library."

"That doesn't pay anything."

"It doesn't matter. It's no one's business. Anyway... I'm *happy*. And I get by. That's all that matters, isn't it?"

"If you say so."

"I do. Anyway... I wouldn't want to work for Rod."

"You could do worse. He's making money and he pays well. Keep it in the family, too."

"That's what I mean."

"I thought you were over all that."

"I am. Can we change the subject?"

She sips her drink. Loudly.

"I'm only saying. That's all. I don't know why you gave up the job at the home."

"I told you why."

"You could have stuck it out."

We continue eating, stabbing at the food like it's trying to escape from our plates.

"You're too much like your dad," she says. Her usual parting shot. There's nothing more to say on it.

She doesn't know everything, of course. The suicide attempts. The diagnosis. Nobody knows in the family. I hate lying to her, but it's for the best. What she doesn't know can't harm her. Can't get her asking questions. Worrying.

After dinner, there's her own apple pie and custard. I find a clove and chew on it... and see nan and grandad eating caraway seed cake, and drinking tea from blue china cups in a clock-ticking room that no longer exists.

I help her to wash up. Then we sit for a while and talk a bit more, and finish the bottle. She trims up the tulips and puts them in her favourite glass vase, then places them on the sideboard amongst the photos.

"There," she says, touching their petals. "Lovely."

She goes to the loo, and there's my chance. I open the cupboard where she keeps the tins. I find the ones I want, in her 'favourites' tin - an old McVitie's biscuit tin with scenes of London in the '50s: red buses, black cabs, bowler-hatted men. Wedding photos. Babies. Family. Michael. Dad. Copies of the ones on her sideboard. Some holiday snaps, too - including one I'd forgotten about: in Dorset, outside the caravan we were renting. Late '60s, at a guess. Mum is sitting in a deckchair in her bathing costume and sandals, shielding her eyes against the sun with her hand. Her expression seems more surprise than smile. She's shelling peas. There's a bowl of them on her lap, and a pile of shucks on the newspaper beside her. Her hair is dark and long - longer, strangely, than I ever remember it. It trails down over her shoulder and comes to rest in the crease of her elbow, giving her a Mediterranean look. Dad is standing apart from her, over to the right, shirtless in light trousers and socks. His arms and chest retain their definition from his Army years, but the slippage was setting in even then: the stoop in his bearing, his stomach sitting on his belt buckle like a risen loaf. More conscious of the moment, he has his left foot resting jauntily on the bumper of whatever car he borrowed that year. A Ford Popular, it could be. His left hand is cupped over his raised knee, while the other hand - a cigarette clenched between the fingers - is poised level with his chest. In almost every photograph existing of him from his youth onwards, he is holding either a cigarette or a drink. Often both. Between the two of them, kneeling on the grass, are Karen and me. I'm about 5, her 3. She has a ribbon in her hair and a big gap-toothed smile. If it wasn't for the ribbon, you'd think she was a boy in her shorts and shirt. I'm dressed the same. We could almost be twins with our smiles - our arms around each other's shoulders, holding close. Michael's in the shot, too. His shadow, falling just short of my knees. And the tip of his finger - over the lens at the left-hand edge. I could take that out easily enough. But I won't. It needs to be there. Behind the caravan, perhaps a hundred yards back, the land slopes away to a cliff edge. Beyond that, a finger of sea points off to the distance. Anyone looking at the photo now would never recognise any of us from it.

I hear her flush the loo, so I slip the box quickly into my rucksack. I'm just hoping she won't miss it and get worried. As soon as I've scanned them in, I'll sneak it back. As I shut the cupboard door, the bottles rattle in their cabinet. I can see them through the glass, with dad on sentry duty there.

Halt! Who goes there? Drunk or abstainer? Look where she's put me, boy. The lunatic standing guard over the asylum. Go on... you can pass if you want to. I won't say nothing...

She comes back in, yawning, saying she didn't sleep well last night. So I leave her to have a nap - the words not mentioned again. I walk back across the park and through the empty streets in a wet-breath of rain, and the leaves twisting down like parchment butterflies from a sky the colour of slate.

Indoors, I close the curtains and sit in the chair, and take out the photos. I look at those faces. I look at myself as I was - my own photo and his. Our face. So similar. The shape and expression.

Too much like your dad.

Michael there, too. He took more after mum in looks, as Karen did. I can see it in him. The good skin. The proud face under that beret. Disdainful, almost. Defiant, certainly. *Just you try it*, it seems to say. *Just try it and see what you get.* With dad's, as with mine, there's the undertone. The suggestion. Things aren't always as they seem. Something else lies underneath. Not too deep, either. It wouldn't take much. Just a push.

I feel it building up inside, pushing against the seams, pushing and pushing...

I put the lid back on the tin and place it beside my desk. Then I sit for a moment, in the quiet, and close my eyes.

The words are there again. They still sting, as they always do. I shouldn't let them, I know. She means well. She doesn't think.

And maybe I think too much. Maybe that's the whole problem.

I think too much.
But I can't help it.
I just wish people would leave me alone.
Leave me *alone*.

~

Monday

I woke with a start at just after 7 this morning. I heard the street door slam, then two heavy sets of footsteps coming up the stairs. They stopped briefly at the first floor landing and I heard the dull tones of a man's voice. Then they continued up to the top floor, where I am. Who were they? What could they possibly want at this time of day? What had I done? I hadn't done anything.

Had I?

They reached the top and stood outside my door. I waited for the knock. It wasn't a dream. I was awake. There was light in the room and the shadows were grey.

Then I heard my neighbour's door open, and voices as they were let in. I didn't catch what they were saying. I wondered what had happened. Had there been an accident in there? Had someone suffered a heart attack... his wife, or her father? I heard thumping in the room next to mine - the father's bedroom, I think. Then their front door opened again and there were voices on the landing, and the sound of something heavy being manhandled. I got out of bed and went to the spyhole. I could see the men. They were dressed in light blue overalls and were trying to get a wardrobe through the door. There was a name in yellow lettering on their backs. I went through to the kitchen and rolled up the blind. Down in the car park, I could see their wagon with the back open.

They hadn't said they were moving out, but I didn't see much of them anyway. They kept themselves pretty much to themselves, which suited me because so do I. A hello in passing. I knew they'd been looking for somewhere else, though. Her father was struggling with the stairs. Then there was the fact that the landlord never did anything about the problems: the damp, the ill-fitting doors, the broken windows, the worn-out kitchen cabinets, the leaking taps. And there was also the noise. All around us. The pub, the nightclub, the all-night take-away, the neighbours and their loud music and rows, the boy racers every night in the car park over the road - revving and racing and blasting their horns until late. Better at this time of year. During summer weekends, though, it can get so bad that I get in the camper and drive out to a quiet side-street somewhere. Complaints don't seem to get taken seriously, but there's nobody to complain much anyway. There are 6 flats here, and 4 will be empty when they go. There'll be no one below me and no one opposite. I'll be the only person on this side of the building, with just one person on the other side, and she's at her boyfriend's most of the time. There'll be just me.

Apart from these things, I like the flat. There's much more room than I had at the bedsit. It wasn't far to come - just across town. I'd been there since the divorce (apart from the two months in the camper). It was my sanctuary then. Just one small room, with a tiny sectioned-off kitchen space and a bathroom shared with the chap next door. I slept on a fold-down sofa. Apart from the camper, it was the smallest space I'd ever lived in. Smaller than a caravan. It wasn't meant to be for long. Just until I got settled again, and I'd recovered from it all, and the settlement came through from the house sale. Everything in my life was new. New space. New job. New status (single again).

New life. The start of one.

But I was there for 4 years. It was hard to leave. Until the landlord sold up, and I no longer had any choice.

I moved into here on my own. I didn't have much anyway. My only big stuff was a fridge, a wardrobe, my bookcases and sofa. Most of it came to pieces. I used the camper to shift it all. I started at 9 in the morning and finished at 11 that night. It took 12 trips in total. 12 trips-worth of stuff from a tiny bedsit. Each trip meant between 8 and 10 times up and down the stairs, carrying boxes and bags and even the fridge, a stair at a time. So, an average of 9 times up and down on each trip. There are 50 stairs from the car park to my door. 50 x 9 x 12 trips = 5,400 stairs I climbed, carrying heavy weights. Then the same number down again. Then, at the bedsit, 18 stairs x 9 x 12 trips = 1,944 stairs down carrying the same heavy weights. Then the same number up. Total stairs up for the day = 7,344. I made some extra trips, too - to make sure the old place was empty, to put the camper away, to check the meter - so I can probably round that up to 7,500 and be about right. A stair riser is about 7 inches. The stairs here are, anyway. 7,500 x 7 = 52,500 inches, which is 4,375 feet. The summit of Ben Nevis above sea level is 4,409 feet. In moving that day, I climbed almost the equivalent of the height of the highest mountain in the British Isles.

It reassures me to know this. I climbed more than a physical mountain that day.

I slept that night on the sofa-bed, surrounded by my boxes of things, and woke the next day to a different light from a different window. I still had my clothes on. Getting up felt like pulling myself out of mud. After breakfast, I went back to the bedsit. I filled in the holes where the shelves had been. I cleaned the sink. I vacuumed the carpet and pulled down the blinds. Then I stood in the middle of the floor and looked around. The faded bit of carpet by the window. The bright squares on the walls where my pictures had hung. This place that had been my little home for a longer time than expected. But it had been safe and warm and quiet. The quietness. Like a church. My sanctuary.

Then I dropped to my knees on the carpet and cried. I cried for the first time in years - something I wasn't even able to do on the last day I saw Lucy, or the day when I kissed dad in the Chapel of Rest and wet his lips from the can I took with me (the can I still have in a kitchen cupboard, the last drink we shared). I know he smiled. I could see it on his face - on his waxen lips.

I didn't think I would ever stop crying. It was like a steel box inside my head had burst its rivets, and everything came flooding out. I cried for it all. For Lucy, and for me, and for us and for what had become of us, and for all that had happened. The mess that I'd made. I cried for that. And I cried for dad, and for Michael, and mum on her own, and even for Karen - for the sister I'd known, and wasn't sure that I knew any more, though I wanted to. And I cried for my life - for still having it, even though I'd tried to finish it so many times. To wipe it out.

I cried for my life and for hers and for theirs, and for things I didn't know I could cry about - for the hurts and the angers, the bad words, the regrets. I cried for it all. I cried until there was nothing left. Then I picked up my vacuum and bucket and tools, and opened the door, and left to start once again.

Which is where I am, or where I'm supposed to be. Home. Where I'm meant to be right now, this day, at this time. Everything I have done and not done, and everything that has been done to me and not done to me, has brought me here. And here's where I am, and where I begin...

I switched on the boiler to take off the chill. Monday. My work day. Just 3 hours, that's all. All I had to worry about. A morning in Hackbury library, helping beginners to learn computers. Silver surfers or special needs. People looking for a new hobby, or trying to keep up. I can manage that. *Now*, I can manage it. It's taken me a long time. I wonder if they know that I'm getting as much out of the deal as they are. Helping others, and helping myself at the same time. As far as they know, I just have time on my hands to give. Maybe I'm very-early retired. Maybe I have independent means. Maybe I just have Monday mornings off work and want something else to fill in the time. I don't worry about what they think, really. I'm done with worrying about what people think.

But people like to tell you, anyway. People always want to tell you what they think - even if it's none of their business. They still like to make it so. They still like to say.

Which is how it was with Mrs McNelly, the woman who was my 'client' today. As soon as I met her and shook her hand, I could sense something about her. Not a pre-judgment - more like an instinct. She was in her late 60s (so I'd been told), but looked nowhere near it. She was tall and upright, and impeccably dressed: trim bottle-green trouser suit, crocodile-skin boots, quality dress jewellery, chiffon neck-scarf (held in place with a fat silver ring). I couldn't help thinking of Diana Rigg in *The Avengers*. She was almost too smart for the occasion - though some people never like to look casual. Fair enough. It made me a little conscious, though, of my hoodie, jeans and Doc Martens. Her hair had been coloured (though not too darkly, which never suits older people) and was stylishly cut. It was a young cut, but it suited her. She'd clearly taken good care of herself. Her face belied her age - fresh-seeming, and made up with care and subtlety. I suspected some surgery at some stage, too. It just seemed too smooth and youthful.

Her hands gave the real clue. It's always in the hands. Even here, though, close attention had been paid. Her nails were carefully manicured and had no need of varnish. They were naturally pink and buffed to a shine, and a sensible length - none of these stuck-on talons and chisels that younger women seem to go for. She was wearing several rings - all gold, with a generous smattering of stones. One particular one, on her wedding finger, was an emerald as large as a pea, surrounded by tiny diamonds. I'd never seen a ring flash and sparkle so much. Her handshake was firm - as was the set of her face, and the way she held my eyes with hers. It gave me the unsettling feeling that she could see right inside, and had sussed it all out. She meant business and was used to efficiency - that's what it all seemed to say. The clothing, the style, the bearing, the look. *I want the best, so don't give me less.*

Her *'Hello, Mr Seagrave'* was stiff - like a bank manager greeting a loan applicant - and my *'Please call me Tom'* invitation was met with a half-smile and a raised, precisely-shaped eyebrow. There was no return invitation. Mrs McNelly she was, then. I felt wrong-footed already, like I wasn't the instructor at all. I was the one awaiting instruction.

We sat at a terminal and she filled me in on her requirements. She'd never used a computer in her life ('Never *needed* to,' she emphasised, as if she knew better ways of doing things, or someone else had always done the computing for her). She'd read Bill Gates's book, though, and was suitably impressed by the man and his vision, and was curious about *'all this dot-com thing'*, and wanted to know what all the fuss was about. I asked her if she thought she might be interested in other computer applications, like word-processing or accounting.

"Oh, I leave it to you to tell *me*," she said, "whether you think I might benefit from these things. You're the expert in these matters."

I thought it best not to mention games. MILF sites could probably wait, too.

I got her logged in and explained the desktop, then opened Mouse Properties and got her practising double-clicks. At first she was too slow, and then she was too fast. I tried adjusting the settings to suit her style, but it didn't seem to help. She would get it for a bit - and then lose it again. She became impatient and started pressing harder on the mouse and thumping the button. Each time it failed to work, she muttered *'stupid'* in an undertone, or snorted heavy breaths out of her nose. They weren't far short of the force of a sneeze. At last she pushed the mouse aside and growled with exasperation. She clearly wasn't used to being disobeyed - especially by something so small.

"There must be something wrong with it," she said.

Of course. Whenever a thing doesn't work properly for impatient (and heavy-handed) people, it's because there's something wrong with it. I could just imagine her on the flightdeck of a nose-diving 747, berating the stupid control yoke because it wouldn't pull back.

"Just try a fraction of a second longer between clicks."

"I *am!*"

Who is this fool who can't make this thing work for me? I could sense her thinking. I started to think she was right. It was my fault, of course.

And then finally, she *clicked*. Or she *double-clicked*.

"Ah... it's working properly now," she said.

With that established, we tried a few other things. I showed her Google and explained what it did. Then I got her to search for various things that interested her. The Old Bailey. The Loire Valley. The National Trust. The Royal Family. Mantovani. Oddly (but who knows?) Extreme Wrestling - especially the images. I showed her YouTube (*'Hm'*), FaceBook (*'I really don't think so, thank you very much'*) and Wikipedia, which set her interest alight. She searched for some things on there - pecking tentatively at the unfamiliar keyboard, taking sometimes thirty seconds to type a single word. She seemed to be enjoying herself, though. I showed her how to print things off, and when she clicked the button and the printer buzzed, she got positively animated.

"Wonderful! Just wonderful!"

I was pleased to see her reaction. The buzz is always good. She asked then about computer prices, and getting the internet, and where was the best place to go. I showed her some things on Amazon, and some ISP sites. Finally, she looked at me.

"I'm most grateful to you, Thomas. Thank you."

Thomas. Okay.

"I intend coming back again tomorrow, so make sure you're free."

I explained my arrangement. She seemed surprised.

"So... what else do you do, then?"

"I just do this. One morning a week."

She seemed perplexed then.

"But what about *work?*"

As always, it felt like an accusation. And there were things I could have said, of course. Things that would have shut her up.

But I told her the truth. The recovery from illness - though I didn't specify the nature of it. I didn't have to. She knew. I could see it in the expression on her face. And then I felt it - in the jewel-encrusted hand that she laid on top of mine on the desk, and the squeeze of it. And the level stare.

"Think positive, Thomas, and positive things will come to you. Think negative, my dear, and they won't. It's as simple as that, whatever anyone may tell you."

As simple as that.

Of course.

I should have known.

I came home from the session feeling down about the whole thing, which was unusual. It was just her. She meant well. Don't they all? All the sooth-sayers and pull-yourself-together types. It's funny how it is with mental illness, though. If you've got a broken leg, or a bandaged head, or pneumonia, or a cactus growing out of your arse, it's obvious. If you've got Alzheimer's, no decent person is ever going to tell you to buck your ideas up, or tell you to keep your bloody hands still if you've got Parkinson's. But tell them it's depression, and it's *'think positive'*. Tell them it's a personality disorder, and they're backing away politely, as if you'd casually mentioned you enjoy wanking to images of donkeys or camels. Tell them it's bipolar or schizophrenia and they're checking for the axe you've probably got behind your back. It's best to say nothing, really. *Leukaemia*, maybe. *HIV - but don't worry, I'll wipe the mouse off before you use it.*

I'd only been home a few minutes when Carly rang. She wanted to check I'd remembered our appointment on Friday. Of course I had. Date and time. I never need to write these things down. She knows that, anyway. She asked me some questions and I gave her the answers. Why hadn't I been to group much lately? Was everything okay? I told her what I'd been doing. I told her I'd been to a meeting, and that it had helped. I told her I went to mum's for dinner yesterday. I told her I'd just finished work. I told her I'd tell her more on Friday. And we left it at that.

In the evening, I sat down and did some writing for a while. I wrote a bit more of that story - about the couple in the failing marriage. I wasn't sure what was going to happen in it. I didn't have a plan. Which is how it felt when it was me. I thought writing about it, even in fiction, might help me to make sense of it all. Carly had suggested it many times - as a way of getting some perspective on it. She thought it might enable me to leave the whole episode where it belongs - in the past. Something that happened and that I've moved on from. Going forwards by looking backwards - that kind of thing. It can't be forgotten, but it can be laid to rest - like so much else that had happened. It's always said that people should learn from the mistakes of history. That's what I was trying to do.

They weren't all mistakes, though. They weren't all my fault. I don't think so, anyway. It's taken me a while to learn that.

So... I wrote for a bit. Then I did my journal.
And then the day was done.

~

Tuesday

Colder today. Not cold enough to see my breath, but colder. There's a mist on the sea. Thicker than Sunday - like the clouds have settled there. I woke at 7 and should have got up then. But I lay back for a while and thought about things. Things I shouldn't be thinking about, but can't help. No job. No money. No prospects. 50 next year and nothing to show. And once that door's open, in they all troop, like unwanted visitors, come to take over with their dirty feet and body odour and bad teeth and piss-stained trousers and reek of tobacco and drink. The regrets. The missed opportunities. The wasted years.

50.

I remember dad's 50th birthday. We'd moved here by then - away from London. It was summer. I'd just started work at the farm - my first job. I came home and we all went along to the pub in the evening. I bought him a pint - another first. We stood at the bar, father and son - me already towering over him - and had our first pint together. We drank to Michael, though we didn't say it. The one who should have been there, but wasn't. Mum sat in the corner with Karen, who already looked old for her age. We all did. That's what it does. I was 17, and he was 50. And we were together.

Michael's death had nearly wrecked us. Dad's drinking took off after that. He blamed himself, as he did for everything. Bringing him up with the army. Encouraging him. Pushing him. That's what he said. He'd pushed him into it - liked he'd pushed him in front of a train. Michael wanted it anyway. He always did. He followed the route, all the way - cadets at 12, regulars at 16. And once he was in, he was off. He wanted to get away - see the world. Escape from home. But dad took the blame. The fault was his. And the drink was his punishment... and his comfort, too. The drink and the drink - while mum held it together for our sakes. Karen and me... and for his sake, too. For all of us. She was our ship and our anchor. Her baby had gone - the one she'd carried and birthed and suckled. The one who had grown and become his own man, and escaped from the fold and gone out there. Had started to do things for himself, keep himself right, behave like an adult, make something of it. For Queen and Country. His strength and independence were what she'd given him. The determination and practicality. And all dad had done was set him up to die. So he'd believed. It was all his fault, and he deserved to be punished. The sins of the fathers. But she held onto him and kept him together. She held all of us together. She got us through it - this woman who'd lost her baby.

Moving away was the renewal. The shot at redemption. Starting again. The escape from London and all that it held: devastation, destruction, the drink and the debts, and the death. And it worked, for a while. It brought him back. It brought us together. For a while. Some things are always there, though. Some things can never be escaped. You can run, but you can never hide. They're always there. Always waiting.

The next time I look at the clock, it's 8:00. *Snap out of this*, I say to myself. *Move!*

I get up and pull on my socks and track bottoms, then a t-shirt and sweat shirt and hoodie, and trainers. I go to the kitchen to make a coffee and pack my gym bag. Then I sit in my armchair and listen to the tick of the clock. Just the tick of the clock - and sometimes a car passing down in the street. A gull mewling. Apart from that, nothing. The spaces between. The empty spaces between. And the tick of the clock.

There are my things. My shelves of books, lined up in their rows. My desk and chair. My pictures, and personal things. An oil burner. Juggling balls. My lanterns and candles. An old pipe tobacco tin, hand-painted in oils, showing a pale sun setting over dark trees and an empty lake. A carved wooden angel, given to me by a woman I saw for a while, two years ago, before it got bad, then worse than that. She didn't help, but I keep her gift. And then, on my desk, beside my dictionary, a small plaster figurine: *Guanshiyin*, an enlightened one, seated with her legs crossed in yogic posture - her feet resting on the tops of her thighs - cupping a lotus flower in her hand.

Guanshiyin - bodhisattva of compassion in Buddhist belief - whose name means *'observing the sounds of the world.'* A wedding gift to Lucy and me from the Priestess who made our handfasting. It came to me afterwards, with everything else. She wanted none of it. The photographs. The posy she held (dried in a box). The cards. The poems. The band she wore in her hair that day - the tiny blue flowers, threaded together, like stars in her hair as she stood by my side in the woods that day, in cold February. The silver and gold braids that bound our hands as the vows were spoken: *'For as long as love shall last.'*

How long does love last? How long does it hold? Is it always there? Does it ever fade? Can something shared like that simply go, like a day that passes and cannot come back? If love is a memory, can memory be love?

I pick up the figurine. Frozen she sits, observing the sounds of the world with me. The clock. The gulls. The traffic passing. The sounds of the day slipping by. I think about Lucy. I wonder where she is, and what she's doing. Nearly 5 years since that final day, when I hugged her close and watched her walk back along Market Street and mingle with the Saturday shoppers there, until there was just a glimpse of her hair in between, and then that was gone too - as if she'd been absorbed by them, back to atoms, vaporised, gone. I don't even know if she's still alive. I think she must be. But I don't know for sure.

The café downstairs has opened for the day and the chap from the kitchen has just been across and scattered some scraps from yesterday to the gulls on the promenade. They fall on it like screeching bombs - crying out to others to alert them, then fighting them off in the scramble to get it.

Come here... Go away... Come here... Go away...

Is that the same as loving someone and not wanting to be with them? Wanting them there, and not? How can that be? How is it possible?

I don't want to be without you. Leave me alone. Don't go. Go. I want you here with me. Leave me alone.

Leave me alone.

Alone I am here, now. My neighbours had gone by yesterday evening. They knocked to say cheerio. I barely knew them - but they had a ginger cat who came in sometimes, if they were all out and he was waiting, on the stairs outside the door. Spice. He'd come in and wander around my rooms, rubbing his face against chair legs and doors, lying in the shaft of light from the window, licking his legs and winking, and leaving a spoor of fur behind, like a tuft of sun. They had him now, in his carry-cage - ears flattened down and howling. I said goodbye and wished them luck, and they went. So there's no one here now in this part of the building. Just me.

I wonder what they thought of me. I told them I worked in care. They must have realised I was home a lot. Her dad was there most of the day. He would have known. Three hours in the middle of the day, for group. Sometimes at night, for a meeting. Trips to the gym or the supermarket, or to pop in on mum. Hackbury Library on Monday morning. Nothing else. They must have noticed. I saw her recently in the newsagents. She asked how work was going. I said I was doing home work, now - on the computer. Same as I told mum. It kept me at home. Just so they knew. As if it mattered anyway. It didn't. And even if it did, it doesn't now. They're gone.

It's comforting in some ways to know I'm alone. I like to think there's no one else. I can always go out and find people if I need them. The gym and the shops, the groups and meetings. Mum. There are always people.

There aren't even any ghosts here. I had a ghost in a flat years ago - the one I had before I met Lucy, over on the other side of town. It was quiet there. My table sat in a bay window, which overlooked a long back garden. Beyond it was a path, then the backs of the houses in the next road over. It was quiet all year. I was happy there. Just me... and my ghost. A benign presence. Doors would close, or doors would open. I'd smell sweet pipe tobacco smoke sometimes. I'd wake some mornings and sense it there, looking down at me. My watcher. I didn't believe nor disbelieve, but I knew what I felt. I knew that doors don't just open and close by themselves - that smells come from somewhere.

Out of curiosity, I went to a medium. She described a photograph I have of dad - even though he was still alive then. The one on my wall. The one on mum's dresser. She described the things I did - things that no one else knew about: my notebooks, my writing, my thoughts, my moods, my drinking (even then, it was there). She told me I was sensitive. She described a place where I was going to live - a house with white walls, and a garden with fruit trees. There was someone else there with me. Someone I loved. I was happy... but there was something else, too. I remember the look on her face. She placed her hand over the back of mine across the table and stared out of her window. Then she turned back and looked at me, with not quite a smile. An understanding. A knowingness. She said it was something I had to go through, and I would. I would find a way. The way would show itself when the time came.

I don't know what she saw - except the photograph, and the notebooks, and the things I carried in my head. My secrets. I spoke of the ghost, and she nodded. And that was all. It was a long time ago. I went back to my flat, and my ghost, and my thoughts, and my life. It all carried on as before.

And then there was Lucy. Lucy, with her witching eyes and silver-dangle earrings, and secrets she needed somebody to share. Lucy, who I gave my life to. Whose hand was bound to mine in the woods that day, on our chosen sacred spot, in cold February. Who returned with me to the house we'd found. The white one, with the garden and wild berry bushes, and a plum tree for making my wine. And the tabby cat that was hers, and ours.

A place where we could be. Until we could no longer be.
For as long as love lasted.
And now I'm alone here. Not lonely. Alone.
Observing the sounds of the world.

~

Wednesday

Each day has a mood - like each day has weather. Some days are bright, with a warm breeze. Some days are bright, but cooler. Some days are overcast, but mild and still. Some days are cold. And some days, as people say, don't really know what they want to be: bright and warm, then clouding up, then cold, then bright again. On some days, there are storms. Like the weather, too, the mood of the day can never be known until it arrives. Forecasts get it wrong. A freak front sweeps in and shifts it around. A gale whips up, lifting the tiles, rattling the windows, raising the sea to a fury. Or a blizzard sets in and smothers, envelops, freezes down, suffocates. No day is the same - except in its span. It comes, it passes, it leaves. And then there's the next one. What's gone is gone. What's coming is coming. What's now is what's now, and is all there is. What's now is right here.

In the day.

Structure and routine. They're the important things. I take the day, and work out what I need to do. Eat. Exercise. Shop. Sometimes a group. Sometimes a meeting. Work on Monday morning. No hour without something in it. At night, a film or a book. Some writing, maybe. And then sleep. 8 hours. I must have 8 hours. Without it, the plan goes awry. The map gets torn. The servers go down. The weather changes.

Yesterday was good. I put a bit of variation into it (Carly said I should) and went to the gym in the afternoon instead. I did my best time on the rowing machine - 7 minutes 38 seconds for 2,000 metres. My average stroke per minute was 41.

...then I go on the treadmill. I feel something stirring now. The energies coming together. Every 100 metres, I increase the speed. Then every 50 metres. I just keep it going, powering up, faster and faster. 4 minutes 36 seconds per kilometre... 4:30... 4:22... 4:16... Sweat sprays off of me, onto the screen and the floor. I see myself in the mirror in front of me - my arms and legs pumping. I look in my eyes. I see it in there. The power. I feel it in my chest - everything fusing. I feel my feet off the ground and my body in the air - feel myself apart from everything. I push up the speed further and further... 4:00... 3:52... I'm flying, right up at the limit. My legs, my arms, my heart, my blood. I can feel eyes one me - everyone watching. I can see it in my eyes. It's there. It's all there. Every bit of me, up at the limit. I'm flying. I'm fucking *flying*...

...and then it changes. I feel myself going - edging backwards, the machine taking over. I'm losing it. I push the red button and grab at the bars. The plane descends. I come back down. I touch the runway. I slow to a jog, then a trot, then a walk, then a stop. I look at the screen. 5 kilometres in 22 minutes and 32 seconds. The world comes back in. The soundtrack music. Pop diva anthems. Pretty boy hip-hop. It's all still there. The machines are there, making their noises, the whirring and buzzing, as the users keep going. Pushing forwards, but staying in place. As I did. I've run over 3 miles, and I'm in the same place. I never left. I was always here. I didn't go anywhere.

I sit on a mat in the corner by the door and cross my legs, and put my towel over my head, and close my eyes. I can feel my sweat running down under my t-shirt. My heart and blood are thumping. I'm invincible now. Anything's possible. I'm strong. I can do anything. No one can hurt me - not any more. Not as they have done, all the way back. The playground. The classroom. The street. The jobs. Those bastards. People still out there, walking around, waiting to do it. Let them try it today, the bastards. I'm ready for them. I'll take them all on. Let them fucking try it now, the cunts...

I slip the towel down to my neck and open my eyes. The bodies working - pushing, turning, lifting, pumping, moving. A caveman on the bicep curls looks at me, until he sees me looking at him, then looks away again.

What was that fucking look for?

His ears are plugged into his phone. He stops his set and looks at the phone and presses some keys. His t-shirt is too tight, which is how he wants it - to show it all off. Tits of muscle. Arms like sides of meat. Dark blue flames or tongues or something snake down them from under his sleeves. They twist and coil around his elbows, trail down to his wrists in tendrils and feelers and squiggles. It looks like something growing out of him. It looks like a skin disease. It looks like his veins are filling with ink, pumping through from his heart, taking him over, consuming him - like knotweed, spreading, invading, engulfing, strangling. He's fucking infested with it. What the fuck does he want to cover himself with that crap for? Why does he think it looks good? It's a load of fucking shit. Why did he pull that face at *me* when *he* looks like that? Well, he can fuck off and take all his shit scribbles with him. Just try looking at me like that again, with his fucking toys and tatts and his fucking distorted body, the wanker...

I finish off with my swim, as usual - ploughing through the water today, weaving past the breast-strokers with their funny little sideways waves. Why do they get in my way? Why won't they let me through?

Why does everyone get in my way? Keep asking questions? None of their business. Fuck off. Just fuck off and leave me alone.

When I left the gym, it was getting dark. I bought some apples in an empty greengrocers, then went to the library to see if she was there. I was going to speak to her. I didn't know what I was going to say, but I'd made up my mind.

But she wasn't there again. I sat at a table and looked at a newspaper, waiting. I wanted to see if she would come. Maybe she was on her tea break. I turned through the pages quickly, scanning them, not really looking. *China sets out demands. UN launches global conversation. Small savers are biggest losers.* It was quiet in there. A couple of people on the computers - looking at Facebook, playing games. One of the regulars - a middle-aged chap in a deerstalker hat and parka - sitting arms-crossed on the table in front of him, chin on his wrist, staring like a schoolboy at a large-print book. The woman behind the counter - not her - fiddled with a box of index cards. I turned the pages. She still didn't come. Maybe she'd left. Maybe she'd been transferred, or had found something else. Maybe she was still on holiday. Maybe she was sick.

What difference would it have made, anyway? What would I have said? What would I have done? What I always do? What would have happened? What would she say? What would I do?

It's always the same. Always. I see them. All the time, I see them. The woman from the gym, for instance, who works in the café up by the station. Too young, though. What would she say? *'Fuck off, you dirty bastard. You're older than me dad.'* She speaks to me, though. If I pop in for a hot chocolate, or I see her in the gym. We speak. But that's all it is. All it will ever be.

Then that woman at the letting agency - the one who showed me the flat. More my age. She let me in and showed me around. She liked it herself. She could have just been saying that... but I think she meant it. It was cool and damp that day - the first signs of autumn in the air. She was dressed in a black raincoat, black skirt, black shoes. Jesus, she looked good.

"Which room will you have as your main room?"

"The other one," I said.

"So... this will be your bedroom."

"Yes. Do you think that's right?"

She stood at the window and looked out - over the jetty and across the sea.

"What a wonderful view to wake up to."

"Yes."

I walked back with her afterwards, to sign the papers. She smiled a lot, seemed coy. Unusual for a woman like that. She made some chat, though. She was being professional. But there was something else. Something I sensed in the way she walked, hands in her pockets, eyes fixed on the pavement just ahead. Then the look on her face as she handed the papers across the desk to me. A kindness. The way she sat. The way she spoke - partly patter, but more than that, too. A warmth and interest. *Tom*, she called me. She asked what I did. I was still in the job then. When I told her what it was, she smiled. A knowing smile, I thought. As if she understood. And the things on her desk. There was nothing on her desk. Her computer, her mug, her papers and pens, her phone. Nothing else. A trace of red on the lip of the mug. *'Party Girl'* it said - though a coffee stain ran down through the *'y'*, obscuring it. *Part Girl.* Her face was youngish - just smoker's lines around the lips. She didn't, though. She smelled clean. And her hands told the truth, as they always do. They were older. Her hands were long, with darker skin and knots at the finger joints. No wedding ring. No rings at all. They were hands that had held on tight sometimes. I could see it in them, as she handed me the papers across her desk with nothing on it, and pointed to where I should sign.

She stayed in my head. During the first week, I went in there most days on some pretext. It was easy enough, with things to check out and clear up. I always saw her. She remembered my name. *'Hello, Tom,'* she'd say. She'd seem pleased to see me. She was being professional. But I think there was something else.

And then, one day, she was gone. Her desk had been taken. Someone else was there in her place. Photographs were there. A plant was there. Things were different. And she was gone.

What would have happened? What usually happens. What's happened before. And that's what stops me. I want something... someone. But I don't. It scares me. I can't cope with it.

Probably for the best, then. *Party Girl.* Parties and clubs, out with the girls, out on the razz. Not for me. How many more years would she do that, though? Why would she do it? Good time girl? Let-my-hair-down girl? Or was it a front? To fill in the space? The thing that was missing? The space on her desk? She had a space, I know it. Something was missing. The voice was a front and so were the clothes. Part of the job. So was the smile. But not all of it. You can't fake it all. Something was behind it. Something was there. Something was there. Something was missing.

I put the paper back on the rack and headed for the door. I stopped at the book display by the photocopier and looked at what was there. Mostly novels by authors I'd never heard of - the kind with bright, whimsical covers showing cartoon women in party dresses, carrying shopping bags, getting in taxis, filling the space. The space on the desk. Or the ones with women in Edwardian clothing, standing at the end of a cobblestone terrace, with children in sailor's hats rolling hoops in the background. There was one, though, that caught my eye. A dark cover, showing hands holding a leaf. *November*. Gustave Flaubert. I picked it up and opened it at random, and my eye caught a line. '*Oh, how intensely I would have loved, if I had loved...*'

I went back and checked it out. Then I went home. I put my things away. I made some dinner. I cleared it away, then lit some candles and sat in the quiet. I thought of the woman. I thought of the women.

I thought of them all. I counted their number, back through the years. I saw their faces, in the glow of the candlelight, floating like wraiths. Jane. Sarah. Cathy. Jill. Sue. Then Lucy, the woman I married. Even Billie, who messed my head so much I wanted to die. They were all with me. I was alone with them. I spoke to them all. I asked for forgiveness and understanding. I told them the things that had happened, and why, and what I'd discovered, and why it had come out the way it had.

I thought of the woman in the library. And the one with the dark clothes, and the desk that spoke for her, as she stood by my window and looked at the sea.

I wondered where she had gone. Where they had gone.

I picked up the book again. *November*. On a page I turned to, another line...

'*It is so pleasant to imagine that you no longer exist!*'

I wonder if I no longer exist to them.

Sometimes I feel like I no longer exist. Like nothing's left.

Today is like that. A good day yesterday. But today I'm not here. I've disappeared.

I no longer exist.

~

Thursday

I got the knife out last night.

I held it in my hands for a while, turning it around, feeling the surfaces. 22 ridges along the handle. I pushed out the blade and ran my finger along its edge. I pushed gently, until I could feel it biting, then stopped. I looked at my finger - a tiny nick, like a paper cut, a rind of red showing through. But no blood. I held it there. It was the first time I'd held it that way for almost a year. One night alone, over the Christmas, drink in my head, it came up inside me like always - like a spark in my head, and a flame catching. And the relief of it. The cut. The blood. The relief. The relief of knowing I was real.

I put the knife down and rolled up my sleeves. I ran my fingers along my arms - each one, along the inside. I could feel them faintly, like the grain in wood that hasn't been planed. The scars had healed well. Just pale bands, like I'd been leaning against a wire fence, and the skin was evening out again. Like striations in rock, worn smooth by the sea. I'd not done it much, anyway. Mainly since the divorce. There had been other ways, too. The burning, sometimes. And the drink. Always the drink. The best and the worst of it. Always the drink.

I rolled my sleeves down again. Then I put the knife away, at the back of the drawer, where it had been and where I kept it, always there, always known about, out of sight. My hands were shaking.

Where did it come from? I don't know. It just comes. It never really goes.

It can work like that, though. A day of highs and lows. The changeable weather of it. The writing. The thing at the gym the day before. Then the emptiness later. Being alone. A bad night. The plane coming down over trees.

And then yesterday, I'd taken out the photos and scanned them in, and started to work on them. Cleaning them up a bit. Cloning out the creases and spots. Adjusting the contrast. Sharpening the features. I didn't want to make too many changes. I wanted them to be as they were - as she remembered them. But I wanted them as good as I could get them. And I wanted them bigger - to bring out the detail and fill up the album. The main ones. Their parents. Their brothers and sisters. Their wedding - and their Silver and Ruby (the last one together). Their children - me, Karen, Michael - at various ages: babies, toddlers, teens. Later years for me and Karen. Karen on her wedding day. The twins, Adam and Chris, then Natalie - again, through the years. With Michael, all that we had. The uniform one blown up to A4 - a page on its own. 23. Him as he was and would always be. Ageless.

There were photos, too, of mum and dad on their own - babies, kids. Mum at the beach in a polka dot frock, high heels, bobbed hair. 18 or 19? At Wandsworth. Riding a bike. At home, on her 80th, surrounded by cards. Then dad. In the army. In Egypt and Palestine. On the lorry. Outside a pub somewhere. At Karen's wedding - pint in one hand, cigarette in the other. One in his last home, not long from the end. Shiny white hair with a nicotine streak. Bloated face - but pink and smiling. And the dress uniform one. The one she has by her drinks cabinet. The one I have on my wall. The barracks. The sword and helmet. The white gauntlets. The jack boots, straps and spurs. The youth. Him as he was.

So, I worked on them. For most of the day, I worked on them. And then I stopped. And the next thing I knew, the knife was out. Stuff in my head already, then all that. I should have know.

Control yourself. You have a choice. You don't have to do it.

But it's good. It makes it better. The pain takes the pain away. It takes it away...

I shut the drawer. I went to the bathroom and rinsed my face. I put on my jacket and trainers and went out.

I walked in the dark, down the alley and across the car park, then along past the flats to the High Street. Outside the *Admiral's*, some men were standing, pints in hand or at their feet - smoking, texting, shouting, coughing. Music was playing. The TV was on, almost filling a wall. Football. It looked warm in there - lights against maroon walls, people pressed in around the bar.

I crossed over and went into Morrisons. Just a handful of late evening shoppers wandering the aisles, stopping, looking, picking. A woman sweeping the floor by the checkouts. No one I knew.

Why was I there? What had I come for?

I went to the 'Reduced Items' section. Packets of ham and chicken slices, meals for one, rump steaks, yoghurts. All of it would be going in the skip in half-an-hour, when they closed. Pounds of food, unwanted. I picked up a plastic dish of dips for 50p. Then I went to the next aisle for a bag of tortilla chips to go with them. I walked along to the other end, turned right, turned right again. Into the alcohol.

Misery Aisle.

I wandered down the tunnel of bottles. The beers and ciders first, with their colourful labels and names. *Legless Ale. Old Thunderer. Tanker. Santa's Brew. Bandy Coot.* Wine lined up in military rows. French wine. German wine. Spanish wine. Italian wine. New World wine. English wine. Mulled wine. Red, rosé, white, sparkling, fortified, bianco, rosso, rouge. Low alcohol. No alcohol. Green bottles, brown bottles, clear bottles, round bottles, fluted necks, screw-tops, corks, squat necks. Vin de pays, AOC, Premier Cru, Temperanillo, Shiraz, Cabernet Sauvignon, Chianti, Merlot. Champagne, Chardonnay, Bordeaux, Spätlese, Valpolicella, Spumante. Damson. Cherry. Apricot. Oporto, Amontillado, Medium, Pale, Cream, Special Late Vintage. Oaky, spicy, tangy, blackberry, smoky, zesty, fruity. Good with pasta. Good with red meats. Good with fish. Good with friends. Good on its own. 9%, 12%, 14%, 20%. 2 units per glass. 10.5 units per bottle. Be drink aware. Take alcohol-free days. Easy-drinking. Drink anytime. Less than half-price. 50p off. Three for a tenner. Take home a box. Pick one up. Pick one up. Pick it up. Turn it around. Look at the label. Put it back. Turn away now...

...turn away... turn away...

...rum whiskey brandy gin vodka scotch cognac... blended, distilled, triple-filtered, single malt, Kentucky straight, smooth, spiced, original, French, Spanish, matured in oak, London, dark, white, 100%. Tequila, Sambuca, Advocaat, Jägermeister, Baileys, Pernod, Midori. Serve on the rocks. Serve with your Favourite Mixer. Smooth as a board. Savour the flavour. Feel it go down. Feel it go down. Offer ends Sunday. Buy it Now. Buy it. Buy it. Buy it now. Buy it now buy it now buy it *NOW...*

I look up the aisle. I look down the aisle. I take one down. I look at the label. I look down the aisle. I look up the aisle. Savour the flavour. Feel it go down. Buy it now

BUY IT NOW!

I go to the checkout. I take out my card. I put in my PIN. I take my receipt. I say goodbye. I go out to the street. I walk past the pub. I go back to my flat. I put it down. I open the dips. I open the chips. I dip the chips. I lick my lips. My lips. I look at it. I look at it. I look at the bottle. I pick it up, I put it down. I look at it.

How long is it? How many days? How many weeks? How many months? Nearly a year. Soon. A good length of time. Cause for a celebration. Cause for a treat. You deserve it. A treat. Been a good boy. One won't hurt. No one will know. Just the one, just for a treat, and no one will know. What harm can it do? Just think of it, think of it, feel it go down, feel it settle, feel the effect. Feel that feeling. Nothing like it. Feel it. Filling the void. Why wouldn't you want to feel it? You only live once. What's life for if you can't have some fun? You can't drink when you're dead. Go on, my son. Can't trust a man who don't drink. Go on. One won't hurt. Do you good. Behaved yourself. Been a good boy. Settle you down. Settle the stomach. Settle the head. Calm you down, boy. Make you feel good, boy. Make you feel good again, make you feel better, make you feel right. What's the harm in that? None at all. Go on, son. You know you want to. You know you're going to. You might be dead tomorrow. You're going to anyway. Might as well be now. Good a time as any. Go on, my boy. Go on, my

*son. Give yourself a treat. Might be dead tomorrow. What you
waiting for? Open it up. Open it up. Open it up. Open it open
it*

OPEN IT UP!

I look away. I look at the walls. I see my pictures. I see
my books. I see my room. I see it all there, the way it is. All
my things there. I see it. And I see him. I see dad. I see his
photo. The same one that mum has, on her dresser, by the
drinks' cabinet. Like she was teasing him. Putting him with it.
I look at his photo. I look at his eyes. Me as I was. Me looking
at me. I take it down and look at it. A good-looking bloke. Me
as I was. Him as he was. I look in the mirror. Him as he was.
Me as I am. Him and me. The smile on his face as I touched
the drop to his silent lips. He took it with him. He passed it to
me. He passed on and left it to me.

*Off you go, boy. All yours now. My gift to you. Good lad.
Good lad. You can't take it with you. You might be dead
tomorrow. You only live once. Live for the day, boy. Live for
the day. Can't trust a man who don't drink. You know who said
that? Sinatra said that. Frankie boy. I did it my way. You do it
your way. You only live once...*

I put the photo back on the wall. It swings to the left,
askew. I take it down again, adjust the hook, put it back. It
stays straight. Straight as his eyes. The look in his eyes. All
that life. All of that life. You only get one. You can't take it
with you.

I look at my watch. 8:53. I pick up my bag. I put in the
bottle. I run down the stairs, along the alley, across the street,
past the pub, through the door, up to the desk.

"Excuse me. I'm sorry. I bought this by mistake. A
present for someone who isn't supposed to drink. I'm sorry."

She takes out a form. "Have you got your receipt?"

I take it out. I give her the bottle. She takes it. She
checks the seal. She fills in the form. I sign the form. She
refunds my card.

"I'm really sorry."

She looks at me. She smiles. Maybe she winks. She goes to put the bottle back.

"It's alright," she says. "It isn't a problem."

It isn't a problem.

I walk home again, past the pub. Still a few stragglers. I get indoors. I take off my shoes. I get undressed. I turn off the light, and go to bed.

~

11th November

The sea is a cloud.

There are five oceans, but one sea. One sea, which covers over two-thirds of the earth's surface, with an area of 139,400,000 square miles. The average depth of the sea is 2½ miles. The deepest point, in the Mariana Trench in the Western Pacific, is around 6¾ miles - almost 1½ miles deeper than the height of Mount Everest above sea level. The volume of the sea is roughly 325 million trillion gallons.

But today, the sea is a cloud. There are no edges. It doesn't have breadth or depth or volume. It is a cloud, enclosing the world, enveloping the world, bringing it to silence.

I saw Carly, my key worker, today. I took the bus over after gym - the one that goes the long way around, along the coast and through the villages, into the city from the other end. Half-hour longer that way, but more scenic - and more time out, too. More of the day spent, so less time to fill. I could have cycled, or taken the camper or bike, but I felt like a bus journey. Like trains, I missed them - the noise notwithstanding. Top deck, back seat. Warm and cosy. A nice place to think and look out on the world. A nice place to drink, too. One of my favourites. Middle of the day, the bus mostly empty. Up in that back corner with a few cans. The long way around. An hour's session. I had a can of Pepsi with me, though, to keep up the association. Some habits are hard to break like that. Like when I go to the cinema. Dark place + good film = drink. Now, it's Pepsi again. Still a can, like on the bus. People can hear it being opened. Beer cans sound different, though. You can always tell.

The driver was the he-she. I used to see him a lot, when I bussed to work. One day, I noticed the nails when he handed me my change. Then I noticed the line of a bra. Later on came the hair and make-up. I wondered what it must be like - a public transformation like that. The school run. Jesus! The cruelty of kids. The other lads at the depot, too. Full marks to him. To *her*. The courage it needed. And the honesty. Not hiding this anymore. Everyone can see it. Think what you like - but this is *me!* No more lies. No more fear. This is the truth. A lesson for all of us, I thought. A lesson for me. And she was doing it, too - driving a bus. The transformation complete. The true person at last.

A lesson.

When I got to the Centre, I bought a coffee and sat for a bit until Carly came out to get me. I had my voice recorder with me. I could keep it hidden. So many things usually got said, and I found it hard to remember them all. I shouldn't do it, I know. But I thought it would help.

We went to the small room, next to the group room. She was wearing a track suit, too. She'd changed her hair. It suited her - made her look younger. I didn't mention it. I don't know why. Maybe I should have, but I didn't. I'm glad she's my key worker. She's been around a bit. Knows her stuff. Apart from that, she's really nice. My type. Shame, really. She knows more about me than most. More than Lucy knew. More than mum knows. More than my GP. She doesn't know what dad knew, though – the shared knowledge. She doesn't know everything I know, either. Most of it, but not all. I have to keep some to myself. The things I write in my journal. My secrets. She knows things no one else living knows, though.

She sits sideways on to me and turns her head, as always. It sets up a distance - at least, I think that's what it is. There's nothing in between us, but the body language does the work. She has her notebook, but she puts it down on the floor, then clasps her hands around her knee. There's a nice firm thigh under there. She looks at me and raises her eyebrows.

"So, Tom. How have you been keeping?"

I look at my hands. There's a tiny end of dead skin on my finger, just near the tip. I pick at it. My nails look quite ragged around the cuticles - tiny pink areas of deeper grain. I can feel the edge of the cut. I press it and it stings slightly.

"I got my knife out the other night."

She says nothing. Looks.

"I didn't act on it, though. I wanted to, but I didn't. I just took it out. I looked at it. Then I put it back in the drawer."

She smiles.

"Well done. That's the main thing. You didn't act on it. That's a huge achievement. Well done."

"Thanks."

She looks at me intently. I can't meet a gaze like that. I look at my knees. The piping on my track bottoms is royal blue. I had to have them specially made because of my height. I don't understand it. The longest track bottoms you can buy in the shops are huge around the waist. Why is it? Why do they think that all tall people who wear track bottoms are also clinically obese? What do they think is the standard size - the standard physique? Who do they think is the standard person? Just who the *fuck* is the standard person? Standard size, standard looks, standard abilities, standard intelligence, standard views, standard behaviour. What is the standard? Who sets the fucking standard?

"So, tell me... what was going through your head at the time? What made you get that knife out after all this time? How long is it, now?"

"Ten months."

"That's a helluva time, Tom. You've done so well."

"Yes."

"So... why now, do you think?"

I wipe my nose. There's a piece of breakfast between my teeth - the left incisor and the molar behind it. I keep pushing at it with my tongue, but it won't budge, and my nails are too short. It's a piece of oat flake, or wheat flake. I've got a plastic bag in my rucksack. I can use that to floss it out. When we've finished.

"There was stuff in my head. Lots of things."

I rock forward - the chair is too low for me and my knees stick up. I must look like a grasshopper or something.

"But that's not the end of it. Then I did something else. I went over the supermarket and got a bottle of whisky. I wasn't intending to buy it. I just went out for a walk. To distract. And I went in there... and there it was, in my hand. I took it home, and I was going to get fucked up. I put it down and I kept looking at it. But I didn't open it. And then... I took it back and got my money back. Another couple of minutes and I'd have been too late, and then I definitely *would* have drunk it. But I didn't. I bought it, and then I took it back again."

Her face is a picture. She looks like she wants to kiss me. She turns towards me now - elbows on her knees.

"That's absolutely amazing, Tom."

"But I bought it. And I was going to do it. Same as with the knife."

"But you *didn't!* Give yourself some credit. You didn't act on either of them. And I mean... you *paid* for a bottle and took it home... and then you took it back again for a *refund?* What's that all about?"

I nod. Her face looks like it's going to split across. Christ, she's hot.

"Am I missing something here? I mean... are you aware of the significance of what you're telling me?"

I nod again. "I guess so."

"Think about where you were a year ago today. What were you like then? What would you have done then, with the knife and the bottle of whisky?"

I don't want to think about it. I think about it.

I shrug. "I dunno."

"Come on... don't give me that. You *do* know. You know very well, because you were doing it then."

I sniff. I think there's something in my eye. My nose itches. I rub it.

"What you've just said is tremendous. Those two big things, both at the same time, and you beat them. You came through it. You beat them."

"Yes. But... "

She puts up her hand. "No buts. You beat them. Full stop."

I look at the wall. Standard colours. Institutional beige. Neutral. Calming. I often wonder what she thinks, when she's sitting there and we're talking. What she thinks of this person in front of her. Intelligent? Over-sensitive? Immature? Sick? Sexy? Does she think that? Does she just want to, one day, in a different place, get me to fuck her brains out? I could. But I can't, so it's pointless thinking about it.

"So... coming back to the question. What do you think was behind it all. The knife. The bottle. You said there was stuff in your head."

I look at my hands again. My fingers are really long. Lots of people comment on it. They're probably proportionate to the length of my legs. That's another problem I always have - finding gloves to fit. They never cover my wrists. It always looks like I'm wearing a child's size. My feet are big, too. Proportionate, again. I always have to send away for shoes. There's nothing standard about me. Nothing at all.

"Just thoughts. I'd been feeling low for a couple of days. It's the usual stuff going through my head. The things that had happened to me, and where I am now in life. Feeling stuck and useless. Thinking about Lucy and where it had all gone wrong there. It was all spinning around inside. But then I started messing with some family photos. Cleaning them up on the computer. I'm making up an album for my mum's birthday next week."

"Uhuh."

"Yeah, well... it just reinforced it all. Looking back on the past. Wondering where it had all gone. And it brought all the other stuff up, too. Family stuff."

"Like?"

"All of it. It all seems such a mess when I look at it, you know. My brother dying so young. I mean, it was years ago, but it's still there. And then what it all did. Dad going off the rails. The way that all ended. Mum and the way she is now."

"I thought you said she was alright now."

"She is... but what it's all done to her. It's just all so fucking sad. Years of it. Never having anything. All the stress and worry, and the heartache. Losing Michael, which was bad enough... but then having to cope with all the fallout from it. And now there she is, getting near the end of her life, and what's it all been for? Struggle. Supporting an alcoholic for the best part of it. And then there's all the stuff with dad, anyway, and all the grief that caused. My sister thinking I was taking his side over mum, taking after him, and the bust-ups we had. Always when I was drunk, too. I needed it to let the anger out. But, of course, it just reinforced all that stuff for her. Made her look right. She doesn't get it and she isn't really fucking interested, I don't think. And it also feels like I'm always getting compared to her because she's the one who's done so well. Like that's the standard I'm supposed to aspire to. Which makes me feel even more fucking worthless. I mean, all she did was marry a rich bloke. How clever's that? And then it's like, I'm not sick - I just need to pull myself together."

Yeah. That was it. That's what it was all about. Same as always.

I stop, and she looks at me for a moment. I can feel it all, pushing outwards behind my face, and she just sits there quietly, looking at me. I stare at the floor. Dark brown carpet tiles, butted together neat and square. Furrows running across them. Like tiny ploughed fields, laid out in a grid. Stretching across the gap between us. I see her head nodding slightly. Like a breeze has nudged it. I wish she'd say something. She does.

"That's an awful lot of stuff twisted up inside there, Tom."

I nod, too. With the weight of it.

"Tell me what your feelings are, right now, having said all that."

My hands are clenched. I open them and look at my nails.

"Anger. Frustration. And sadness, too, I suppose."

"Resentment?"

"Hm. Maybe."

"That's what it sounds like to me," she says. She sits forwards a bit and crosses her legs, cupping her knee in her hands as if to hold herself up. "Anger, frustration, sadness... yes. But resentment, too. Against your sister. Against your mum, too, it sounds like. All very valid feelings. Feelings we all get for valid reasons. But for you, the job's harder. For you, they can be triggers. And if you had them that night, with the knife and the bottle, then you managed them fantastically well."

"I don't resent my mum."

She turns her head slightly, looking at me sideways.

"Well, that's a point. What was that stuff about how you're made to feel?"

"I don't think she means it that way. It's just how I pick up on it."

She lets go of her knee and opens her hands towards me.

"Which hits the nail right on the head, doesn't it? It's how you pick up on it." She waggles her fingers, like she's sifting flour. "Like you've got all these little antennae, sticking out everywhere, picking up the slightest vibrations. And *especially* the ones that tend to enforce the way *you* feel about yourself. Now, you might be perfectly right about all those things. But you know how that stuff can get twisted and distorted. Again, we all do it. But with someone like you, it can become difficult to separate it all out. To know the difference between what's *actual* and what your head is *telling* you."

"So, you're saying I'm making all this up?"

"No, of course not. I'm saying that you might not always be interpreting things objectively, though. You might be picking the negative stuff and concentrating on that... until, pretty soon, it all becomes negative. You know what they say in AA. Feelings are feelings. They're not necessarily facts."

Yes. I'd heard it. Many times, I'd heard it.

"They feel like facts when you've got them, though."

"Of course. *Feelings* again, though. Just as we can make ourselves *feel* unwell if we think hard enough about it, when there's nothing wrong with us at all."

I grinned. *Willness*, I thought. A condition that won me a pen.

She shifted back to sideways on and showed me that thigh again. That's a fact I wouldn't mind feeling. I hope I don't make it too obvious.

"These things with your past... and with your mum, your dad, your brother, your sister. They're big things. They'd challenge anyone. With you, though, it's a much bigger challenge. But you *are* dealing with them. You're making huge strides. What happened the other night is testament to that."

"Yes. Maybe."

"I don't think there's any 'maybe' about it. And look at the other things you've achieved. You've made peace with your sister, haven't you."

"We can tolerate one another now. I still don't think she understands."

"And maybe she never will. And maybe tolerating one another is all you need to do, and all that you ever *will* need to do. That's families. I know you don't believe in God, but there's a saying that God gives us our relatives... so *thank* God we can choose our friends."

She brings her hand up to her knees again. She has standard hands. Standard knees. She also has a standard tattoo, just above her wrist. Four stars in a curving trail: small, medium, large, extra-large. Cartoon stars. Yellow, pink, orange, red. I'd not noticed them before. They must be new. She looks good. An off-the-peg body. One size fits all. The standard model.

"The other thing is... I know this stuff upsets you. All of what you've said. But you can't change it. Your mum, your dad, your brother dying, your marriage. *All* of your past, with the bullying and abuse. You can't change it. What you *can* change, though, is the way you deal with it. Which is what you're doing. Not drinking any more. Not harming yourself. Going to the gym. Keeping yourself fit. *Respecting* yourself instead. At the end of it all, does it matter what other people think, anyway? What's important, surely, is that what you're doing now is the *right* thing. Think what that must mean to someone like your mum, who saw the way your dad went, and then had to stand by and watch you going down the same road. She lost one son, and I can't begin to imagine what that must be like. It's the natural order turned upside-down. And then this thing with your sister. You say... she's done well for herself. But that's by one set of standards. The standards that many in our society like to judge people by. Money, and things like that. But you need to understand and appreciate - and I don't think you do quite yet, but you're getting there - that you're doing well for yourself, too. In your own terms. You're getting better. Again, think what that must mean to your mum. It doesn't matter that you're not your sister. It matters that you're you, and you're getting well, and you're being there for her. Just think how much worse it could be, Tom."

I pick at my fingers. Rachmaninov had long hands, too. He could span a 13th on the piano - one hand, making a chord 12 inches long. I can span an 11th, at a stretch. But only with one note in between. It's still a chord.

"The other vitally important thing to remember, too, is that you're not just doing it for her or other people. You're doing it for *you*. Because you're worth it."

She shifts her legs forwards again, so her feet are pointing towards me. She switches them left and right. New trainers. Off the shelf. If my feet and hands were as small as hers, I'd look odd. Odder than I look now, anyway. *Sans-serif.* As odd as she'd look with big hands and feet.

"So. These photos. Do you think it's a good idea to be doing them at this time? If they're bringing stuff up?"

"I want to do them. I've almost finished, anyway. Mainly it's resizing them. I think it'll mean a lot to her."

I'm not sure she's convinced. She arches her eyebrows.

"I have to learn to deal with this stuff sometime, anyway. You said it's good to challenge myself occasionally. Do something that induces these feelings."

"Yes... as long as they're things you're sure you can manage."

I can. I'm sure I can. I *know* I can.

"I can manage it."

She nods. "Okay. Fair enough. Anything else?"

I look at the window. There are blinds up - the vertical kind. Wide fabric slats linked by a chain made of tiny silver balls - like a bath-plug chain. They're open enough to let the light in, but the angle's too narrow for me to see out. I can see the shadow of a tree on them, though. It's like looking at one of those Chinese screen pictures. It moves in the breeze. The slats move, and the tree moves. The shadow looks like it's reaching. Fingers. Long fingers.

"There's just the normal stuff."

She's waiting. I glance at her, then at my hands again.

"The stuff that's always there. The fear. Fear about everyone going, and being left alone. And what I'm going to do with the rest of my life. I can't carry on like this forever. Something has to happen. What will it be? And then there's the... usual thing."

She knows. But she's waiting again. She's well trained in this. She knows her stuff - fuck knows, does she. But it's still like trying to explain to someone why you like atonal music. Why you like the taste of coal. Why you see the face of Stalin when everyone else sees a satellite picture of Essex.

"The void. The nothingness. Like I've been emptied out, and there's nothing left."

She nods. Her mouth is tightly shut, and she twists it - like her face is itching and she can't move her hands to scratch it.

"You may disagree, Tom, but I think that's all bound up in the same thing. I think our sessions, and your response, and your recovery, all show that. It may never completely go, but you can learn to cope with it without destroying yourself. Who was it said about fear... 'the only thing you really have to fear is fear itself'?"

"Roosevelt. It doesn't stop you feeling it, though."

"No... and again, it's a feeling, and it's a natural feeling. And if you look at the things you're fearing... well, like we said just now... they're not really things you can control. The same as none of us can control what's going to happen. As clichéd as it sounds, life must go on. And what matters most is what you choose to do with it, and what you're doing with it *now*. Not what you should have done in the past. What you're doing with it now, and where it will hopefully lead you. The other way wasn't leading you anywhere. Well, it was... but not a good place. At least, this way, you have a chance. What you're doing now is laying the groundwork for the future. Taking time out for you. Getting yourself ready for these challenges, so that when they come you'll be able to deal with them. As for the emptiness... if it's part of your condition, all you can do is find strategies to manage it - the same as you are with your other behaviour. If you can't figure out where it comes from - and, like I said, I think it's all part of the same thing - then maybe you should stop trying to figure it out. Try instead to accept it, and work with it."

The sun goes in briefly and the room is filled with shadows. Her face is half shadow.

"Yes."

"What do they say in AA about keeping it in the day?"

"Yes. Yesterday's history, tomorrow's a mystery, all that stuff."

"Exactly. And it's corny old homilies. But it's true as well. Keep it in the day, because that's all you have. Until you're better."

I stretch out my legs towards her and she sits back.

"I've got a better one."

"What's that?"

"Life can only be understood backwards, but it has to be lived forwards."

She smiles and picks up her pad.

"I like that. I'm going to write that one down. Who said that?"

"Kierkegaard."

She's writing it down. She looks up, grinning.

"How on earth do you spell that?"

When we've finished, I go and sit in the group room alone. It's still half an hour before group. Time to sit quietly. Drink another coffee. Eat an apple I've brought with me. Think about what we've discussed.

I like the group room. It feels peaceful. There's a picture on one wall showing a view of the sea, looking down a narrow cobbled street of small white houses. It's a foreign country. Spain or Italy, or possibly Greece. Somewhere hot, anyway, because there are people sitting in shaded doorways, crouched up, with their heads sunk down. Like they're on a siesta. It looks restful, as it's meant to. I wouldn't want any Picasso or anything. No jagged edges or broken faces, like a jigsaw that doesn't fit together - even if that would be more appropriate, maybe. I like the view of the sea. I like the fact that it's there. Surrounding us. Deep and wide and vast. I like the fact that there are huge parts of it that will forever be hidden, mysterious, unknown. A secret.

I drink my coffee and look at the picture, and wait for the others to arrive.

The cloud has lifted, and there's a glimmer of sunlight again.

I'd told her about the inquest I had to attend next week. The client who had died at the home. I said I wasn't looking forward to it - another challenge - but I'd take it as it comes and worry about it then. Try to be positive about it. A chance to get stuff off my chest. Draw a line under that whole thing. Move on from it. I'd talked about the writing, too, and what I was doing. The story. Putting it down, trying to make sense. She told me not to worry if I couldn't. Make sense. What I'd worry about more, though, is if I couldn't write. If it stopped again. That's the big fear - being empty of words. All the while I have something to say, there's a reason for going on. It's when it stops. When it stops, and there's nothing, then that's what there is. Nothing.

But for now, the cloud has lifted.
And the sea is still there...

~

12th November

It's colder today. I went out for a cycle ride this morning, at 8. I cycled along the sea wall and out to Lantern Reach. Lots of dog walkers. Lots of Saturday joggers. It was low tide, and bait diggers were out on the flats. It was still and clear, and the pier head shimmered like a fairytale castle. It looked so close today. Close enough to swim to. A perfect day, right on the cusp of the seasons. I had a good sweat going, and it felt good to be out. To be alive.

Alive.

I had a strange dream again last night. Some people were calling me to come quickly. *She's drowning*, they cried. *Hurry... she's in the water. She's going to drown.* I found myself by a river then. I looked along it, to where they were pointing, and could see the body under the surface. She was wearing a long white dress, from her shoulders to her feet, like a shroud - though her head was exposed. I could see her hair - dark and flowing in the current, like seaweed - and I knew. I didn't need to see the face. I knew it was her. Lucy. She was there, under the water, drifting under the water. Ophelia. That's what I called her sometimes. Just being playful. Ophelia. *Get thee to a nunnery, wench!* She'd grin. *Whatever you say, my troubled prince!* Troubled. Yes. And there she was, under the water. And I knew it was too late. I knew she was already gone.

And then I awoke. *The past is prologue*, I thought. Just that. And I couldn't remember who said it, though I was on the right track all the time.

I met mum for lunch. We went to the little café by the station, near where she lives so she didn't need to walk. 86 next week. I still can't believe it. 86. Where does it go? I'll be 50 next year, and I can't even begin to think what that means. Nothing, probably. Just another number.

I asked her what she wants to do. Karen had rung her and asked the same. She thought it would be nice for us all to go out for a meal. A chance to get together. A neighbour had told her about a pub where the food's good. She thought maybe we could all go there.

I can't remember the last time I was in a pub. I didn't drink in pubs much, anyway. Home alone - that was me. She doesn't know. Not all of it, anyway. The same with Karen. It wouldn't be easy, being with her. It never is. In a pub, too. Challenges.

"Whatever you want to do," I said. "It's your day. You choose."

"I think it will be nice," she said. She looked at the menu board by the counter, where everything was listed. "Now... what do you want to drink?"

Yesterday had been a better day. Seeing Carly. Talking always helps. And then the group afterwards. It was a good group. Seven of us - a nice size. A smaller group means it's more intimate. There's more chance for everyone to speak.

Molly and Lisa were there, and Max. And Geoffrey and Elaine. Max has had almost 2 years, but still struggles. As he says - he's had to retrain his brain. How do you cope when you're coping mechanism's been shot to shit by vodka? When your coping mechanism *is* vodka? I'm always a bit wary with him, too. He gets a bit spiky. Confrontational. I'm never entirely relaxed with him in the group. But we're all sick, so you have to make allowances - and he does speak a lot of sense. Lisa had a relapse a couple of weeks ago and is really struggling. Her family has cut her off. Her ex has the kids. She couldn't handle them. She's always going on about what a complete bastard he is, but I've heard people say he's okay. Try living with it and see what it does. Molly still drinks off and on. Days sober - a week sometimes. Then it's there again. It never goes. She's only 25. She has other problems, but most of us do. You wouldn't know it to look at her, but you can't go by looks. This is what people don't understand. *'You look so well'* - as if *'There's nothing wrong with you really, is there. It must be in your mind.'* Well, guess what? It fucking well is. *'Look at that Maserati GranCabrio over there. Christ, that looks fast. That must go like shit. Hang on... it's out of petrol. The plugs are missing. The gearbox is shot to fuck.'*

Geoffrey is the group's 'old timer'. He's been coming for years. I guess he's about 60, but it's hard to say. The drink has defined his face - shaped it and coloured it. Deep valleys run down to his chin and across his brow. His cheeks are like rock faces flecked with red lichen. He might have hung out with dad, back in the day. I've asked him, but he doesn't remember. He doesn't remember a lot of it. He usually comes up with Elaine because she has a car and she lives close by him. She used to be a solicitor, until she was disbarred. She was a functioning drunk for years. A bottle of vodka in the briefcase, down the back of the drawer. And then she stopped. Functioning. You can't outrun it. It always catches up in the end.

The other chap there was new. Early 30s, but hunched and thin. The drink had defined his face, too. He was on the ambulatory detox. It was like something inside him thrashing around to get out. I remember it myself. He kept his hands between his knees and looked at the floor, but his shoulders were shaking.

Maggie took the group, which pleased me. Tough Maggie. Plain-speaking Maggie. No nonsense Maggie. Don't try bullshitting a bullshitter Maggie. She's been there too, unlike most of the other workers. She has that extra qualification. The inside knowledge. She's been there and come back again to tell the tale, and set things straight.

"Good afternoon, everyone."
"Hello, Maggie."
She rubs her hands together vigorously, like her numbers have just come up.
"And how are we all today?"
Murmurs and nods.
"Thank you, Maggie," says Geoffrey. "Nice to see you, darlin'."
"Always a pleasure, Geoffrey," she says.
He chuckles.

She looks around at us all. She sees the new chap.

"I don't think we've met."

He looks up. "I'm Keith."

"Hello, Keith. I'm Maggie, as you've probably heard. I'm the group facilitator today. Is this your first group?"

"Yes."

"You're on the detox." It's an observation, not a question. "How's it going?"

"Not easy."

"I'm sure it's not. Getting near the end of the week."

"I think I'm over the hump."

"Well, let's hope so. Welcome, anyway. Shall we do the introductions?"

We say our names in turn.

"Can someone explain the rules for Keith, please?"

Geoffrey sits forward and clears his throat. "Group starts on time, Keith, so if you're late you may not be allowed in. You must be alcohol-free. You'll be breathalised if there's any doubt. No smoking, eating or drinking while the group's in session. No bringing drink into the group, either. Feel free to speak, but don't feel obliged to. You can just listen, which is just as important. Try to keep what you say to drinking, and the problems it's caused you. Once the group's started, if you leave you can't come back in. No being abusive to others, but be prepared for challenges. We challenge each other. As long as it's constructive, not aggressive."

Keith nods.

Geoffrey looks at Maggie. "Anything I've forgotten, Mag?"

With her thumb and finger, she mimes a phone call.

"Yes... I always forget that one. Switch off mobiles. And no using them during group."

Everyone immediately takes out their phone and checks it. Except Geoffrey, who doesn't have one. Except me, too.

"Thank you," says Maggie. She sits back in her chair and pushes up the sleeves of her jumper. She has forearms as thick as my legs. She sweeps her eyes around the room. "So... what are we discussing today?"

"Booze," Max quips.

A few low chuckles.

And then there's silence. Mostly, someone will start speaking straight away, but sometimes there's nothing. There's nothing now. 30 seconds. A minute. I glance at Lisa. She often kicks things off, and once she starts she keeps going. Not today, though. She just stares at her legs, stretched out in front of her, crossed at the ankles. Geoffrey clears his throat again. Seats creaking. Breathing. Human sounds. Elaine sits forward suddenly and wipes her hand across the front of her skirt, like she's brushing off ash or something. A siren sounds, way off on the bypass, then stops again. When it sounds again, it's much further away. Nothing.

"Cat got your tongues?" says Maggie.

I decide to mention about the knife and the bottle. I raise my head, but at the same time so does Keith. He looks at Maggie.

"Do I have to say that I'm an alcoholic?"

Maggie gives him one of her looks, like she's not sure what he's made of and is trying to weigh him up. Like she's waiting for him to answer his own question.

"You don't *have* to say anything, Keith, as Geoffrey said. You certainly don't have to say you're an alcoholic. It's not an AA meeting."

Keith nods. "Sorry."

"Don't apologise."

Max leans in. "Do you think you're an alcoholic, then?"

"I don't know. I mean, I know I'm having a detox and that..."

"Do you think that might be a clue?"

"Well... probably. But I don't know. I always drank normally before. It's just been the last year it got out of hand."

Max sits back and peers at him. "And why was that? What made it get out of hand, if you don't mind me asking?"

"I had a lot of stuff to deal with. Divorce, then my mum dying. Things were bad at work, too. Lots of stress. And I just started drinking more."

"And now you're going through a detox," said Max. "I hope you won't mind me saying, but we can all see how tough you're finding that."

"Right."

"So... do you think you might be sitting there, like you are now, if you'd just been drinking a bit too much?"

Keith looks down. Max can be intimidating, but it's probably a fair question.

Elaine breathes in sharply and everyone looks at her.

"It's the old question, isn't it," she says. "Definition and degree, I mean. We've probably all thought about it. When is it *too* much drinking? When is it *problem* drinking? When is it *alcoholism?* Is it all the same thing, anyway? And how much of it is just in your head?"

Keith is still for just a moment - a brief moment. "How'd you mean?"

"Well, I mean... someone who, say, drinks half a bottle of wine a day might not think they have a problem. It might not even occur to them. They might have done it for years without any ill effects. Half a bottle seems a piddling amount, anyway. A piss in the ocean. I used to have the best part of a bottle just to face work in the mornings. But add it up and that's still a lot of booze a week. Probably twice the healthy limits for men, which means three times for women. So, what does that mean? Is it too much? Is it problem drinking? Is it alcoholism? What is it?"

Maggie crosses one foot over the other and leans back in her chair. "I don't think that's too difficult a question, Elaine. There's no mystery about it. It comes down to, could they get through the day *without* that half-bottle of wine? If you took it away from them, would it affect them? Would they crave it? Would they get withdrawals, and so on? Find themselves thinking about it all the time? Obsessing? Or would they be able to say 'Okay, fine... I'll just switch to tea or Pepsi'? It's at that point that we start getting into the realms of addictive behaviour, problems, and so on."

"That's what I mean," says Keith. "If I feel like that, if I get the shakes and that, does that mean I'm an alcoholic?"

"I'd think it's a pretty good possibility, mate," says Max. "Wouldn't you? I mean, I don't know what you're like, but when I was drinking... well, that was it. All bets were off. I drank 'til I either blacked out or passed out, and then I woke up and did it again. There was no buggering about with half-bottles of wine, either. Christ, no."

Keith shakes his head. "See, I wasn't like that. I didn't drink like that."

Max is lighting up now. You can see it in his eyes, the way he sits. "But hang on a minute, mate. You're going through a detox. You're sitting there looking like you've just spent the morning drilling up the roads with a jackhammer. Sorry, I don't mean anything personal... but that must *suggest* something to you."

Geoffrey comes in. "Tolerance is a word we haven't heard yet. We all have different tolerances, Keith. What Elaine's saying. What Maggie's saying. And look at me. I used to start off the evening with four large whiskies before I went onto the pints. Ten pints a night. Every night. I did that for years. Your body gets used to it. It builds up a tolerance."

Max looks at him. "I don't know what that's got to do with anything, Geoffrey. What I'm trying to say is... if Keith's sitting there shaking and he's on a detox, what sort of a question does it become if you then say 'Am I an alcoholic?' I mean, perhaps a better question might be 'Am I in denial?'"

Keith's looking agitated now. I'm worried that he's going to get up and leave, but to his credit he sits there. "I still think it's a reasonable enough question to ask."

Maggie puts up her hands. I'm relieved about that. We can all see the way it's going.

"People... people. Can we come back to the point I was trying to make about alcohol use... i.e., can you get through the day? Can you take it or leave it? Geoffrey's point about tolerance is a good one because yes, we *do* build up tolerances. It's whether we can maintain a level, or whether we then start to increase it, rack it up further, so the half-bottle becomes a full one, then two, etcetera."

"That's what I meant, Maggie," says Geoffrey. "Thank you, darlin'."

Max is annoyed, but keeps it in. He sits back in his chair and looks up at the ceiling, like he's been deflated.

Maggie takes us all in again with her eyes. "The bottom line, anyway, in all of this is - none of us are here in this room today for the fun of it. Even I'm only here for the pay."

A ripple. Smiles. Just what's needed.

"On that level, it doesn't really matter what the quantity is that we drink, or used to drink, or the type of drink. Nor is it really about what we might choose to call ourselves - though I'll be after any of you who refers to themselves as a pisshead." She chops the air with her hands. "If alcohol has become a problem for us, if it's having a major effect on our lives or the lives of those around us, if it's at all detrimental to us in any way... then, if we don't want to get ill or die or lose our families and jobs, we need to do something about it. And so..." She opens her hands then - *da-da* - the end of the trick. "Here we all are."

There's a silent pause. We've probably all got a point to make, but what she's said is the main one.

Keith stirs again. "So after that... after we've done something about it... then what?"

"What do you mean?" says Elaine.

"Once we're better, I mean. When we've recovered. What then? I mean, I'd like to think that I can go back to... drinking normally again. Like I used to."

Max puts his head in his hands. We've all heard it before.

Keith goes on. "I just don't want to think about going through the rest of my life not drinking. I want to be able to go back to it and be alright with it. Not now. But when things are alright again in my life, and I'm over it."

"I don't believe I'm hearing this," says Max. "I'm sorry, Keith, but you're talking about this like it's a cold, or a sore throat. What we're talking about is more like cancer, mate. It's a simple as that."

Keith's got the fire in his eyes. Max does that.

"So... tell me why I was drinking normally before, then."

Max throws up his hands. "I don't know, Keith. You tell me."

Lisa comes in. "Keith, you know... I can tell you, if I had a fiver - a quid, even - for the number of times I've tried to go back to normal drinking, I wouldn't have to worry about working again. What the *fuck* is normal drinking, anyway, if you'll excuse my Anglo-Saxon. A glass of wine with dinner, then a cup of tea afterwards? That doesn't make any sense to me at all. Why the hell would I ever want to drink like that?"

Keith looks like he might just shake himself to bits. Or explode.

Molly speaks. She doesn't often. But it's good to hear some soothing tones.

"Keith, listen. I think what people are trying to say is... we don't know if you're an alcoholic or not. Perhaps it doesn't matter. The thing is, as has been said... you're on a detox, you're having physical withdrawals, you're finding it a struggle. Clearly, drink has become a problem for you now, even if it never was before. There are no hard and fast rules about this. Not every problem drinker started in their teens and has never stopped. Some started later in life. I did."

"Me too, mate," I say.

"The point is," she goes on, "it's a problem for me. I know I can never drink normally. And I know my drinking will wreck my health eventually, even if I do look well now, as people always tell me. Maybe you'll be different. But do you really want to take the risk of trying it again to find out?"

Keith puts his head down towards his knees and runs his hand through his hair. When he looks up again, there are tears in his eyes. Tears of frustration.

"I just don't want to think of going through the rest of my life without it," he says. "I used to enjoy it. I still want to enjoy it."

That prompts me again. "I find it helpful to think about it positively instead of negatively, Keith. Instead of thinking 'I *can't* drink ever again', try thinking, 'I don't *need* to drink ever again.'"

He looks at me like I've simply not been listening.

"But I *don't* need to drink. I *want* to drink."

We look at him. Everyone's got something to say. Everyone's trying to find a way of saying it. Everyone's been there, too.

Lisa, who's sitting next to Keith, lays her hand gently on his arm.

"I think you might have to look at your wants and needs, Keith, and decide what they really are. It's what I struggle with, too. My last binge was two weeks ago. I drank then because I *wanted* to. But it pretty soon became *needed* to. Once I'd started, once it was inside me... it's like a poison. It takes you over. It's what it's done to you already, and it'll do it again, believe me. It might be alright while things are okay in your life. But how long do things stay okay in your life? If things go arse up again, and you're still drinking, what are you going to do?"

There's silence for a moment as Keith thinks on that.

And so do I. It's a question I've often asked myself. Can I manage it now? Is it alright? Is it worth the risk? Christ knows. And I can see where Keith's coming from. All the way.

"It's like grieving, Keith," says Geoffrey. "Part of what you're feeling. Grieving 'cos you're losing a friend. That's how it felt for me."

"Not for me," says Max, sitting up. "All it was was a fucking relief. It was like killing this bloody monster that had been on my back for years. I didn't grieve at all."

"I'd grieve if it ever came back," says Elaine. "And it's not dead. It's never dead. It's always lurking there, waiting for you to let it in."

Molly puts her hand up to the side of her face. She looks incredibly sad. "Well... all I can say is... *I* grieve."

Everyone looks at her. And I know what she's going to say. I just know it. I'm right there with her.

"I grieve. Because I know that alcohol is a terrible thing for me. It'll wreck my health. But without it... life feels..." She wipes her eye. I can see the tremor in her hand. "...it just feels... so *empty*. Meaningless. And alcohol... alcohol takes that away."

"But does it?" says Maggie. "Are you sure about that?"

"Yes, I am," says Molly. "I'm sure because I've had periods of sobriety. And when I've been sober, life has just been... *unbearable*."

Max leans towards her, elbows on his knees. I think he's going to go into one again, but he keeps it low. "But how long have you given it, Molly? What's been your longest period of sobriety?"

"Four months once."

"And it didn't get any better?"

She takes a tissue from her sleeve and wipes her nose.

"No, it didn't. It just got worse. And that's what people don't understand. For some of us, it doesn't make life better to give up. It makes it worse, if anything."

Max nods his head thoughtfully. "I just wonder if perhaps four months wasn't long enough to find out. I mean, I've been two years now. I still get bad days with depression and that - but they're not anywhere near as bad as they were. And it took me a while before I started to realise that, actually, life isn't so bad - once I'd learned to deal with the bad stuff without alcohol, which wasn't easy."

"Please, Max... it's not that I didn't try hard enough."

"I'm not saying you didn't."

"It sounded a bit like it. You have to remember that I have other issues. And sometimes... sometimes just stopping drinking doesn't solve them. I can't explain what it's like to wake up every day and feel... *empty*."

"You don't need to, Molly," I say. "I know how it feels."

Max turns to me. "But you must be coming up for a year, Tom. How have *you* managed?"

How? How have I managed?

"I don't know," I say.

And I don't. Not really.

"I just have. But I know what Molly means."

She smiles at me. Yes... I know.

"I think," says Maggie, "the point about grieving is valid. Yes, for many, it's casting off a burden. But it's also about having to live without something that, for whatever reason, you've always turned to when you felt there was nothing else."

"That's what I mean," says Keith. "That's why I can't even begin to think yet about how I'll do it."

"Or even if you *want* to," says Elaine. "Maybe it just hasn't done enough damage yet. I hope it doesn't. For me, it took losing my licence to practice law, losing my husband, losing my home... and then almost losing my life. Waking up in hospital one day with tubes coming out of me and skin the colour of parchment. Even *that* wasn't quite the end of it."

Keith nods - staring at nothing.

"I just... I just don't know if I can go through the rest of my life without drinking again. That's all."

"Well," says Lisa. "There's a sure-fire way to find out. In the end, it's up to you. No one can stop you. It's your choice. It's all about that, after all. Choice."

Choice. Yes. That's the nub of it. What it's all about.

And what do I want to drink? What do I *choose* to drink?

"I think I'll have a hot chocolate. What about you?"

"I think I'll have the same," mum said.

And the waitress - the one from the gym, who's much too young - was suddenly there with her pad, smiling at me. Waiting.

~

Sunday

I went to the meeting again last night. The candlelit one. It's the only one where I can feel relaxed now. There aren't any evangelists there. No Big Book bashers. No one to tell me that I won't stay sober if I don't get a sponsor and get on the programme, start doing the 12 Steps. It's the moderate wing. Non-conformists. Struggling recidivists. No one judging or shaking their head. No one lecturing. Just hugs, handshakes, chit-chat. Tea and biscuits. Candles. Warmth. Human warmth, on a damp, misty night in a church hall.

I took the camper over. I hadn't used it since the summer, but it started first go. I can't really afford to run it now, and I should have sold it, but it's come in useful. Weekend nights, when the noise invades, and my head's filling up and I can feel it coming, I grab my pillow and duvet and go. I get out and away - along to the park or up the hill. As far as a puddle of diesel will take me. Find a side road. Shut it out. Hide.

That's why I took it last night. And that's what I did. After the meeting, I drove out to Eastgate and got some chips. Then I turned down a back street and pulled up in a spot where the street light was out. I sat in the shadows and ate my chips, listening to the tick of the engine cooling. Smells of hot vinegar, cooking oil, old leather, damp. Smells of an old campervan on a Saturday night on the coast.

Childhood smells.

I bought it after the divorce, and lived in it for a couple of months until I got the bedsit. I didn't have much to bring with me. A couple of bookcases, a fridge, an armchair, a computer, books, the few small boxes that were all that remained of a shared life. I put it in storage until I found the bedsit. Mum said I could sleep on her sofa, but I didn't want it. I wanted to be alone. The weather was warm anyway. I drove to different places each night, drank until I passed out, somehow got up for work next day. It had been my home. It had a gas hob and a fridge. A fold-down bed. A sink. All I needed. I didn't want to lose it. But it was coming up. Tax and insurance in December,

MOT in January. It all went together. The brakes were squealing. Two tyres were low. The rust was bad on the passenger side - around the door and the wheel arches. I couldn't use the side door because of it. I could sell the Honda - but who wants a motorcycle in the winter? It still wouldn't be enough, anyway. Nowhere near. Something would happen. Something had to. There wasn't much choice about that.

Carly had said about managing things. Taking time out. Keeping it in the day. It's like the AA thing: don't project.

But I can't just disregard the future. Some things have to be planned for. Some things can't be ignored, because they're just *there*. Waiting. It's not a void I'm moving into. It's what happens next.

Keep it in the day.

It might be your last, anyway.

That was dad's philosophy. *'Live for today, boy, 'cos it might be your last.'* And that's what he did. The last night I saw him, there in the hospital, in the side room, on his own, wheezing like a bellows, his chest heaving, his body wracked, his last night alive. *'I'm wishing my life away, son.'* Finished with it now. This is the day. There's no tomorrow. His head against the pillow there - the rise and fall of his breathing, his desperate breathing. Like he was running. Trying to catch it - to get there quicker. His last breaths in that room in the hospital, 70 miles and 78 years from the place he was born in - a single road, looping off into the past like a tape, the miles and miles, through all those places, through all those things that had brought him to here. To this. The end of it.

I finished my chips, put up the blinds, closed the curtains. I found the plastic cider flagon I kept in the back and had a piss. Cider it looked like. All piss. I made up the bed. I took off my jacket and trainers, and got in. It was just after 10. The bed isn't long enough for me, so I had to lay crouched. Foetal. I lay still and listened to the night. The distant static of traffic on the A road. An alarm going, somewhere far off, rising and fading in the shifting wind. The occasional car passing - the van rocking gently in the wake. A voice calling out, once.

I closed my eyes. The candlelit faces at the meeting. The warm glow. I sit on the edge of it, listening. A part - but apart.

The night settles in. And the voice again, calling. Crying out. Crying out in the night. Calling...

'Hello, pretty baby...'

It's sunny and warm, with a breeze as gentle as mother's breath. Outside the house. The pram creaks on its springs as he rocks in it, tugging at the reins. Birds there, on the pavement, pecking at the pieces of rusk he's thrown out. He watches them as they flap and jump - their beaks pecking and jabbing, jabbing and pecking and jabbing...

'Hello, my pretty...'

The birds erupt. The sound is enormous. All of the world. The woman, coming closer, looking down at him - her face, the scarf on her head. Like hers. Not her, though. Dark eyes. Funny skin. Marks on her teeth. Her huge head and her eyes.

'Who are you, my pretty darling?'

She reaches down and touches the straps, pulls at the buckle. The smell of her breath. The cry building up inside him, swelling up, ready to burst. The fingers on the straps, on the buckles. The pram rocking on its springs. The strap giving...

...and then she's turning. Someone is there, coming out of the door at her, shouting. She turns away. The pattern on the back of her scarf. Like a face. Another face.

The scream coming out of him. Bursting out of him.

The primal sound.

The sound of fear in the night.

Birds again.

Bigger birds. In the park. By the river.

'See the gulls, Tommy.'

'Goes.'

He giggles as they flutter and babble around him. She looks in the pram while he stands there, the birds all around, pecking and squabbling.

'Greedy gulls,' she says.

' 'reedy goes.'

She takes his hand as she pushes the pram towards the railings. The river out there. The boats. The big bridge there. The cars going over. The bus going over, the people inside. The river flowing under. The sun flashing on it. She pushes the pram along the railings. The river flicks between them... flick - flick - flick...

She stops and leans into the pram. She makes a sound. A sound he remembers. She turns to him. She does up the top button on his coat.

'Shall we go home and get Daddy's dinner, then?'

'Da-ee!'

She smiles again, her teeth bright behind her lips. She kisses his cheek.

'That's right. Tommy, Karen and mummy go home and see Daddy. And get Michael from school.'

' 'ichael.'

'That's right. Get Michael. Then go home to dinner.'

She licks her handkerchief and wipes her lipstick from his face, and he squirms.

She takes his hand again and pushes the pram towards the gate. He looks back to catch a last glimpse of the river. The river, sparkling in the sun.

The heat of the fire in the late afternoon, flashing on all the shiny surfaces. She sits there next to him, on the sofa, sewing a button on a shirt. Michael at the table with his plastic soldiers, his feet swinging under his chair. Karen in her cot in the corner.

The snap of the fire. The ashes dropping through. The tug of the cotton as she sews. Her arm working. The shadows hulking around the walls. Her face in the firelight. The clock ticking on the mantelpiece.

She puts down the shirt and gets up. She checks in the cot. She touches something. She slips out to the kitchen.

The key in the lock. The scrape of the door. The bang as it shuts. The steps coming up. Then he's in the room. He's *filling the room. The smell on his clothes. Hay. The winter air. Cigarettes.*

He touches the boys' heads. He looks in the cot. He sits by the fire and takes off his boots. He pokes the fire. The coal breaks open and orange stars fly up the chimney. He sits back and rubs his eyes - rubs them hard, digging his fingers in. He takes out a cigarette and lights it, and throws the match onto the flames. He looks at the boy sitting there. He touches his cheek. Then he gets up and leaves the room.

From the kitchen, the rat-tat-tat of a spoon on a plate.

The rat-tat-tat of their words...

Darkness. Empty darkness. The orange glow at the edge of the curtains. The sound of singing from the pub. Loud voices, late in the dark out there. A whistle. A whoop. Doors slamming. A car starting up and driving off. Gear changes fading off into the night. A window dropping shut.

The key in the door. The steps in the hall. The door opening slowly, quietly. Him standing in the doorway in the light from upstairs, looking in - a dark shape, cut from the light. The smells. The sour smells and the sweet smells.

A whisper. 'God bless, boys.'

The door closes and he's gone again. The darkness again. The night again.

Later, the voices. Upstairs, the voices.

The loud, angry voices...

The bike shed. The corner. The faces crowding. Grinning. The hand at the neck.

'Where'd you think you were going, you cunt?'

'Fuckin' 'it 'im.'

Tightening.

'Where's that fuckin' money you owe me?'

'Just fuckin' 'it 'im, Tel.'

Tighter.

'You better fuckin' bring it tomorrow.'

' 'it the cunt, Tel. Rip 'is fuckin' trousers off.'

'I want my fuckin' money, Seagrave, you cunt.'
'Blakey's comin'. Fuckin' do it.'
Done.

I woke early. For a moment, I didn't know where I was. I sat up sharp. My heart was pounding so hard it sounded like someone knocking. And then I saw the light at the edges. The shapes emerging. The head rest. The steering wheel. The curve of the dashboard.

I lifted a curtain. The window was steamed up. There was light in the sky, but just. I checked my watch. 6:45. I pulled on my trainers, then opened the curtains and took down the blinds. The street was empty and quiet. I could see the sun glinting on a skylight further along, and the sky looked clear. I folded up the bed. Then I started the engine and got going.

I drove back on the A road, past mist-shrouded fields. The day was coming, and looking fine. The sun flashed white in my mirror, and I switched it up. At home, I ate breakfast as I sat at the window. The tide was high, and cars were arriving at the jetty, boats in tow. Men in waders were loading rods, checking tackle, standing in small groups smoking and chatting. A day out there, on a rippling sea the colour of ancient slates.

Remembrance Day.

A day to remember.

A day. Another day.

~

Monday

I see the world in fragments - like pieces of a puzzle I fit together. The sky, the sea, the earth. The places I go. The faces of the people. Fragments. Some days they come together, they fit in place, they fix. The picture is there and whole. Some days.

Some days, the fragments are all I have. The bits of the day, like a shattered window. I can see through to the other side, to what's there, but the image is fractured. I try to reach through it, but it catches against me, tears through my clothing, lacerates my skin. Or a shattered mirror. I see myself in pieces. The pieces of me. Smashed.

I see life in the same way, mostly. Fragments. What has been, what will be, what is. What has been has brought me to what is. What will be is where I will go from what is, guided by what has been. Between moving away and moving towards is where I am. In the day. I have this day. I am alive today, and have one opportunity to live it. The challenge it gives me is in finding a way to accept what has been, to take what I need from it and let the rest go, to endure. And each day that passes is another to add to those I have lived and cannot change. I cannot ever change what is past. All I can do is interpret it. Use it to work out a way to live. A way to be. To continue to be.

Fragments...

A gull settles on the lamp post opposite my window. I pick up my toast crust and throw it out of the window, where it lands on the roof projection below. The gull sees it and flies down to get it. As the gull lands, a black cat appears on the balustrade, ready to pounce. The gull sees the cat and flies off again. The cat jumps down and sniffs at my toast crust, looks up, looks around, sniffs the crust again, licks it.

A young woman walks along the promenade. Well-dressed. Plaid jacket and skirt, scarf, maroon woollen tights, high-heeled shoes. She stops by the bench opposite my window, where an old man is sitting, smoking, his dog waiting by, looking at him. She speaks to the man, then crouches to the dog. She runs her hands over its head and through its fur. The dog stands, wagging its tail. It tries to lick the woman's face. She straightens again and strokes its head. She speaks to the man and he replies. She continues to stroke the dog's head. The man continues to smoke. They speak. I turn from the window for just a few seconds. When I look back, the bench is empty. The promenade is empty. Just the gull there.

The pier head shows through the mist like a phantom ship. Marooned out there - dark, derelict, disconnected. A place which is no place. Form without content. A part, but apart. Even as I watch, it vanishes - lost in the ash-grey swirl of the day.

Those among us who are not among us. Things which are there, but not.

After work this morning, I went for a haircut. I hadn't been for months, and I wanted to look smart for the inquest. It was curling up from my neck and tufting out around my ears. A parting had formed - the start of a quiff, like dad had. It needed brushing again. I keep trying it long, like I used to have it when I was younger. But it never lasts. Years ago, it looked good that way. Now, it makes me look ragged and untidy. It makes me look older. It makes me look *old*. I don't enjoy getting it cut, though. In the spotlight, unable to move, with a stranger right there, touching my head. I find it too intimate. It leaves me exposed.

I sit in the chair and hold my breath, looking at my face as she snips away, reframing it. The tiny tucks at the corners of my eyes. The lines that run from the sides of my nose to the corners of my lips, looking deeper in the slanting light from the window. The jowls beginning - like a pattern beneath that was starting to emerge, to redefine. The hair falls down my front, soft and grey as ashes - tumbling, settling. Something of me that is no longer me. Dust and ashes.

The face. His face. The curve of the brows, the shape of the nose, the eyes. Even the ears - one sticking out more than the other. A feature we all shared - Karen, Michael. Even Karen's children have it. Chris and Adam. Natalie. I never really noticed it until the first time I had my hair cut really short. Like it was cupped. I checked all the photographs to make sure. All of mine and all of theirs. There it was - like a cup handle. Like a shell, opened up.

Observing the sounds of the world.

"Day off today?"

The questions. I dread the questions. If I give the wrong answer, will she drive the scissors into my neck?

"Yes."

"Not very nice, is it. Cold."

"It is, yes."

I feel the need to say something, but I never know what. I'm always at a disadvantage in this situation. I don't do this kind of thing.

The pieces keep falling, like feathers.

The phone starts ringing. The other young woman, sitting behind me, doesn't move. She sits with her magazine. There's no one else.

"Sorry... excuse me a minute."

She goes off to answer the phone. Someone for an appointment.

"I'll just get the diary."

I bring up my hand from under the cape and take some of the hair in my fingers. So fine. I rub it between my fingers. It feels like grains of salt. I hold up my fingers and watch it fall in silver scintillas, gently settling in the folds of the cape. His was the same. He was white at 50 - his hair like tufts of cotton, except for the orange streak from the cigarettes. The orange in his hair. The orange on his fingers. On the ashtrays, the window ledges, the basin rims. The marks in the paintwork. The marks on his lips. The tang of it, wherever he went, whenever he was near. In his clothes, on his breath, in his rooms, in his hair. In his laugh. In his cough. In his voice.

"Sorry about that."

"That's alright."

She's noticed what I was doing.

"It's a lovely colour, your hair."

I look at her in the mirror. She looks at me in the mirror. We look at each other by looking away from each other.

"Grey?"

"Yes... but it's a lovely shade. And you've got this dark band at the back. It's really black. It must have been your natural colour."

She picks up a hand mirror and holds it up to the back of my head.

"See?"

I see.

"Yes. It was my natural colour."

"It, like, fades into it. Very grey. Then dark grey. Then black."

"It used to be further up."

"That's how it goes. It's working its way down. In a few more years, it'll be completely gone."

"I suppose so."

She carries on snipping away, her eyes tightly focussed. She has a nice face. Round and well-featured. A small nose and hazel eyes. Pale lips. Smile lines. About 30. She glances at me in the mirror and I shift my eyes back to me. She pushes her fingers into the hair on the top of my head and pulls it up, like she's kneading it. It feels like a playful thing. Like a parent would do. Or a lover. She combs up a length and starts to snip it. The soldiers, all in a row, cut down. Watch them go. Snips of my hair cling to the front of her jumper, where it rises.

"Did you start going grey young?"

"Yes. 19 or 20. I dyed it for years."

"Don't dye this, will you."

"I won't."

"It never looks right on older men."

126

I raise my eyebrows. She sees it.

"On any man, really. It's always obvious."

"I know what you mean."

"All those celebrities. Brad Pitt. Ronnie Wood. And Bono and that. When their hair's in the light, you can see it."

"Right. Tom Cruise."

"Oh God, Tom Cruise. But who cares with him. I wouldn't."

"They don't all do it. George Clooney. Richard Gere."

"Oh no. Grey suits them. It suits men. Men more than women."

She picks up her clippers and begins to trim my sideburns.

"At least you've got plenty of it. You'll never be without it now. My boyfriend's only 27 and it's nearly all gone from the top of his head."

"Saves having to brush and comb it."

"He'd sooner have it back. Even if it was grey."

She switches off the clippers and picks up the mirror again.

"How's that?"

"Lovely. Thank you."

I always say that, however it looks.

"Anything on it?"

"No thanks."

She brushes down my face and neck, then removes the cape. My hair is in piles on the white-tiled floor. Grey, with some black. When I was a kid, mum had some grey squirrel-skin gloves dad had bought her once for a birthday present. I used to take them out of her drawer and put them on, and pretend to be a bear with huge furry paws. I loved the feel of them - soft and fine. I used to run them over my face, smelling her perfume in them. I loved the colour of them. Grey, with black. Grey, fading into black.

I put on my jacket and go to the till. She looks different. Smaller.

"That's nine pounds fifty, please."

I give her a tenner.

"Keep the change."

"Thank you very much. You take care now."

"I will. You too."

"Have a good day."

"And you."

"See you soon."

"Bye."

Back home, I take down his photograph. The hair dark then. Regulation length. Greased and neatly parted, with the quiff. He looks like Clark Gable, without the moustache. 18 or 19. In full dress uniform, his sword at his side, his parade helmet tucked in the crook of his arm. A fine-looking man. You can see what she saw in him. Yes, you can. Him as he was. Knightsbridge Barracks. 1944, thereabouts. The country still at war.

At 10.30 yesterday morning, they came along the seafront and went past on their way to the memorial in the park. The Sea Cadets band, with their drums and bugles and bell lyres. Marching with them, the Army Cadets, the Sea Cadets, the ATC. And then came the veterans. Ranks and files, marching in time, arms swinging in unison. Caps and badges and berets. Medals and buttons. Jackets and boots. And the poppies. A parade of poppies - the splotches of red, like blood stains or bullet wounds.

Remembrance Day.

Off they marched, and the drumbeats faded.

Each day is a remembrance. Each day, I remember.

There is no forgetting. Just passing on. The drumbeats rising. The remembrance coming. The beats of it, loud and heavy.

Returning...

~

GHOST TRAIN
a tale

They're still a long walk from the common when they first hear it - the distant music, jangling through the evening air like the sound of an approaching band. He is leading the way, tugging at his older brother's hand like a dog on a scent. In his other hand, he feels the coins - the hard, hot shape of them pressing into his palm like a promise. Like the key to the secret of the excitement ahead. Cars are passing them, heading that way. He thinks of all those people going, getting there first, getting on the rides ahead of them, stealing their fun, using it all up before they arrive. He pulls harder at his brother's hand.

"Come on, Michael. I want to get there. I want to get there."

He feels the older boy pulling back. Slowing. Teasing. He tries to wriggle out of the grasp, but it's too strong.

"Don't! Come one."

They begin to move faster.

"What do you want to go on first?"

"The bumper cars. And the Ghost Train."

"You can't go on them both at the same time, nitwit."

"I want to go on the Ghost Train."

Michael pulls back again. He strains against it, but Michael's hand is too tight and too strong.

"Let me go!"

"When we get there. Remember what dad said."

Michael slows, laughing each time his brother tries to pull free.

"Please stop it, Michael. I want to get there."

Then Michael stops and holds onto a lamp post. He squeezes the small hand harder, until he knows the scream is coming. Then he starts running, pulling his brother behind him, running so fast that the smaller boy can hardly keep up. He slows to allow it, then spurts again.

"Stop it! I'll tell dad!"

"Yah! Cry baby! I thought you wanted to get there. Come on, or we'll be late and miss it all."

Michael slows for his brother and they run together, side by side, until they reach the pub on the corner. The noise is much louder now - they're almost close enough to see. The jingling and clanging and whooping. And the music. The magical music. They turn the corner and cross the road between some parked cars, and onto the common, and there it is, over in the farthest corner, bright and bustling in the early evening - like a rollicking pirate galleon on a rough and tussocky sea of green. He slips his hand free at last and the two of them run, seeing the spectacle build before them - the shapes and colours, the spinning and flashing and screaming, the figures moving across the lights like imps dancing around a blaze. The hum of the generators. The cables curling like snakes in the grass. The roar of the machines. And then finally they're over the threshold, and the energy grabs them and pulls them in, into the vortex. The jolts and blurs and voices and eyes. The eyes, watching them. Beckoning them.

"Give it a go, boys. Three goes a tanner."

They stop at the Rifle Range and Michael hands over some change.

"Watch this."

He cracks open a rifle and slips in a pellet. He aims and fires.

"Bullseye!"

He does it again - one after the other. The man takes it down and looks at it. There is one big hole, dead centre.

"You should be in the army, lad."

"I'm going to. I'm in the cadets."

"They won't stand a chance against you!"

The man picks up a bag and hands it across, giving Michael the target as well. Michael holds up the bag. A goldfish - a sliver of orange in silvery water, circling - its body lucid and incandescent against the light.

"What shall we call it, Michael?"

"Goldie. I'm calling it Goldie."

He stares at it - its eyes like rivets, its fins as fine as tissue paper.

"Can we go on the Ghost Train now?"

"What?"

"Please."

Michael hands him the bag.

"Hold him a minute. There's something else I want to do first."

They move across the neon-gilded grass - the stalls blazing like a Christmas grate - towards the Dive Bomber.

"I'm not going on that, Michael."

"Why not?"

"I don't want to go on that. I don't like it."

"You've never been on it."

"I don't like it. I want to go on the Ghost Train."

"Well, I want to go on it."

"Can't we go on the Ghost Train first?"

"No. I want to go on this. If you don't want to come, you'll have to wait for me."

Michael grabs his brother's hand.

"Come and wait by the ticket office, where they can keep an eye on you."

They go to the booth. The ride has just stopped and the people are getting off. Some of them are laughing. Some of them look sick. Michael gives his money to the man, then turns to his brother.

"You just stay right there and watch, alright? I won't be long."

He stands there, holding the bag with the little fish, watching as his brother steps up on the platform and goes over to the capsule. He turns and calls back.

"Remember, just stay there, alright? Don't move. I'll only be a few minutes. Then we can go on the Ghost Train."

"Alright."

Michael gets in the capsule with some other people. Then a man closes the door on them. The whole thing turns slowly until the other capsule is on the platform. He tries to look up to

131

*see Michael, but can't.   He looks again at the goldfish,
swimming to and fro in the bag, bubbles popping from its mouth
as it goes.   The Dive Bomber is full now and starts to turn, very
slowly at first.   Somebody screams.   Then there are more
screams as it turns faster.   He can hear the swoop of each turn it
makes.*

*He looks away, across the crowded grass to the Ghost
Train.   He sees a car move along towards the doors.   They look
like the old shutter doors in the western films that dad's always
watching.   They swing inwards as the car as it goes in, and
beyond it there's just darkness.   He hears the screams of the
passengers as the car rattles its way through the innards.   He
looks back at the Dive Bomber, which is going much faster now
- so fast that it makes him dizzy to watch it.   He looks away
again, then takes a couple of steps towards the Ghost Train.   It
draws him - the lurid pictures, picked out in lights: a skeleton in
an open coffin, a dark hooded figure holding up a claw, huge
bats with Dracula teeth, a broken skull with an eye dangling
from its socket.   A ghost voice whirrs and rises inside the thing,
like a police car siren.   He steps over closer, wondering how
frightening it could be in there, wondering if the people will ever
come out.   What if it swallowed them up, and they were trapped
forever in there in the haunted darkness?*

*He looks at the people milling around near the ride - the
loud teenagers, the kissing couples, the kids and sisters and
uncles and dads.   He thinks it will be alright to stand with them -
to wait with them until Michael comes back.   There's a man
standing by the ticket booth, smiling at him.   A smart-looking
man in a hat.   An old man.   Older than dad.   Not as old as Mr
Sewell next door (the one Michael calls Mr Sewage because of
his smell), but almost.   He looks at the man shyly, then back at
the Dive Bomber.   It's really going now, the passengers
screaming - though not as loudly as the ones in the Ghost Train.*

*The man has his hand up - waving.   Waving at him.
Smiling and waving.   He looks at the empty car there, waiting.
He steps closer, clutching the bag tighter in his hand.   Then he
looks at the man again.   He thinks he knows him from*

somewhere, but he doesn't know where. Maybe one of dad's friends in the pub - one of the men who sat in huddles at the bar when dad was there, in their caps and coats, with their pints and cigarettes, talking in loud, cackling voices, laughing at one of dad's jokes, while he stood in the doorway with a bottle of Pepsi and a packet of crisps - outside looking in. Yes... he was one of those men, he was sure. His hat and trousers, and his smart brown coat with the white fluffy collar, and the buttoned-up shirt with a tie. There's a badge on the coat, too - small and round, with a stripey design - like dad's one from his army days, on the case he keeps his darts in.

The man keeps smiling as he steps closer. He wants to look at the badge to see if it's the same. The man stops waving and holds out his hand, as if to touch his shoulder - like dad does sometimes, when he comes home. The car is still there empty, waiting. He looks back at the Dive Bomber. It's turning so fast it looks like it will crash. He feels the man's hand on his shoulder.

"Do you want to go on the Ghost Train, son? I'm going on it. But they won't let me on on my own."

He looks up at the face. His nose is large and red, like a clown's. He has a moustache, and tiny grey tufts of hair are poking out from under his hat. He looks very hot because he is sweating.

"Are you scared of it, then?" he asks the man.

The man's grip tightens on his shoulder.

"Not really. But they won't let people go on on their own."

"Can't your wife go with you?"

The man looks sad all of a sudden.

"She didn't want to come with me. She doesn't like funfairs. But I always like coming here. Don't you like it here?"

"Yes."

"It's fun, isn't it."

The man smiles again.

"I'll tell you what... if you come on the Ghost Train with me, I'll pay for you."

He moves back a step, though the man's hand remains on his shoulder.

"I have to wait for my brother."

The man looks up and around.

"Where's your brother?"

"He's on the Dive Bomber."

The man looks across. He looks, too. The machine is still moving very fast.

"He'll be a long time on there yet. It goes on for ages."

He looks back at the man again.

"Your brother won't mind. You can come on with me and I'll look after you. And when it's finished, your brother will be here waiting."

He looks at the man, then at the empty car.

"Come on. I'll pay. It won't take long."

Before he even knows what's happening, he's sitting in the car while the man hands some change to someone on the boardwalk. Then the man is there beside him and the car is moving, rocking, turning, swinging through the doors and away from the light.

At first, all he notices is the darkness, spiked with the odd splinter of light as the car rattles past cracks in the walls of the tunnel. After a few moments, the car starts to climb, and a red light suddenly flashes on, revealing a hooded figure with a skeleton's head. He shrinks down in the seat as they pass the figure, which wails at them as they go. He feels the man's weight against him. He feels the man's hand on his leg.

"That was scary," the man shouts. "I didn't like that."

In the glow of the light, he can see the outline of the man. He feels the hand moving up his leg, getting higher. He tries to move, but the man's too heavy against him.

"Don't worry. It's alright."

The car reaches the top of the climb and swings around sharply, and he feels the full weight of the man's body again. A siren whirrs close by, followed by a loud cackle of laughter. Another red light flashes on and off and a body looms out of a gap in the wall - one hand holding the severed head, all bloody, one eye missing, a stump of bone sticking out of the neck.

The man is using both hands now.

The light goes out and it's dark again, and the car swings along another gallery where flickering lights show strange creatures dangling from above, and a wailing spook with blood-dripping fangs and glowing eyes. He tries to push the man away, but he's too strong and heavy. The man grabs his head and pulls it down, down to his lap. He feels something there, in the man's lap.

"Put it in your mouth," the man shouts.

It hurts to struggle. He wants to scream, but the thing is there, against his mouth. The man is shouting at him - pushing his head.

"PUT IT IN! PUT IT IN YOUR MOUTH!"

He feels something on his face. Something warm and sticky, like snot. He tries to wipe it away. The man is screaming at him. He sounds like he's dying. He sounds like a ghost.

The car turns another corner and starts to go down, and the man lets go of him. He feels the weight lift, feels himself coming free. Then there's a hand at his face. The man is wiping his face with something. A handkerchief or something. Like she does, when his face is grubby.

"You keep your mouth shut, alright?" the man shouts, right next to his ear. "If you tell anyone, I'll come and get you. I'll rip your guts out. Do you hear me? I'll kill you."

The doors crash open and they're out in the noise and bustle and blare of the night again. The car rattles to a stop. His eyes are closed. When he opens them, the man is gone. Off in the crowd. Vanished. He stands up and steps out onto the boardwalk, and sees the people. The faces there, closing in and moving away, bustling past as if he's not there. Like he doesn't exist. Clamouring around him, like figures in a dream - bending, distorting, massing together and coming apart.

And then, all of a sudden, they're turning towards him. Looking at him. Their strange faces. Their questioning eyes.

Their laughter. He feels the tears coming, sees the faces turn to fragments of light. Then a hand grips his arm again and he yells.

"Where the hell have you been? What did I say to you?"

His legs buckle. The tears erupt from him.

"What's the matter with you? For Christ's sake, tell me what's the matter. What did I tell you to do?"

"The man," is all he can say.

"What man? What are you talking about?" Michael's holding him like the man was, digging his hand into his shoulder, pulling him.

"The man..."

Michael keeps holding him - by both shoulders now. Holding him up as his legs go weak. Shouting.

"Ah, look what you've done..."

He feels the wetness on his trousers. He looks down at them. The stain has spread down his legs. His trousers are soaked. He looks at the bag, still clutched in his hand. But it's alright. The fish is still there, darting around, its eyes agog, its mouth opening and closing, opening and closing. The bubbles coming out. The people are closing in around him. Their faces everywhere, looking. Their blank eyes looking at him. Their legs.

"You dirty bastard."

Michael pulls him up, drags him back to his feet.

"Wait 'til dad finds out about this. Just you wait."

~

Tuesday

Numb. Empty and numb. There's no other way to describe it.

People say '*You must be able to say why you feel the way you feel.*'

Why *must* I? I can't.

'*Do you feel sad, upset, unfulfilled, depressed, melancholy... what?*'

I feel empty.

'*But how do you mean, empty?*'

Just that. Like there's nothing inside. No emotions. No feelings. No happiness, or especial sadness. No sense of well-being and balance. No equilibrium. Nothing.

Pain.

'*What kind of pain? Physical pain? Emotional pain? Headache?*'

The pain of nothing. The pain of being empty. Of feeling that there's nothing. That everything is pointless.

'*I don't understand.*'

No. You don't. I don't expect you to. That's why it's pointless asking. There's nothing you or anyone can do. Nothing.

'*So... what can you do about it?*'

Try to live with it. Try to live, and accept it.

'*Is there nothing you can take?*'

Nothing that will really make it any better. There are things I can do, though.

'*Like what?*'

I can hurt myself.

'*Hurt yourself? But why would you want to do that?*'

Again, you wouldn't understand.

'*Try me.*'

Because...

'*Yes.*'

Because... it brings relief.

'*Relief? Hurting yourself brings you relief?*'

137

Yes.

'You mean... like masochism?'

No, I don't. Nothing like that. It gives me no pleasure.

'Then why on earth do it?'

Because it reminds me that I'm real. It validates me.

'I don't understand.'

I said you wouldn't.

'What does your family think about this?'

They don't know. But they probably wouldn't understand, either.

'And what about your doctor?'

Neither does he.

'Does anyone *understand?'*

Yes. I do. I understand.

And tonight, I did it. Tonight, it all got too much. The stuff in my head. I tried to write it down. To get it out. To see it there, in words, and look at it, and try to make sense. But it wouldn't work. The words wouldn't come. Nothing was there. No way of expressing it.

I didn't know what to do. There was nothing else to do.

So I did it.

It was a difficult day. The day of the inquest. I went to the gym first thing. On the treadmill, I pulled a muscle in my leg. It stopped me dead, but the machine kept going, which made it worse. I couldn't even swim afterwards.

I hobbled home in pain. I wrapped a bandage tightly around it, which made it easier to walk on. But I won't be able to run for while, and I hate that. I hate being incapacitated like that. It makes it all seem pointless. I can't even do that now.

I had some breakfast and got myself ready - shirt, tie, jacket, trousers, shoes. I looked at myself in the mirror. I had to face this. It was important to do it and get it out of the way. To get these things off my chest. Do the right thing. Defend someone who could no longer defend themselves, and couldn't do it even when they were alive. It meant facing those people again - being in the same room as them. But I wanted to see justice done. I'd seen things. I knew things - things that I'd lived with, that I'd tried to pretend I didn't know, hadn't seen. I wanted to see it put right. I wanted it for him and for his family, and for the others still there. I wanted it for me, too. So that I could move on.

I put some fruit in my rucksack. I put on my leathers. Then I got on the bike and set off.

I arrived early and waited in a side area, out of sight. I watched everyone else go in first. Then I went in and sat on my own. I didn't look at anyone. I didn't look in anyone's eyes. I waited and listened, and went to the stand when I was called. I answered the questions I was asked. And when they were finished, I got up and bowed to the coroner, and then I left. I don't know how many people were there. Forty or fifty. But while I sat there, answering the questions, I knew all their eyes were on me. All their blank eyes, looking at me.

"You said in your statement at the time, Mr Seagrave, that there were things going on in the house that you didn't agree with. The behaviour of some of the other staff members. Can you say what some of those things were, please?"

I looked at the counsel who asked the question. I told her some things. The shouting. The bullying. The threats. The deprivation. The abuse, yes... the abuse. She asked for the names of individuals. I said there were various people. She asked again. She reminded me that I was under oath. I gave her the names and told her what I'd seen and heard them do. Specific incidents. Pushing. Punching. Slapping. Swearing. Taking food away. Locking people out of their rooms or inside their rooms. Ridiculing. Stealing. Provoking fights.

"What did you do when you witnessed these things? Did you report them?"

"Some of them."

"*Some* of them. Not *all* of them?"

"Not all of them, no."

"What about some of the more serious incidents? Did you report *them?*"

"Again... not all of them."

"Why didn't you report them?"

Why? Why didn't I do it?

"I was afraid."

"Afraid of repercussions?"

"Yes."

"Afraid you might lose your job?"

"Mainly afraid of being victimised."

"Has that happened to you before, then? In other jobs?"

"Yes. And in other circumstances."

"So, you were afraid it would happen again?"

"Yes."

"Were you aware of the whistle-blowing policy?"

"Yes."

"But despite that, you still didn't report these things?"

"No. I had no faith that the whistle-blowing policy would protect me."

"Oh? And why was that?"

"Because I know of people who've been victimised, bullied and hounded out of their jobs after blowing the whistle."

"I see. But did you ever feel that, by saying nothing, you were complicit in what was going on?"

"Yes."

"And did that bother you?"

"Yes. I felt very guilty about it."

"But still you didn't do anything?"

"Yes... I did."

"Oh. You haven't mentioned anything in your statement to that effect. What did you do?"

I looked at the coroner.

"Must I answer that question?"

The coroner peered at me over the top of his spectacles.

"Yes."

I picked up the jug of water in front of me and poured some into the glass. I took a sip. I put the glass down again and stared at it. Their eyes were all on me. The whole roomful of people was as silent as a church.

"I... "

Everyone was looking at me. I could feel the sweat dripping down inside my shirt. I could smell it.

"Take your time."

"I became sick. I became ill because of it."

"It made you ill?"

"Yes."

"How long were you ill for?"

"I was off for six months. But I never went back."

"You didn't return to the job at all?"

"No. I resigned on the grounds of ill health. Last November. I haven't worked since."

"And was all of this ill health brought about by these things that you witnessed?"

"No, not all."

"There were other things?"

"I had pre-existing health conditions. These things made them worse."

There was a pause. The counsel looked at his notes. I picked up the glass again. Then I brought it down on the table hard. I didn't mean to, but I did. It sounded like I was hitting a gavel with a hammer - drawing them all to order. Water splashed across the table, but the glass didn't break.

"I swallowed a month's supply of anti-depressants with a bottle of port, then I cut my arms open. That's what I did about it. That's what it led me to do."

The water was dripping on the floor. The coroner looked at me. Everyone looked at me. They'd never stopped looking at me. I kept my eyes down. I saw the puddle forming on the floor where the water was dripping.

"I have no further questions for the witness," said the counsel. "Thank you, Mr Seagrave."

I came home through the late evening traffic. I rode the bike fast - 75 - 80 - 90 - 95. The road was straight. I passed everything. When I got home and took off my helmet, my teeth were clenched so tightly they were hurting. I'd only eaten the fruit since breakfast. I went to the toilet and put my toothbrush down my throat until it came up. Chyme and saliva. Thick ribbons of it. The colour of coffee and egg yolk.

I rinsed my mouth out and washed my face.

Then I went to the drawer and took out the knife.

And I made it feel better again. I made it go away.

I made myself feel real again. I saw the blood, and it made me feel real.

Do you understand?

Do you?

~

Cold, and I'm sitting here with my tracksuit on under my clothing, with a coffee, and I need to put the heating on, but the meter's nearly out, so I'll have to go out soon and get a top up, but I only have a tenner, and I don't have anything left in my account until my benefit goes in, and then I'll have to make a payment on the credit card, so I'm going to have to do something pretty soon, because there's the camper to tax and insure, and Christmas is coming and I just don't know what I'm going to do, I don't, I really don't, I don't know what I'm going to do.

You'll find a way. Don't project. Keep it in the day.

But I'll be 50 next April, and I don't have a job or the prospect of one, and Carly and my doctor are telling me it's far too early to think about full-time work again yet, that I'm a year away from trying to end it, the stuff that was going on in my head, which is why I drank and self-harmed, and I'm trying so hard not to do those things anymore, I'm trying so hard, trying to keep it manageable, trying to keep it in the day, trying to stay focussed in the day and leave the past where it belongs and let the future take care of itself, because the day is all I have to worry about, the day is all I have, all I have to do is worry about the day and get through the day, just get through the day.

That's right. Keep listening to that voice. Keep it in perspective.

But it's hard to shut out. I can't shut it out. No one can shut it out. It's always there. Even with dementia, it's still there in pieces that connect together, like bits of dust that collect in balls. But I don't have dementia. My memory's clear and my brain is sharp, despite my disorder, which is order to me, which is my way of seeing the world and understanding the world, my way of finding order in the chaos of the world, and it doesn't make me a freak or a psycho or a nutter or a schizo or a pervert or paedophile or rapist or attention-seeker or loony or pisshead or masochist or goofball or spazz.

Of course it doesn't. It means you're you and nobody else. There's nothing wrong with being you. You can't help what happened. Try to shut it out.

I try to, but it's always there, even though I can't change it, because all of the things that have happened to me and not happened to me, and all of the things that have been done to me and not done to me in my life have brought me here, where I am, and nowhere else, and if those things hadn't happened, if none of it had happened, I might not be here, I might be somewhere else, I might be married and I might have children, and I might be successful with a nice house, and not have to worry about money or the noise in the street that keeps me awake at night, and those people I worked with, the ones I ratted, who know where I live, and will see me on the street or in the supermarket, I might be free of all that and be happy and carefree like everyone should be, if it hadn't all happened and things had been different, and I hadn't fucked everything and messed it all up, and started all the drinking and cutting and trouble and grief and destruction, it might have been different, it might have been better, I might have been better, I might have been happier, I might be enjoying life, and if mum and dad hadn't met I might never have been born at all and none of it would have mattered anyway, none of it, I might never have been born, never have existed, but they did and I do, I do exist, I'm here, and I might have been dead, I might have been dead or never existed, but I'm here and alive and I might have been dead.

Which is all that matters. You might have been dead, but you're not. You're here. In the day. You might have been dead. But you're not.

But I might as well be. Because death is the only true end of it. Death removes it. Death takes it away. The booze takes it away, but not altogether. It's still there to come back to. The Great Remover - Alcohol. Removes your health, removes your money, removes your friends, removes your family, removes your home, removes your job, removes your future, removes your past. The Great Remover. But it still comes back. Death removes it altogether. Death the Final Great Remover. Death removes it, takes it away, the past doesn't matter and the future doesn't matter and the day doesn't matter, because all of it's stopped and all of it's finished and there's no remembering any more, and no more pain, and no more emptiness, and no more cutting or drinking or pills, and no more hurting, no more anxiety, no more noise, no more people, no more threats, no more upsetting anyone, no more destroying any lives, no more money, no more hospital, no more worry, no more anything, nothing, finished, done.

Nothing.
The end.
Nothing.

Nothing. No life. But you have your life. So you have something. Something of value. Something worth keeping. Keep your life. Keep it. Keep it here. In the day.

~

Wednesday

Today was the first anniversary. A year to the day. A whole year. Just before mum's birthday, too. Christ! What a present that would have been.

So today, I went to a daytime meeting. I'd never been to one before. I could have gone to group, but that wasn't until 1 and I wanted to be somewhere earlier than that. Somewhere safe. Somewhere I could share and be listened to and not questioned. Somewhere with people who would understand, who would listen and not judge. Somewhere with people who live on my planet. And it was a year, too, which I needed to mark.

I knew a couple of people there. We shook hands and hugged. A woman called Katerina made me a coffee, and I took a seat in the circle and ate some biscuits. It was in a small room in a social centre. Comforting pictures. Plants on the window shelves. A piano in the corner. I lifted the lid and started to pick out Chopin's E minor Prelude, but couldn't remember it without the music. It was too sombre, anyway. There was a tiny garden outside, where a few people stood smoking and chatting. A lot of us smoke - another addiction - but I never have, really. A cigar now and then. Dad cured me of that. He gave me one of his cigarettes when I was 12. A Woodbine. It made me puke. I didn't do it again. The same thing didn't happen with drink. We shared plenty of those together. All the way through.

I listened to the others. A few people shared about relationships. How hard they found them. And how hard they found it living alone, too. Katerina said how her partner had come at her with a knife the other night, and then tried to strangle her. I thought about my own relationships. My own difficulties. My own failures. How did normal people manage it? I couldn't imagine it ever again. It was too difficult.

When I shared, I told them about my cutting. Then I told them that today was the anniversary. I told them what had happened a year ago. The normality of it. The *banality* of it.

147

How I'd got up as normal, and popped into mum's, and had a coffee and a sandwich with her, and kissed her on the cheek as I left. How I'd gone for a walk along the seafront, and breathed in the day, and gone home for a nap on the sofa. How I'd been online and gone to some forums, and told the depression one I was feeling low, and read the hugs and take cares in response. How I'd gone to the supermarket for a bottle of port, and gone home and drunk it while I wrote all the notes and put everything in order, and posted a status update on FaceBook to say the world was completely fucked up and there was no God and people were evil and I hated AA, and all the bastards who'd hurt me in my life and damaged me and caused me to be the person I was, and how I'd be better off out of it. How I'd finished the bottle with a load of pills, and taken my knife out to cut myself free, and passed out, out of life, out of this world, out of it all, everything gone and forgotten, for ever and ever, and amen to that.

And how I opened my eyes on the other side. The lights above me. The face above me. The voice asking me *'Are you alright, Steve?'* And me saying *'I'm Tom, not Steve.'* And the same voice saying *'He responded to the incorrect name.'* And then sleep again, and its all being over. Until it wasn't over any more, and I saw the bed next to me, and the things stuck onto me, and the bandages, and the sound of the machine going *bleep... bleep... bleep...* over and over, telling me where I was, telling me I was still here, and feeling like I was somebody else, not me. I wasn't me. I was somebody else.

The mug of tea. The talk with the nurse. The suggestions for help. The telephone numbers on a slip of paper. The waiting area. The street outside. The cold of the day, in just a sweatshirt and jeans, without any money, and twenty miles from home. The bracelet on my wrist. My name, on the plastic bracelet on my wrist. The walk to the station in the cold. The hiding in the carriage toilet. The arrival home and finding the bottle, and the letters still there, and everything there.

And my face in the mirror.

His face.

His son. Still here
One year ago to the day.

After the meeting, we hugged and kissed, said a few words. Katerina gave me a long hug - this woman I'd never met, but who knew me. I picked up a leaflet from the literature table: *The Loner - Staying Clean in Isolation.* Then we all said our goodbyes.

And then I came home in isolation.

And here I am. In isolation. Another day.

Another day to keep it in. Yesterday's history. Tomorrow's a mystery.

Today's all I have to worry about. I have today.

I still have today.

~

Thursday

You are the product of your life. The person you are is the person your life has made you. And the person you are is the person who's in your head. The brain you're born with, the genes you inherit, the life you come into, the things that happen - they are you. You are also what you do with those things. How you choose to use what you've been given. The way you behave and the way you react and the way you feel and the way you think, and the things you do and don't do - they are what you are.

He knew that. My father knew that. Limited by birth and education, he did all that he felt able to do, felt equipped to do, and it was never enough for him. He hadn't the strength or the will to break through, to overcome. His life hadn't prepared him for it. He surrendered to it. He surrendered to drink. It pumped him up and made him big, made him better, made him able, gave him the confidence he lacked. Drink was the cure. Drink was there. It was always there. He lived for the drink. Drink gave him life. Throughout his life, it gave him life. Then, like the Judas it always was, it took it away. It took him away.

He could never live with his life. He could never accept his life. Never see that what he had was good - that he could be good, in himself, intrinsically, inherently good. He couldn't accept it. And he took the blame. For every mistake and every problem, he took the blame. For his oldest child's death, he took the blame.

I pushed him into it. Like I'd pushed him in front of a train.

And then it took hold. It gripped him harder. In making him the man, it broke him down. I laid him in pieces. It laid him to rest.

And he gave it to me. I was the one. I took the baton and carried on running with it, after he fell at the line. I carried it on.

Today. Today is Thursday. I must go to the gym. I must go shopping. I will go to the group today, too. I will tell them what I've been doing. I will mention the cutting. I will mention the anniversary. I will come home and have dinner. I will spend some time finishing the photographs. I will do some writing. I will sit and read a book, or watch a film. I will go to bed afterwards. I will keep it in the day. My day is there and I know what I shall be doing with it. There are no empty minutes. I have the structure. I have the routine. I have the day. I need to remember, it's only a day. The future's a mystery. The past is history.

History.

When she finally put him out, after 43 years of it, he had nowhere to go and nothing to take. There was nothing left. The man was a husk. Just the clothes on his back and a few bits in a carrier bag - his tobacco and lighter, his cans, a wallet of photos, the few quid she'd given him. It was early summer, so he'd be alright. He'd done it before, many times - spent nights in the cab when he drove lorries, in buses when he drove those, in store rooms when he was a caretaker, in offices when he was a security guard. Nights at pubs, nights in shelters, nights with friends, nights in parks, nights under bridges and bushes, nights behind walls, nights behind bars, nights under bars. All through those years. Nights when he'd been paid and had spent it all - in the pub or the bookies, or both, or paid back loans to people he owed (rarely), or lent to people who wouldn't return it.

'You'll have it on Friday, Nat. I promise.'
'Don't worry, mate. When you've got it.'
'No... you'll have it Friday. Monday at the latest.'
'Pay me when you've got it.'
'You're a diamond, Nat.'
'Don't mention it. You'd do the same for me.'
'You're a pal, Nat. One in a million. Let me buy you a pint.'
'Put it away. I'll get it.'
'You're a life-saver, Nat.'
'Don't mention it. Cheers.'
'Bless you, mate.'

He borrowed and lent like a profligate government - spent more than he had, gave it away, gambled it away, drank it away, drank it away. He gave it away. Like the life he had, he gave it away. And then he'd go missing. A day, a weekend, a week. Afraid to come home because nothing to bring. She'd look for him. She'd traipse through the streets, around the betting shops and pubs, and go to his friends, and go to his haunts - dragging the kids with her, all the way through. The big lad, and the two little 'uns.

'That poor woman. The life he leads her.'

'It doesn't make sense. He's such a nice fellah. Do anything for anyone.'

'Except his family. Look at them. She does her best for them.'

'It doesn't make sense.'

'What doesn't make sense is she sticks by him.'

'But he's such a nice fellah. He never lays a finger on her, either.'

'He doesn't have to. It's everything else. Just look at her.'

'It doesn't make sense.'

'Nothing makes sense with the drink.'

He slept in shop doorways. He slept in rubbish skips. He broke into beach huts and slept in those. He climbed over fences and slept in sheds. He slept in buses parked up at the station. He helped out a friend and slept in his van. He came back every now and then and rang the bell - asked for a sandwich or a coffee, or some money.

'You can't just throw 43 years away, girl.'

'I didn't throw 43 years away. You did.'

One day in late autumn, when it wasn't so good, she took pity and let him in for a hot drink. He was shivering (probably withdrawals) and looked feeble and thin. He wouldn't hurt her. He never hurt her. Not that way, anyway. She sat him down and went to put the kettle on. When she came back, he'd gone upstairs, taken his clothes off, got into bed. She rang up the boy to come and get him out. He came straight from work. He pulled back the bedclothes and woke him up and told him to leave. He didn't argue. He was too weak to argue. He shuffled back into his clothes and went. He shouted obscenities out in the street. The neighbours were watching. His own wife and son, kicking him out in the cold! You have to live with it to know. He went to the beach and got some stones. He went to the police station and smashed a window. They took him in - a night in the cells, a hot drink, a meal. They didn't press charges. They gave him some numbers. They sent him off on his way again, to do something else, in another day that he had to get through.

I've done my stuff and eaten my dinner, and it's 8 o'clock. It's been mild, so I haven't needed to have the heating on, which saves me some money. I've done everything I needed to do. I went to the gym and the supermarket. I went to group. I said what I had to. I finished working on the last of the photographs. I wrote some things. I laid on the sofa for a while and dozed. I'm sitting here now. I'm focussing on the day. The here and now. This very second. And I feel alright. I've achieved a lot. I've gotten through the day. I shall do some writing in a bit - a few more things. And then I shall go to bed. My arm is still sore, but it's okay. It wasn't bad. Just a couple of plasters. It didn't even bleed at the gym - though I couldn't go on the treadmill because of my leg. I used the cycling machine, though - pushing hard, legs pumping, heart pumping, blood pumping.

I'm drinking a glass of water now. A nice, cool, clean glass of water, and it's making me feel good. The only drink necessary to man. The basic drink. Odourless, colourless, tasteless, virtually incompressible. Eau de vie. We couldn't survive without it. We wouldn't ever have existed without it.

Water is a wonderful thing. Water is the only natural substance that can be liquid, solid or gas. It becomes solid at 0° C (32° F) and gas at 100° C (212° F). Its freezing and boiling points form the baseline by which temperature is measured. Water is unusual in that its solid form is less dense than its liquid form, which is why ice floats. It can absorb a great deal of heat before it begins to get hot itself, which is why it is invaluable to industry and why it is used as a coolant in vehicle engines. It is also this property that helps to regulate the rate at which air temperature changes, which is why the temperature change between seasons happens gradually rather than all at once - particularly near coastlines.

Water has a very high surface tension, making it sticky and flexible, with a tendency to hold together in drops rather than spread out thinly. The capillary action this creates allows water to move through the roots of plants, and through the blood vessels inside us. At birth, our bodies are 70% water. In adulthood, our bodies are still over 50% water. It is able to dissolve more substances than any other liquid, which means that wherever it goes - through the ground, through plants, through our veins and arteries and capillaries and organs, it carries the vital chemicals, nutrients and minerals with it.

Pure water has a neutral pH of 7, which is neither acidic nor basic. It falls from the sky as rain or snow, it arrives as a gas in mist or fog. It runs off of mountains and hills, and down valleys, in drips and trickles and rivulets and streams, which then form rivers, which flow into seas, which become the ocean, which nucleates clouds, which start the process all over again. It collects in ponds and lakes and puddles. It drips down gutterings, fills up tubs, comes out of a tap or a well or a fissure or an aquifer. Societies and civilisations grow up around it, and because of it. Wars are fought over it. Boundaries are formed by it. Countries are divided by it. People die because of it, or through lack of it. The first life began in it.

In its distilled form, where most impurities are removed by boiling it and condensing the steam, it has many important uses: the manufacture of chemicals, medications and syrups, to prolong the life of wet cells in batteries, to flush wounds during surgery, and - because it is tasteless - the manufacture of liquids processed for consumption: milk, juice, squash, syrup, Coke, Pepsi, Dr Pepper, alcohol. A few simple ingredients. Barley malt, sugar, hops, water. Rice, water. Potatoes, water. Grain, water. Grape juice, water. Apple juice, water. Pear juice, water. Made with pure water, spring water, triple-filtered water, distilled water. Ethanol, water.

All you need. Water.

They take him in, they give him a place, a room of his own, 3 meals a day, some clean clothes, and a set of rules: no drinking on the premises, no bringing drink onto the premises, no coming onto the premises drunk. Everyone else is in the same boat. Everyone has to pull together - help yourself, help each other. Three strikes and you're out. He manages it. AA meetings, days in bed smoking, pacing around, smoking, drinking lots of tea and coffee, smoking, playing pool, smoking, reading books and papers, watching DVDs, smoking - all the time, it's there in his head. It won't go away. Fifty-odd years of drinking won't just go away. He gets the shakes and the sweats and the dry retches - but he doesn't wet the bed anymore, and he has enough money. He gets it together. Christmas comes. The family visits - Eve, Tom... even Karen. They bring him presents. Chocolate. Tobacco. Bottles of flavoured waters. Cans of ginger beer. Good coffees. Lighters. Novels. Bags of sweets. He wants the sugar. He crunches sweets the whole time, and smokes. He is always smoking now. Rolling tobacco, bought cheap from a bloke who goes across on the ferries a lot. He saves the dog-ends, breaks them open, collects up the bits, smokes it again. Sweets and cigarettes. And coffee. Strong coffee. His fingers are brown, like he's rubbed them in shit. His hair has an orange streak. Some of his teeth break up and fall out. But he manages it. He makes it through. He's on the way. Everyone's proud. He's doing it. The days become weeks.

And then comes the spring. The temperature rises, the buds come out, the birds are singing, it's nice in the park on a good day. He goes to the park. He sits in the park and talks to people, and feeds the birds. He loves the birds. He talks to other drinkers. He can't keep away from them. Once a drinker, always a drinker. Never trust a man who doesn't drink. Have a swig, Nat. Go on, mate. One won't hurt you. No one will know. Just have the one, Nat - for old time's sake. Go on, boy. Do you good. That's the stuff. How does that feel? Fancy another? Got any money? Why don't you join us? This is the life. Life without it? Call that a life? Call that a life? Fuck that for a game of soldiers, mate. What's life for if you're miserable? Stick with your own, mate. Fuck the rest. Have another one, Nat. That's it, mate. Why don't you join us? Come and join us. Have another one. When'd you get paid, Nat? When'd you get paid?

And he's out again. The cold weather's gone. The three strikes are gone. Fuck it - who gives a toss? He's out again.

He's out.

~

Friday

I slept badly last night. The pub along the seafront was blasting out music until midnight. Then the take-away downstairs took over - the constant stream of cars and drunk people calling in for an over-priced shit-food snack. Even with earplugs in, I could hear it. The car doors, the stereos, the revving engines, the loud pissed-up conversations. I shouted out the window a couple of times, and got abuse in return. In the end, I dragged the duvet into the kitchen and tried to sleep on the floor. I would have gone out in the camper, but it's out of diesel and it was too late to get any, and it was too cold anyway. I'll have to sell it. I have no money. I feel trapped here. I don't know how much longer I can put up with this. I can't keep losing sleep. I can't take the stress of it. The noise of pubs and drunk people - everywhere, drunk people. I don't want to end up drinking again. I can't drink again. I can't. I don't have to.

I can't.

I went to see a film tonight. On the way to the cinema, I passed through the middle of town, across the High Street and the park. Teenagers were out in force, stalking around in hoodies like urban monks. They take over the town on weekend nights. All of them drinking. All of them pissed. Screeching and staggering and running. Chucking things at each other. Cans. Bottles. Chip wrappers. Stones. Muck from the planters at the roadsides. I cut through side streets and alleys to avoid them and what they were doing. Everywhere, the smell of alcohol, like the stink of cheap scent in a chain store clothes shop. People collecting in the doorways of pubs, around trees and benches, in the washes of light from the windows of offies.

'Can you get me a can of K if you're going in, mate?'

'I'm not going in.'

'Can you get me a can of K anyway?'

'I'm not going in.'

I wanted to tell them. I wanted to stop and tell them. But what was the point? Would they listen? Would *I* have listened?

'Fuck off and get a life, cunt.'

They'd have to find out for themselves.

At the cinema, I saw *We Need To Talk About Kevin*. It held me until the closing credits. I couldn't move. I wanted to get up and go to the toilet after an hour, but I couldn't move. I felt every internal scream of the mother in her struggle. Her struggle to love her disturbed child. The stress coursed through her every move, every gesture, every action, every emotional response. The stress was there in the black of her eyes, the set of her mouth, her voice. Her incomprehension at it all. How can you love a child like that? How can you *not* love a child who is also your own? Despite what he does - however horrific and hateful and evil - how can you ever stop loving? And how can a child stop loving a parent? What must a parent do, how far can they go, what level of abuse must they inflict, before they forfeit love? Before they surrender the right to be loved by those whose love should be unconditional?

Can love ever be unconditional? Are there always conditions for love? And if there are, can it ever *really* be love? *Can* it?

She carried on loving because she was his mother. She carried on. He took everything away from her - everything she held dear - but she carried on loving. He came into life in her womb. Her body nurtured him. He grew and became strong through her, became a man through her. He took all she had and cared for and left her with nothing. Left her with pain and misery. Left her bereft. But she kept being there. He was all she had left. She was all he had left.

And when she was alone, she drank. The only other thing left was drink. Drink and memories. Memories and drink.

This afternoon, I went for a cycle ride along the seafront - along past the beach huts and the sailing club and theatre, and over the roughs and along to where the sea wall ends and the cliffs take over. In a small cove there, on the shingle, a dozen years back, a whale was beached. It had strayed off course, swum in too close, got stranded by the tide, and was trapped. A life born in the sea and solely adapted to the sea, washed up out of it and left to die. A young whale, it seemed. Ripped from its mother. A memory to her now. Nothing more.

On the day it was found, I was there. I stood with it for a while. Then I went home and sat with a notepad and pen, and I wrote a poem.

"Sixty-six feet from snout to flukes,"
the coastguard said.

As if that was all it was -
something reducible to
human proportion. A scale
more fitting to comprehend:
the length of eleven men
laid end to end.

Dead.

Death as palpable as death can be -
a silent tonnage of it, tossed aside
as easily as empty shells.

Hard to fathom such a life
snuffed out - like a loved one's:
a life too large, too vital to be
spent.

Across the beach, baleen is
strewn like a broken comb,
its purpose done.

Now, no more than a side-show -
a freak to glut the curiosity of
things best left unknown.
A miracle - its secret undone -
exposed in its immense indignity.

The eye, though blind, accuses.
And I, aware of the intrusion,
pick my way back up the rocks
and off

thinking of my father, in his room,
waiting for the end.

I sat there a while, in the fading light, looking back on the town from afar - at the tide encroaching, the seabirds circling, the lights coming on. Then I cycled back. As I passed along the High Street, I thought I saw her. Just a glimpse, in the bustle of shoppers - the hair, the pale skin, the way of walking. A flicker of light between the trees. I kept going for a moment, letting it register. Then I stopped and turned back. I cycled along. I looked in shop windows. I looked around corners. I went further up, then returned, still looking. Maybe she'd got in a car. Maybe she'd got on a bus. Maybe I'd been mistaken.

What would have happened anyway? What would I have done? What would I have said? She'd said she never wanted to see me or speak to me again. I couldn't understand it. There was no animosity. We dealt with it all in a civilised manner. We remained friends until the sale went through. We went for a meal on the day it was finalised. She'd found a new flat and I offered to help her to move. That's when she told me. That was the end. From that point onwards, we ceased to exist for each other. There was nothing else. And that was it.

I could have just asked her if she was alright. If she was happy. Surely enough time had passed now? Water under the bridge? But perhaps enough water could never flow under the bridge for her. Perhaps there would never be long enough. She never said she'd stopped loving me. I never said I'd stopped loving her. I still don't know what happened. I still don't know *why* it happened.

Except I do. The same old reason. The reason that had always been there. She knew only the half of it, though. She thought she knew. But she didn't. And neither did I. Not at the time.

I went home and put the bike away. I made some dinner. And I went to the cinema. I saw a film about love that endures beyond what's reasonable. About human contact that transcends the most testing of circumstances - that remains because there's nothing else left. Then I came home, through streets full of drunken children, and tried to sleep in the horrible human noise that assaulted the night like an alien force.

~

CONSERVATORY
(a scene from a marriage)

I fill up the glasses from the wine box in the fridge. I empty mine, straight back. Then I fill it again. I can feel it kicking in. I take the glasses through to the conservatory, where Lucy sits clipping her toe nails. She's collecting the tiny pieces and putting them on the lid of a paint tin. I put her glass down beside her basket chair, then go and sit in my own.

"Thanks," she says. Very quietly. Not looking up.

It's late August and there's still some light in the evening sky, though she's lit the candles anyway - a small pool of them, floating in a blue glass dish on the coffee table. Maybe she thought it would improve the mood, and perhaps it does. The wine's working on it for me, too, as it always does. After the row, she'd sat in the lounge on her own for a while - left me out here, gave us the space to think. Except I can't think. I can't think anymore. There's too much of it, and I can't work it out.

I take a mouthful of wine.

The thing with the clippers - it's a distraction. A signal that she's prepared to be in here with me again, but she wants to keep her own space. I'm fine with that. I want my own space, too.

The door to the garden is open and I can see Mickey out there - Lucy's tabby cat - huddled up under the plum tree, like a great fat tea cosy, blinking at the midges. My adopted son, I call him. I'm the only male he likes. I can do anything with him. Even her dad's had his hands ripped open. Me, though... never a problem. Lucy was pleased about it when we first met. Saw it as a good omen. Now, though, I think there's jealousy in it. Or maybe something else. Maybe she thinks there's a bit of a Judas lurking inside there. Can cats make choices like that? God knows. I don't think they set conditions like we do, anyway.

The air's heavy and still - thundery, maybe. There was a crackle in the radio earlier, when we were washing up (me washing, her drying and putting away, the tension there in the clatter). There's a sweetness in the air, too. The garden fragrance. The candles. It takes the edge off the mildew smell that always in here. The timbers are black and rotting where the rain's seeped in over the years. The carpet and the furniture have all absorbed it. When it rains, the place becomes an obstacle course of buckets and bowls. I lie awake at night and listen to it... *drip - drip - drip - drip - dri-drip - drip.* A lick of paint's all it can have for now. There isn't the money. Other things come first. The things I don't want to think about.

I take another mouthful of the wine and close my eyes. The click of the clippers. The insect sounds from the garden. A car passing out on the road. I half expect another word, but I'm grateful that it doesn't come. I just want to shut off like this - let the wine do its thing. She hasn't touched hers yet and mine will soon need a refill. I'll sneak some when I go in for a piss.

I hate this kind of thing. The bickering over nothing. The way she sulks. I know what's underneath it all. It's always there. We never talk about it openly, though. It's just the allusions. When will the spare room get decorated? Her age next birthday. All of that. I try to hold it together around the things there are to do, and the money they'll take. The time they'll need. And back it comes to the same thing, and I've opened the trap and put my own foot in. The time. The clock ticking and the days getting shorter, like the end of a season. And that's what it is, really - the end of a season. Things drawing in and cooling down. Things dying away. Don't let them die. Make the most of the light before it goes.

And what about those promises? What about those promises?

It baffles me to think of it all. Me, here, in this house - right here in this decaying conservatory, overlooking this garden, living this life, in the company of this woman. Do I love her? Of course I do. There's no doubt about that. It's why I'm here. But how did it happen? How the fuck did it happen? Almost two years. What was I doing then? Where would I have been now? What would I have done?

How would I have felt?

I had one life. I was happy with it. I thought I was. I didn't want to change it. And then? And then everything was different. Everything changed. Just like that. Nothing would ever be the same again. Didn't even know she existed one day. Couldn't imagine life without her the next. That's it. It's done. Sealed. Promises made.

You go through all those thoughts - making all those connections. We all do it. *If* such and such, *and* such and such. If *this* hadn't, and *that* hadn't... what would have happened then?

There I was - living alone, in that tiny flat. Not earning much, but getting by. Getting somewhere with my writing, too. Poems and stories. The odd piece published. Some small competition wins. Just a few pounds, here and there - but something. And enjoying it, too. Not needing anything else - or any*one* else, come to that. Happy. Alone, yes... but not lonely. I wasn't lonely. Was I? No.

I saw the ad in the paper. The evening class. *Creative Writing - Finding a Voice.* Hah! Finding a voice! I *had* a voice. I had stuff out there, in magazines and anthologies. I *had* a voice. I didn't need to find one. I didn't need creative writing classes, either. Did Dickens have classes to find a voice? Chekhov? Emily Bronte - up on the moors, shut away from the world? No.

But I cut out the ad. I thought on it. A chance to air some of my work, perhaps. Meet other writers. Perhaps there'd be someone there. Someone like myself. A kindred spirit. Not that I needed anyone else, but...

I filled in the form and sent it off.

And so the night comes, and I almost don't go. And then I do. And then I almost stay on the bus anyway. And then I don't. Lives change on the basis of such small decisions. Taking your eye off the road a second. Going in *that* shop instead of the usual. Taking the right instead of the left. Tossing a coin. So in I go. And there she is. Reading her poem out - a bit flowery. But does it matter with that voice? Look at her. Just *look* at her. And listen to that voice. You've found it. Coming to find a voice, and there it is. That voice. The coffee break. The chat. The writers in common. The interests in common. And there it is. The longing for Tuesdays. The weekend meets. The walks. The talks. The trips out. The holiday. There it all is. Amen to that, and here we go. Promises made. Happy ever after. Amen.

"We're a whole now," she'd said one day. "Apart, we were just two halves. Now, we're complete."

I couldn't believe it.

It was right. I was sure it was. As sure as I could be.

She wrote me a poem.

> *Evening, and the breeze comes*
> *as solace - ruffling its skirt-edge*
> *on the shore, stirring late birds*
> *home.*

> *We watch a cloud-bank catch*
> *the sun, ease its decline, lay it*
> *gently to rest in the sea -*
> *one force absorbing another*
> *across the line.*

> *Your fingers, lacing into mine.*

I couldn't believe it. I'd found her. My voice. Two halves. A whole.

Complete.

The clipping stops and I hear movement. I open my eyes just enough and see that she's stretched her legs out in front of her and is wiggling her toes. She takes a sip from her glass - the way she always drinks. Half a mouthful, if that. Not even a taste. Earlier, she'd made a daisy chain and looped it through her hair, and I can see the tiny flowers now, poking through between the dark strands like stars. She's letting her hair grow again, as she had it when I first saw her that night. She'd had it cut shorter for a while, but hadn't liked it so much. Nor had I,

but I didn't say anything. It certainly suits her better longer.
Where her hair touches them, her shoulders are pale and waxen-
looking. She raises the glass to her lips again and holds it there.
I can see the beads of moisture on it. I want to take a sip of
mine - but I want to stay shut off, too. Let her think I'm dozing.
Maybe she'll go to bed or something. I close my eyes again and
wait.

I hear the chair creak as she gets up. Then there's a
shuffling noise as she makes her way across the carpet towards
me on her knees. And now here's her hand on my leg. I turn my
head towards her, put my hand over hers, open my eyes. She's
looking at me shyly, with a half-smile. There's something else
in it, too - like she's trying to see right into my head. It's
unsettling. Then she turns her head and rests it on my thigh.
With the fingers of her other hand, she picks at the threads of the
rug. I stroke her hair.

"What are you thinking about?" she says.

I stare out into the garden again. How do I answer a
question like that? How do I tell her what I'm thinking about?
Refilling my glass? Wishing she'd go to bed? The life I've left
behind? How the hell I'm going to deal with all this?

"Nothing, really," is all I say. I take another mouthful of
wine. The glass is almost empty now. "Wool-gathering."

What the fuck does that mean, anyway? Wool-gathering?
Shit-stirring might be closer to the mark. My head's full of shit
and I'm giving it a damn good stir. Washing machine head, they
call it. Main wash. Maximum spin.

She carries on picking at the rug. "You're always
thinking. Off in that world of yours. I sometimes wonder
what's in that world."

Ah, Jesus! You really wouldn't want to know, sweetheart.
I can't get a proper grip on it myself.

But what I say is

"I was thinking how maybe it would be nice to have
someone around one night, before the summer's over. Get a few
bottles in. Some picky bits. Maybe have a little fire going out
there. Just something."

Which is, actually, what I'm also thinking, so it isn't quite a lie. A party, kind of. A decent session. A good excuse for it.

She moves her head slightly so that she can see into the garden. As if on cue, Mickey gets up, stretches, then steps through the grass towards us in that eyes-fixed head-down tail-up way he has.

"Who were you thinking of asking?"

There was a question. Who do I know? The neighbours at the old flat? The people at work? Rod and Karen? No on all counts. Rod and Karen would be the most likely to accept, and just thinking of it - Rod looking at the state in here, Karen sitting on a blanket in the garden in her Fenwicks trouser suit, the conversation centring on production processes, growth sectors, the world according to the right-wing tabloids. Rod's usual cringe-inducing style of performance comedy. No. So, who else is there? Most of my friends have long since moved away, on to better things. In some ways, they all feel like part of an old life, anyway. Ancient history. I've never really been one for friendships. She's the same. It's another of those things we found we had in common. Since we've been together, no one else has registered very much. Which was fine for a while. All we really wanted was each other. Our neighbours here are mostly elderly - apart from the Baldwins over the road, with their huge cars, loud parties, fashion accessory dogs. They should meet my sister and her husband. But not in my garden, thanks very much.

"I don't know. It was just a thought."

Mickey skips over the step onto the rug and begins rubbing his head around my feet. Then he turns on his back for Lucy to stroke his chest. I pull a strand of Lucy's hair up and rub it between my thumb and finger. It's as dark as a twist of licorice, with a faint glimmer of deep red where the dying sun catches it. I do love this woman. I do. I just don't know what the fuck to make of it all.

"Maybe if we can smarten this conservatory up a bit first."

She holds up her hand and flicks her fingers, and Mickey's fine hairs fall from them like strands of silk. The sun is sinking fast now, and it's light gives a coppery glow to her skin. She stands up suddenly and turns. Then she leans over me, hands resting either side of my head on the chair back, and gives me that look again.

"Well... I'm going to leave you to your deep thoughts and have a bath. Then I'm for bed. Any more of that wine and I'll fall asleep here."

I just look at her. I don't know what to say.

"Are we forgiven?" she says.

I give her the most reassuring smile I can manage.

"Yeah... we're forgiven."

She leans down and kisses me on the forehead. Then she steps back over the rug to the French window, with a tiny skip and chuckle - Marilyn Monroe style - as if she's too tipsy to make it. Mickey gets up, too. He steps after her, tail up, purring. Then he stops briefly and turns his head back to me. And he scowls at me! That's what it is. It's a scowl. It's so striking that I blink - am I really seeing this? But then he carries on after her and leaves me behind on my own.

"Won't be long," Lucy calls, but I can't see her now. She's disappeared behind the curtain, with her scowling Judas cat in tow.

I wait until I can see, through the kitchen window, Lucy pass into the bathroom and shut the door. Then the water starts flowing through the pipes. I creep in and fill the glass again from the fridge, knock it straight down, refill it. I can feel how light the box is getting. It was brand new at 3, when I put it in there. She's had two small glasses. I'll have to figure that one out in the morning. I knew I should have bought two. Maybe I'll get a bottle and top it up. I go back and sit down, and there's just me and the wine and the candlelight at last. I look around at the piles of stuff, the mould around the beams, the cracked glass, the buckets and mop, the damp patches, our bikes propped against the wall, the odd bits of furniture (mainly mine, from the flat) that we couldn't find room for anywhere else. I look at it and I could cry.

It's a shambles. The whole thing's a fucking shambles. Everything.

When we first looked at the bungalow, it scared the hell out of me. The previous owners were an elderly couple who'd been in the place nearly 50 years. The woman had died suddenly, and it cracked the old chap up so much he'd gone into a home. There were no children, and the relatives wanted to get rid of it quickly. So the price was good. But the whole place needed work. They'd both smoked, too, and the smell still lingers even now - after the walls have been scrubbed down and the carpets and curtains cleaned. The water was the colour of strong coffee. You don't notice it until you go out and come back, and then it hits you. The stale, sour mustiness - like it's seeped into the entire fabric and structure. Not just the smoke, either. Something else. That odour you sometimes find in the houses of very old people. Neglect, perhaps. Things left because they no longer mattered. Like the smell in dad's rooms.

There was modernising to do. New kitchen units. A new bathroom. New doors. A replacement gas boiler. Re-rendering. And then this conservatory - original from the 50s, and not used by the old couple once the rot had set in. It'll probably fall down of its own accord in a few years if nothing's done.

We stood there that day, in the middle of the lounge, while the chap from the estate agents went through all the usual crap about potential and scope, and room for expansion, and the good postcode, and the shops nearby - and she was taking it all in and seeing it all, seeing the start, seeing the challenge. Seeing the family home it would become, with this fantastic new man she had in her life now. What could possibly spoil it? What could go wrong? How could I tell her, even then, what I was feeling? Like I was a stranger in my own life. How could I voice those things - thoughts that I hated and couldn't understand, but also couldn't deny?

I remember - I'll always remember - she'd taken my hand and squeezed it hard. She was telling me I wasn't alone in this.

I don't know if she felt the shaking or not, though I'm sure she could sense it.

I hear faint splashes from the bathroom, and the water still running. I see the light from the bathroom window shining across the fence at the side. I see her shadow, then it's gone again.

A few times recently, in the evenings, I've found some pretext to go out (*Why do I need a pretext? I never did before*). Maybe some stuff we've needed from the supermarket. Or to check the tyre pressures at the service station. So I've jumped in the car and driven down the hill and along, and stopped off for a can, then kept going, right through the town, until I've come to the little side road that runs down the back of my old flat. And there I've parked up and opened the can and sat there in the dark drinking it down and looking up at that window. Someone else is in there now. I can see new curtains up and a lamp glowing behind them – on the opposite side to the one where my own lamp used to be. And I just sit there staring at it, feeling the booze getting into my system and settling it down, and wondering what the fuck I'm going to do. I've left that life for one I can't handle, for one I haven't a fucking clue how to handle, for one that's a goddamn fucking mess and a shambles, and I just can't handle. And I just feel fucking awful, because I don't know what to do. I love this woman. I can't imagine life without her. But I don't know what to do.

A breeze blows in from the garden, and there's a moth now, fluttering around the candle bowl. The water stops running and there's silence for a moment. I take a mouthful. There's a flicker of light in the sky, above the rooftops at the back. Silence again. Then a faint, distant rumble of thunder - like someone shifting a wardrobe in the house next door.

I take the glass and get up and step through the door and onto the grass. It feels cool and damp under my bare feet. It's been a scorcher today - like summer's little parting shot - and that breeze, that promise of a storm, is a relief. I walk up past the plum tree to the end bed, which - so the estate agent told us - had once been a thriving kitchen garden. Now, it's more like a waste land. Weeds, brambles, thick clumps of stalks from some prehistoric gone-to-seed vegetables. There's a tiny hollow, up by the fence where Mickey sleeps during the day. Beyond the fence are the gardens of the houses in the next road over. I can see lights on at some of the back windows, shadowy figures moving about the rooms. Lives going on right there, completely oblivious to me. There's the faint sound of a TV filtering out from somewhere - some film music, rising in a dramatic crescendo, followed by a scream. Christ, there's a soundtrack for me. The only other sound is the background static of the traffic on the bypass - like the sound of the sea in a shell. I take another mouthful from the glass.

There's another flash in the sky - closer this time, and the rumble's only a few seconds behind. Seven seconds to the mile, isn't that what they say? If that's so, then this isn't far off. Half a mile? A third? I turn around and step back a few paces to the plum trees. Look at this... these tiny little fruits, growing here. Just a bit bigger than the size of grapes at the moment, but fattening up. That was another of the selling points. How productive the tree was. Lucy talked about jam, but the first thing that was in my head (*all you ever think about*, she'd said, jokingly) was wine. I've done it before. Easy enough. A few basic ingredients, a demijohn or two or a bucket, and a bit of time. You can't rush it, even though you want to. And I've drunk it before it's ready, and it's still a bit sludgy, and Christ does it give you the shits, but doesn't it work just the same? Sometimes, you just can't worry about such things. You just need what it can give you and you need it right *now*. But just look at these tiny little fruits here - these little balled fists of sweet unborn life. Look at them. Perfect. Filling with juice and colour. Fattening up. Getting ready. Round and hard and full of promise. Full of so much promise.

There's that breeze again. Christ... goosepimples. Someone's just walked over my grave. I can see the glow from the candles, lighting the conservatory like a Hallowe'en skull.

The wine's getting the better of me now and I just want to sleep. I just want to get back there and climb into bed and go to sleep. Be asleep before she comes in, so I don't have to say anything any more.

But there goes the water. There it goes, flushing away down the drain at the side, in a tiny bubbly cataract that's just been wrapped around her body, her beautiful body.

Do you love her? Of course you love her. Of course you do. So, what the fuck's the matter with you? I don't know. I don't know anything any more.

The light's gone on in the bedroom, and there she is, wrapped in her white cotton dressing gown I got her for her birthday, with her hair turbanned up in a towel. I can see the heat flush on her face from the bath, even from here. I'm standing here, just outside the range of the light, watching this woman like I'm watching a doll moving around in her own little house. This woman. This beautiful, quiet, special woman who's in my life, who's changed my life, who's like a tidal wave rushing through the streets and alleys of my life, moving everything, washing it down, clearing it away, flooding it.

She pokes her head into the conservatory. She's calling my name. She's peering out into the night, but she can't see me. She calls my name again, once more, louder. Then she turns and goes in again, pulls the French window to, closes the curtain across it. And I feel like a peeping Tom. Ha! Peeping Tom! That's me. A peeping Tom, hiding out here in the night. Spying on my own wife. Spying on the life that's mine. Spying on my life.

I finish off the glass. I creep back towards the conservatory door, like an intruder. A peeping Tom, coming in closer for a better look. The candles are flickering down to their last, and the glass casts and inky blue light on the walls. And there's the moth there, lying still on the surface of the water, floating like a little brown insect raft. And there are her nail clippings, on the lid of the paint tin by her chair. I put down the glass and just stand there. I look at the curtains. I look at her shadow cast against them as she sits at her dressing table, wiping something over her face.

The flash makes me jump - so close and bright that everything lights up around me, and my shadow is hulking there against the wall. The thunder's right there with it, too - that same split second - and the sound is so huge it makes everything shake.

And after it - the total darkness. The power's tripped off. And it's like I've been struck blind. And she cries out once. Then she calls my name again, and I can hear the tremble in her voice. The fear in her voice. She calls my name.

"*Tom!*"

I grope for the handle to the French window, kicking paint tins, knocking my glass over. It smashes at my feet, but I can't see it. I can't see a thing.

"I'm here, love," I shout. "Don't worry. I'm here. I'm coming."

And I can't see a goddamn fucking thing.

END

~

Saturday

A bad night again. But I had a dream. I was the only person left in the world. Everyone else had gone. All the houses and streets and shops and offices - empty. I went to the top of a building and called out. I looked down on the empty streets, the parked cars with no one in them. Nothing was moving. Even the birds had gone. There was no one and nothing. Just me.

I spent the morning putting the photographs in the album. They'd come up well. All were larger than the originals, and better. I grouped them according to age. Grandparents through the years. Then their children. Then their children's children - the extended families on both sides. Then I had a section at the end just for mum and dad. On their own and together. The final two were those of mum and dad in their twenties. Dad in his uniform, mum in her polka-dot frock. They were both taken around the same time. They were engaged by then. At the very front, though - before any of the others - was a photo of mum taken when they'd just met. 18 or 19. It was done in a studio. She'd sent it to him when he was out in Palestine. He'd pinned it up in his armoured car. That day, the car was blown up. He was lucky to escape with his life. The photo escaped, too. They joked about it forever after. The day he pins it up, he's hit. Was it good luck or bad luck? Did it cause it - or would it have happened anyway, and the photo protected him? It was about the size of a playing card. There was a small hole above her head, where the pin had gone. I'd resized it to A4 and cleaned it up. But I left the pin hole in the final image. I could have cloned it out, but I didn't. It was only right to leave it. It was where he'd pinned it up. He liked to look at it positively - that it had saved his life. She had saved his life. Which is what she went on to do for the rest of his life, once they were married. She saved his life. Until she could save him no longer. Until she had to save herself.

At last, worn down by the drink, the months without a roof, without a decent meal, he tries again. He goes into a halfway house. He behaves himself. He keeps to his room. He eats his meals. He smokes and watches television. He stays away from the wrong company. He gets visits. She visits him. And Tom visits him. Tom – the lad. The chip off the old block. He talks of the old days. The old times. The years they share, and the years before. The things he did.

The things he did.

He shakes his head at the things he did. Smiles at some of them. Then it drops again, the eyes look sad. Led her a dog's life. Denied you kids. Gets all tearful when he talks about it. Maudlin. Full of regrets. What a terrible time I gave you all. I wasn't a proper father or husband. My fault you never had nothing. My fault she always went without – you kids always went without. And Michael, bless him. My son. That was my fault. I tried my best. You understand that, don't you? I tried my best. But it was all my fault. Everything. Good for bloody nothing. She did the right thing turfing me out. I don't blame her. It was the best thing for both of us. I still love her, you know. I always will, boy. She was my first and she'll be my last. Known her since I was 18. 50 years. Known your mum for 50 years. Christ.

It wasn't all bad, though, you know. You remember that. It wasn't all terrible. We had some good times too, didn't we? Remember those times in London, when you was kids? It was alright. I did my best. You and Karen. Karen. She never comes now. I'd like to see her, but I can't blame her. And Michael. Bless his heart. My Michael. He comes, you know. He visits me. He's here with me. My Michael.

And the pubs and the clubs, the boozers, the dens, the offies. The nights in the pub. The people from the pub. Everything centred around the pub. The Saturday nights. The lock-ins. The mates at the brewery, the barrels at Christmas – straight off the back of a lorry. The crates of bottles. The bags of cans. The flagons and barrels and jars and casks.

And the parties. Remember the parties? Fuck me, the parties. The parties at Blackburn Street when you was kids. The Christmases. How old are you now, boy? Christ... was it that long ago? Where did it go?

Where did it go?

...the upstairs sitting room, rocking with people, windows steaming, crammed to the gills, stuffed up and snug as a rum-tub's cubbyhole. The heat flowing, the booze flowing, blushing up faces, oiling the wheels, loosening tongues, getting it going, shouting and giggling and screaming and coughing and singing. The chink of glasses. The fume and flare of it. The slop and froth of it. The glints in the eyes. The tinselly blaze of lights and flames. The kisses and pats and squeezes. The clump of shoes on the stairs. The chill of the night at the door. The fumble of footing. The waves and shouts and car-door slams. The rumble of engines. The trail of lights off into the darkness. The hip-hugging, ear-kissing, foot-slipping return to the room and the chairs and the light and the fug and the heat. The remains of the night. The remains of the night. The feeling of it. Like nothing else mattered. Like this was it, and nothing else mattered...

He behaves himself. He keeps it going. They make him an offer. A dry house, shared with another. Self-managing. A chance to do it. A chance at redemption, to prove he can do it. So in they move, and there they stay and live like normal. Just like normal. Shopping. Cooking. Washing. Taking care. Keeping themselves safe. A day at a time. One thing missing, though. He goes out one day and rents a telly from the place in the High Street. They deliver it and set it up. When they've gone, the two of them carry it along to a second-hand shop. They flog it for £30. Money in their pocket, and a nice day. They pack up their stuff. They're off. He's off again. Here he goes, all over again.

When I'd finished the album, I went out to get a birthday card for mum. I wandered around the shops aimlessly, looking in windows, looking at things I didn't want and had no interest in, looking at nothing. All the time, it was there... in my head. I couldn't shake it. Like a virus, moving between brain cells, infecting every thought. Every time I looked at something, it was there. The thought of it. The first taste. The first mouthful hitting the bloodstream, hitting the brain. The feeling. The lack of feeling. The floating off and not having to worry. Not having to feel.

I was wandering closer and closer to the off licence by the bus station. I wasn't really going there... but that's where I was going. Past the kebab place, past the computer shop ('*Need more memory?*'), past the letting agents ('*Working tenants only*'). I could see it coming, just a little further along. The sign outside listing the 4-pack offers ('*Stella - £3.99, Tennent's - £4.50*'). Just the second-hand shop to go. Jimmy's Place. Jimmy... the chap dad worked for when he was homeless. The chap who's van he slept in. Looked after dad. Even visited him sometimes, in the homes. The first person I told outside of family, the day after he died.

And there he was... coming out, seeing me, stopping me for a chat. Jimmy. Long streak of bacon rind, like me. Faded jeans. Cowboy boots. Shoulder-length hair. Crucifix earring. Looking more like Neil Young than Neil Young does himself. Long time since I'd seen him. He asked about mum and how she was. Then he mentioned dad. He asked if I had time for a cuppa - he was just brewing up. I glanced along at the off licence. I hesitated a moment. Then I followed him in. He boiled us up a mug each, got a packet of fruit shorties out of a cupboard. He sat on one of the old sofas in there, and I sat in a recliner. Just like being in a living room. A living room, full of other people's cast-off furniture. Clocks. Pictures. Tables. Dressers. Knick-knacks. Photo frames.

Jimmy settled back in his seat, put his right foot on his left knee, sipped his tea.

"He was a lad, your dad. One in a million. Grafter - but he had the chat, too. Sharp as a tack."

He dipped a biscuit. So did I. Comfortable in there. I could live in a shop like that. A grandfather clock ticking in the background. The muted sounds of the traffic passing. Dust motes in the sunlight. Tea and biscuits.

"I'll never forget this one day. Don't think I ever told you. We went out to this place - elderly retired couple with a big house up Briar's Mead. Having a clear-out they was and wanted to get rid of some stuff. So we arrive there and the bloke lets us in... and he's a bit abrupt, you know? No 'hello' or nothing. 'Oh, yes... come in,' he says, right gruff like... like he's sized us up straight away as a couple of shysters come to fleece him. Your dad looked a bit rough anyway, bless 'im. He was bang on it then, and sleeping in the back of the van, too. But anyway, we follow the bloke in... and your dad turns to me and says 'That was a bit bloody rude, Jim.' That was something about your dad - he could never stand rudeness. I remember once, it was right at the end of the day and we was over in Eastgate, and we was both gasping for a coffee, so we went in this café. But the chap behind the counter was rude - so your dad told him to stuff his fucking coffee, and walked out. So, we didn't get our coffee, and I was really bloody gasping, too. But that was your dad. So anyway, we're here at this house, and your dad says that to me - but we're going in anyway. I mean, this stuff sounds good, and I'm going to have a look - rudeness or not. So, I'm checking it over, and the bloke's there watching, all crusty like, probably to make sure we're not going to nick nothing, and his wife's hovering in the background, too, all done up with her nose in the air, giving your dad the eye because of how he looked. And he's just nosing around the room at all the stuff they've got, too. You could tell it was a fair bit of money. Antique furniture, silver and china, proper paintings on the walls. And I'm just hoping he doesn't say nothing, 'cos you know how he could be if he got the itch with someone like that. But what he does instead... he sees this old photograph they've got on the sideboard. Young chap in an army uniform. Second world war, it looks like. Very smart-looking bloke. Officer. So your dad looks at it for a bit, then he turns to this bloke and says, in this really polite way he had, 'Excuse me for asking, sir, but is this your good self in the photo?' I looks over, and this bloke's really giving your dad the hawk-eye. 'Yes it is, as a matter of fact,' he says. Your dad looks at the photo again and says 'What regiment were *you* in then, sir?' I can't remember what the bloke said. Tank regiment, or something. Whatever it was, your dad must have realised straight away he'd got one over on him. 'I was in the Household Cavalry myself,' he says. Well... you could just see it in this bloke. The change. All that stuffiness... it just goes, like someone's stuck a pin in him and let the air out. Even the missus does an about-turn. *'Really?'* the bloke says. 'That's right, sir,' your dad says. 'Wouldn't know it to look at me now, I know. Old soldier fallen on difficult times. But look at this.' And he gets out this wallet he was always carrying - Christ knows why, 'cos there was never any money it - and takes out this photo and shows the bloke. Him in his uniform, at the barracks. Do you know the one I mean, Tom?"

I nodded. "I've got it on my wall at home," I said.

Jimmy grinned. "Well... he shows the bloke... and the missus has a gander, too. And they're suddenly like two very different people - admiring this photo of your dad as he was. The bloke asks him a couple of questions... and then the woman suddenly says 'Do you know, I should have offered you men a cup of tea. Would you like one?' I'm about to say no thanks... but your dad's straight in there with 'I don't suppose I could bother you for something stronger could I, please?' I'll tell you what... if ever I'd wished the ground would open up, that was the moment. I can't believe he's had nerve to say that to these people. And I'm just thinking 'Oh Christ, he's fucking blown it now,' when the woman grabs your dad's arm and says 'Oh, do *please* excuse me. How rude of me. Of *course*. Whisky alright?' And this huge smile spreads across your dad's face, and he just says 'Well, that would be highly delightful, ma'am. Thank you.' And to top it all, the bloke chimes in with 'I think I may as well join you.' Well, I'm gobsmacked, Tom. No one else could have got away with that. But he had that charm, see... and that twinkle in his eye. And they were reeled in by it - hook, line and bloody sinker."

We sat for a moment and sipped our tea, thinking about it. The clock ticking. The traffic going by outside. Dust. Jimmy chuckled.

"Do you know what? We was there for nearly an hour in the end. The missus makes us all a cup of tea, and brings in some cakes as well, and we all sit there while your dad holds court - scruffy as he was, and them done up like a couple of toffs. He tells them about the number of times he trooped the colour, and how he served on the Queen's wedding, and the scrapes he got into - like when he got put on a charge for nicking coal out of the officers' coal bunker at the barracks one winter night 'cos the lads was freezing, but how his mate who was with him came off worst for deserting a comrade 'cos he legged it when they was caught. He tells them all this, and they're both as gone as last Christmas. Then the bloke tells a couple of stories of his own, and gets out a photo album and everything. Amazing. I'll never forget that afternoon 'til the day I die."

I finished my mug. It was starting to get dark out.

"Anyway... at the end of it all, I made them a decent offer, and they was happy, and me and your dad loaded the stuff on the van, and the bloke helps us, too. And when I paid them, the bloke slips twenty quid in your dad's coat pocket and tells him to stand a round at the mess later. 'That I most definitely will, sir,' he says. And there was that grin and the twinkle in his eye again. And he drew himself up and made a salute, and the bloke returned it, and they shook hands... and that was that."

Jimmy grinned at the memory, shaking his head.

"He turned that whole situation around, you know. There they was, treating us like a couple of toe-rags... and then your dad got them eating out of the palm of his hand. He could do that. He had the knack. What a character."

He got up and stretched.

"Yep... special bloke, your dad was. One in a million, mate." He took my mug and turned his face to the window. "It was just his demons, bless 'im."

Afterwards, I got mum's card. Then I went home and wrote it. Then I went and had a lie down for an hour. And when I woke, it had passed.

Though I could still see the back of it. Not too far ahead of me.

Like a sign along the street.

~

Sunday

No sleep. I shouldn't have dozed yesterday afternoon - but I needed to. It wasn't just that, though. It was the anticipation. It was like a living thing in my stomach. Only one thing would have settled it. I've done the therapy. I'm able to analyse my feelings, to question my feelings. It doesn't stop me feeling them, though. Only one thing does that. And I can't have it anymore. Not after last time.

I went to the candlelit meeting last night. Heard the voices. Heard the words.

'If you're dancing with a gorilla, it's the gorilla who decides when the dancing stops.'

'I drank to forget... but I couldn't remember what.'

'The scary thing is... the really *scary thing is... when you're in it, there's no greater feeling. Nothing matters. There's no greater feeling. And you don't want that to end. You never, ever want that to end. So you keep chasing it. And that's the scary thing.'*

'Transformers. That's what everyone became when I drank. Transformers. It transformed them into bastards and bitches and people out to get me. I was the transformer, though. They stayed the same. It was me who was transformed. Into the meanest fucker under the sun.'

'I thought I'd hit my rock bottom. I didn't think it could get any worse. But the elevator still had a few more floors to go down.'

'It changed the way I felt. That's what I wanted. I didn't want to feel like that anymore, and the drink took it away. It made me feel better. It made me a different person. And that was the problem. It made me a different person. A person nobody wanted to be with. A person nobody wanted to know.'

'I live my life a day at a time. I take my life in day-sized bits. I can manage a day. If I keep it in the day, I can manage. If I keep it in the day.'

I listened to it. I took it in. I knew it anyway. I'd heard it so many times before. I'd said it so many times before. I knew it all. And that's the danger. Familiarity breeds contempt. And the other one...

'Stay out of wet places.'

Stay out of wet places. And it doesn't mean Manchester. It doesn't mean marshes and rivers. It means wet places. Places that are wet. Places where you get wet.

Like pubs.

At lunchtime, we all meet at mum's to take her for her birthday meal. Me, Karen, Rod, and Natalie. They've come straight from church. Baptist. It's the first time I've seen them since the summer. I give Karen a kiss and a kind of hug that doesn't quite make it. Like novice dancers, our feet end up in the wrong places. It's more like I'm trying to hold her back from a road as a lorry passes. Not so long back, I'd have let her fall.

"Nice to see you," I say.

"And you, Tom."

She looks well. She's got the family's good skin (mum's side), and she's kept her figure. She's had her hair restyled and tinted. From the back, you'd take her for a teenager - Natalie's much older sister instead of my slightly younger one. She doesn't look 47, anyway. Not in the way I definitely look 49.

Natalie gives me a warm hug and a kiss on the cheek. She dropped the 'uncle' bit when she was a kid, and I'm happy with that. She looks grown up in her hipsters and jacket. The puppy fat's dropped away, like someone's let some air out of her. I can see her mother more than her father in her. But I can see her grandfather, too. I always wondered with the choice of name. Karen said it was because they both liked it, and they were both fans of Natalie Imbruglia. They always use her full name, too. Christopher is Chris, and Adam is frequently Ad. She's Natalie, though. Not Nat. Never Nat.

"I like your jacket, Tom," she says.

"Thanks. You look smart, too."

"That's 'cos I *am* smart."

That makes me smile. She's right... she *is*. Smarter than her parents realise. She's the rebel, as I was. She calls herself her parents' karma child - there to remind them of what they'd rather forget. It's dad again. It's certainly not anything from Rod's side. Karen didn't take it, either. All she took from dad was the jug-ear and something in the smile. With her, though, it's just the shape her face takes. Some cats look cute because they *are* cute. Others look cute because they want to scratch you.

Rod offers me his hand. It's like squeezing an uncooked chicken wing, fresh from the fridge. He's wearing a check shirt and a maroon sleeveless jumper with grey slacks and shiny black shoes - the kind with the long toe, as if his feet are shaped like trowel blades. He's not got a single grey hair on his head, but there's a hole at the back - like an egg in a nest. He looks half the part of the grand-dad-in-waiting.

"How's it going, Tom?"

"Good, Rod. It's going, anyway."

"Keeping busy?"

"Yeah. You?"

"Can't complain... except to say there's too much work, and I can't really complain about that."

Right.

Rod runs a business producing those cutesy knick-knacks you see in gift shops and airport lounges, and which sell by the truckload. The company sails through every perfect storm the economy hits. It just goes to show there's always a market for tat. Perhaps that's what people do when times are hard: buy something else cheap to dust, to give the impression of shelves of plenty. On the proceeds of thousands of plaster Turk's heads, country cottages and dopey-eyed dogs, they paid off their mortgage, bought their gite and their motorhome, enjoy private healthcare ('*Leaving the NHS for those who need it*') and are sending Natalie through the same public school the twins went to.

It still feels awkward, even though we've made our peace. It's always there. Too much history. Like the night I called her a fucking bitch, and no sister of mine - then fended off Rod with a fence post afterwards. The drink in action. The drink talking. The drink bringing it up. 'A useless pisshead, just like your dad,' she'd said.

My dad. Not hers anymore.

Amazing we'd pulled it back, really. The final chance. They know about the groups and meetings. They know that I'm sober. Toleration is all it is, really. As Carly said, though... perhaps that's enough.

Rod claps his hands together and rubs them - a pantomime parody, perhaps, of a deal with the Japanese for 20,000 miniature Samurai warriors.

"So, Eve... shall we hitch up and hit the trail? This horse needs his oats."

I'd been hoping they'd save the Roller and come in Karen's less 'look at me' Espace - but no. It sits there in the estate's tiny car park, all 17 silver feet of it, like an aircraft carrier in a Cornish harbour. The Honda is there, too - my own little jet-ski, better kitted for riding the waves. Natalie makes straight for it and pats the tank.

"If only you had a spare helmet, Tom."

I hate to say it, but I'm thinking the same. I almost go back for my helmet, anyway. Follow them up or lead the way. Anything but get in that fucking showboat.

"You'll get on one of those over my dead body, young woman," Karen says. She says it with a straight face, too.

Natalie gives me a look that says she's thought about strychnine in the Chardonnay. And then we get in.

As we pull out into the road, passers-by look. Rod loves the attention, of course. The 'RNK' number plate must have been a massive concession. 'ROD' would have been far more appropriate, in all sorts of ways. They bought the Rolls for their silver wedding 2 years ago. Their present to each other. A Silver Shadow. 1980 vintage - one of the last ones Rolls Royce made, apparently. 'Who could resist at £15k?' I wonder what it'll be at 50 years. A Gold Wing each? I've no doubt they'll get there.

We glide along and up the hill to the tones of Susan Boyle's latest, chosen especially for mum. She sits in the middle at the back, like a strange grey child in the huge seats - her head sunk down between her daughter and grand-daughter, her bag on her lap, the light catching on her glasses in a way that makes her look faintly baffled by it all.

"I always feel like royalty in this," she says, grinning. "Like I should be waving at people as we pass."

I can sense the satisfaction that comment brings.

"I always feel like hiding," says Natalie.

Rod glances up at the mirror.

"Plenty of room to hide," he says.

Enjoy The Silence finishes playing. Endure it, more like. Just the seats creaking for a few moments. Maybe a crackle of tension.

"Well, I think it's beautiful," says mum. "Never expected to be going for a ride in one of these at my age."

I should feel pleased for her, and I do in a way. Why begrudge her these little things after what she's been through? Dad never had a car. Never had the money for it. If she wanted to go anywhere, it was bus or train - if there was the money for those, even. He probably drank away the price of a Rolls in his time. More important things, too.

And this is like a kick in the teeth to all that. Which it deserves, of course. But it feels like something else, too. A conspiracy. Pointing the finger. Rubbing my face in it.

It's not far to where mum wants to go - a village pub, about four miles out of town. It's a good choice from Rod's perspective, too: another small car park filled with average family saloons. We cruise in - the tyres crunching the gravel, turning the heads of the people sitting at the picnic benches outside, enjoying the unseasonal sunshine. I can gauge the questions from the looks: *'Who's this with the money, then? Someone famous? Someone important?'* and at least a couple of *'Who's this wanker in the prick substitute?'* Rod simply savours the moment. You can see it on his face. The blissful-eyed satisfaction as he pauses a second before switching off the engine, tilting his head towards me slightly with his eyes fixed on the dash - the whole gleaming walnut sideboard of it - as if listening for the sound of a mouse farting in the distance. *You hear that?* his expression says. *Can you hear that? Of course you can't hear that. There's nothing to hear, that's why.* Then he turns the key, and the difference is barely noticeable - like a breath stopping. His mouth twitches at the corners, and I can see it there on his face. What the moment was about. *That's what money can do, see. It can buy you that silence. It enables you to enjoy that silence. But to get it, you have to work for it.*

"Lovely," says mum, clinching the moment for him.

"Okay, peeps," he says. "Let's go fill our faces."

The pub is quiet inside and there are plenty of tables to choose from. Karen and Natalie take mum's arms and escort her off to claim one, while Rod and I go to the bar. It's an odd experience. A long time since. I did most of my drinking at home, but I sometimes kicked it off in a pub. Either that, or I popped in one already drunk, on my way to the offie for more. So... usually either the first strike, or the second base. Today... neither. At least I had people with me.

I'd been holding onto twenty quid especially for the occasion, and I take it out. Rod already has his wallet out, but doesn't demur when I push it back. Not even an '*Are you sure?*', which is a small mercy.

I order the drinks, and watch as the barman pulls Rod's pint.

"I can have one," he says. "The food will break it down."

"It's alright, Rod. I'm not a cop. I won't keep tabs."

"I know. But I've got to think of your mum."

He means it kindly, I suppose. But it still comes across as '*the rest of you crazies can go through the windscreen.*' He picks up his pint and takes the top off. Just a mouthful - the foam clinging to his moustache like a dip of emulsion on the end of a brush. He lets out a small sigh of satisfaction and puts the glass down again. He looks at it - turning it slightly, then back again, as if trying to decide which angle he likes. The barman then puts my drink down beside it. Soda water, ice and a slice. Rod looks at it while I look at his pint. The bubbles rising through the nut-brown liquid. The creamy layer on top. The drips running down the side of the glass. I can smell it. I can smell it on his breath. As if catching the drift, he takes out a handkerchief and wipes his moustache.

"Looks just like a gin and tonic," he says.

As if it needs to. So it can look 'grown up' by his pint.

I take a sip. I can hear dad's voice. *'Why'd you go to a brothel if you only wanted a wank?'*

"Gin's one drink I could never stomach," Rod says. "Vodka, on the other hand..." He moves his head to make the point - as if remembering those wonderful vodka times he had, back when (as he's often told me) he was an alcoholic himself - before he pulled himself together.

He takes another mouthful of his pint. It saves having to speak - a ploy we're both using to cover the awkwardness. I certainly don't want to talk about booze, and that's where it seems to be heading. Maybe he's just not thinking. Being a bit tactless. Or maybe he's trying to prise me open a bit. Look in the can and see what it holds. I have an image in my head, for some reason. A trigger being slowly pulled.

"She's looking well, don't you think?" I say. "Considering everything."

We both look across to where they've settled, on the far side of the bar by the window - Natalie helping mum out of her coat whilst Karen grabs the menu.

"She's a toughie, alright," Rod says. "They made 'em to last in those days, eh?"

"Yes."

The barman puts down the rest of the drinks on a tray - a sherry for mum, wine spritzer for Karen, diet Coke for Natalie - and takes my twenty.

"I see it in Karen as well," Rod goes on. "Soldiers on regardless. When she broke her wrist that time, she never let it set her back. The kids always had their school uniforms fresh in the morning. 'Flu, stomach bugs, migraines... she just works through them. The pioneer spirit, she calls it."

I take my change, mentally trying to square gastritis and a headache with rheumatoid arthritis, hypertension, skin cancer, Type 2 diabetes, one kidney and glaucoma.

I really should just let it go. I wish I could.

"Comes down your mum's side, Karen's always saying," Rod says, picking up the tray. "All those women have been tough."

Is it a dig? Is *everything* he says - they say - a dig? Or am I just too sensitive to this sort of thing? Is any of it worth worrying about? *Fuck 'em*, as dad might have said. They can think what they like. They certainly seem to like what they think. I pick up my glass and follow him over. There are chairs sticking out everywhere and he just needs to catch his foot accidentally under a leg...

But he doesn't, of course. People like that never do.

We take our seats - Rod next to me - and choose our meals. The waitress takes our order. Rod raises his glass.

"Happy birthday, Eve."

We drink the toast.

"Let's hope there's plenty more of them, eh?" he adds.

She smiles. She's facing the window, and in the light I can see how frail she still looks - how much it's all taken out of her. Not just the illnesses - her life. All the lines of it are there, writ large, like a history book. The stress. The strife. The worry. The struggle. The pain and grief. You looked at this woman and you *knew*.

I led her a dog's life, boy. You know that. What I put that woman through. I don't deserve to be forgiven for it. I don't deserve to see any of you again.

"I hope I've got a few more in me yet," she says. "We were all long-lived in my family. Even my dad, with what happened to him."

"What was that, gran?" Natalie asks.

"The war. The Great War, I mean. He was gassed on the Somme. His lungs were always weak after that. But he smoked a pipe all his life and made it to 80."

"What did he die of?"

"Pneumonia. He had emphysema, anyway."

"Bit of a double whammy that," says Rod.

"Bless him," says mum.

We sit quietly for a moment with our drinks. Natalie, who's sitting on the opposite corner to me, stirs her straw around, making the ice tinkle. She isn't old enough to drink alcohol in a pub, but she could easily get away with it. Not under Karen's and Rod's watch, though - and I guess it's more Karen. A rule's a rule and a law's a law. From what I know of Natalie, I'm sure there's plenty they *don't* know about. Longevity may have come down mum's side, but Natalie has plenty from dad's. Anyone can see that. I can, anyway. I should know.

"I've got a joke," says Rod, suddenly. "You'll like this one, Eve."

I exchange a glance with Natalie. She rolls her eyes. Then she takes out her phone and begins to fiddle with it. Karen puts her hand across.

"*Not* in here, please. I *did* tell you."

"I was going to record dad's joke, that's all. Just so I can play it to my friends later and watch them fall about."

"*Please.*"

"No, that's alright, love," says Rod. "If she wants to record it for her friends."

Natalie looks at him, nonplussed. Then she puts the phone away and glances at me again. We both know what to expect. Rod loves his jokes. Or rather, he loves to hear himself telling his jokes. He's perfected his performance technique over the years. We get all the accents and voices - exaggerated for maximum comic effect. All the facial expressions and gestures. All the wince-inducing stereotypes. We watch him build himself up for the role. Mum's chuckling already.

"Paddy goes on holiday to New York, and he goes into a bar and says to the bartender 'Oi'll have tree shots of da best Oirish whiskey in da house, sorr.' So the bartender gets him his three shots, and he drinks them straight down, one after the other, and then he gets up and leaves. This goes on for about a week. Every day, he goes into the same bar and says 'Tree shots of da best Oirish whiskey in da house.' Alright?"

Mum is quaking now - holding her hand over her mouth, possibly to keep her dentures in. Karen looks at him in either admiration or disbelief - it's hard to work out which. Natalie sits on her hands and starts to rock slowly.

"So one day, the bartender says to him 'Say, pal... doncha tink it wud make more sense if I's put all da shots in one glass fer yuz?' So Paddy says 'Ah, now well you see, sorr... Oi've got two brudders back home in de old countree... Moichael and Sharn - and every toime Oi'm away, Oi goes into a bar an' Oi orders a shot for each o' dem as well as one fer meself. It's a way o' rememb'rin' 'em, loike.' Okay?"

I notice someone at the next table listening in. They seem amused - either at the joke or at the arse Rod's making of himself. He's completely oblivious, of course - wrapped up as he is in his raconteur brilliance, his missing his true vocation, his settling for the manufacture of crap ornaments as a reasonable alternative to global comedy super-stardom.

"So, another week goes by, and then Paddy goes into the bar one day and only orders *two* shots. 'Hey, buddy,' says the bartender. 'Wassup? Somethin' happen to one of yuz brudders?' 'Ah, no... not at all not at all,' says Paddy. 'Me brudders are foine. It's me. Oi've decoided to give up da booze.'"

Mum clutches her mouth and dips her head forwards alarmingly, like she's about to be sick. The veins are throbbing in her forehead. Karen pats her on the back. Her face is straight, so she's heard it before. Or maybe she hasn't. Natalie sucks at her straw. Rod grins over the top of his pint.

"I thought you'd like it," he says, then takes a mouthful.

"Oh God!" mum gasps, regaining her composure slightly. Any second now. I can sense it coming.

"It's the way you tell them, Rod," I say. Yeah, good. Another dig about giving up alcohol? Come on, Tom... surely you've got a sense of humour, no? You must stop being so sensitive, you really must. Must I? Why? Maybe I should tell a joke about a balding prick with a Roller and a tat factory. See who's got the sense of humour then.

Mum coughs. There it is. It always happens. Any exertion like that always starts it off. She coughs again. And again. She cough-cough-coughs. A really hard one, like always. She had pneumonia herself as a child. And then, later on, thirty-odd years of stress-induced smoking... until she was forced to quit. *Cough-cough-cough-cough-cough.* I'm about to go to the bar for some water when it settles again. She takes a sip of her sherry. She uses her handkerchief to wipe her eyes under her glasses.

"Oh dear... that tickled me."

Rod seems entirely satisfied.

My son-in-law. He's so funny. Such a wag.

Dad didn't have quite the same opinion.

What does your sister see in the dopey cunt? Do you know, boy? Fucked if I do. Unless his prick's as big as his bank balance.

I lean forwards.

"I've got one, too. A woman goes into a bar and asks for a double entendre. The barman says 'See that woman over there? I've just given her one.'"

Natalie has a near-disastrous blowback on the straw. Karen just glares at me.

"Fine," says Rod, firmly, unsmilingly.

"I *must* remember that one," Natalie giggles.

"I'd sooner you didn't," says Karen. "I think your uncle should know better."

Fuck off. Po-faced cow.

"I'm not sure I get it," says mum.

"Don't worry," I say. "Sorry. I shouldn't have mentioned it."

Rod harrumphs loudly. "Do you want to open your cards now, Eve?"

Karen fishes in her bag and brings out an envelope. Natalie beats her to it, though, with one from her jacket pocket.

Natalie's is one of those with facts about the year mum was born. 1925. The price of things. 3d for a pint of milk. £850 for a detached house. The average weekly wage for men: £5. 5d for a pint of beer. Famous people born then, too. Paul Newman. Richard Burton. Both gone now. Mum's captivated by it. 1925. Christ.

Rod's and Karen's is more cutesy. A painted landscape with a thatched cottage, smoke at the chimney, a garden full of flower beds, a bonneted girl sitting in a swing chair. Sweet.

"What a beautiful picture," mum says. "I'd have loved a cottage like that. Right out in the country, away from it all."

I hand over my card. I bought it to go with my present - kind of as a clue. A comic one. A couple of codgers in a nursing home, looking at a photo album. One is saying to the other *'They never text or e-mail me.'* Mum chuckles.

"Thank you all," she says, and puts them in her bag.

Next, there's the presents.

The SuBo CD from Natalie

"Thank you, love," she says, kissing her. "But you should save your money, you know."

"Don't be silly, gran."

Some DVDs from the twins. A boxed collection of railway journeys from around the world. She loves trains. And she loves the idea of travel, though she's only ever been abroad twice - once to Rod's and Karen's gite for a week, and once to the Black Forest, about 20 years ago, when a woman she did some cleaning for died and left her £500. It was the most money she'd ever had at once in her life. She never told dad exactly how much it was. They just took the holiday, and she hid what was left under the wardrobe because she didn't have a bank account. He found it, of course. He always did. He had a nose for it.

"Ooh! Now, these will keep me occupied in the winter evenings," she says, running her fingers over the cases. "Bless their hearts."

"They said they'd ring you later," says Karen. "They're both at Adam's new place, getting it fixed up for the new arrival. Only a few weeks now. Looking like Christmas."

Mum smiles wistfully.

"A great-grandmother already, at my young age."

Rod chuckles. "Plenty of time to add another great to that yet, eh?"

Next comes a small, daintily-wrapped and beribboned box from Rod and Karen.

"What's this?"

"Open it and see."

She takes off the ribbon and paper and lifts the lid. Inside is a brooch in the shape of an owl (she loves owls). Silver, with dark stone eyes and a body of feather-shaped crystals in downward gradations of navy blue, turquoise and white.

"Oh, look at that!"

She takes it from the box. The feathers sway with the movement. She holds it up and it sparkles in the light. She looks open-mouthed from Rod to Karen.

"It's beautiful. Thank you."

"That's alright," says Rod.

"We thought you'd like it," says Karen.

"I do. I love it. "

She gives Karen a kiss, then leans across the table to meet Rod's cheek half-way. Karen takes the brooch and unclips the safety chain. Then she pins it onto mum's cardigan.

"There you go."

She looks down at it, smiling. She touches it and watches the feathers swing.

Then I hand my present across to her.

"I'm doing well today," she says, picking at the Sellotape. She pulls the strip slowly, trying not to tear the paper. One of her things. If she likes the paper, she saves it. She's got a drawer at home full of saved bits of wrapping paper, ready to use on something else. She never uses them, though - as far as I know. Maybe she keeps them for another reason.

She peels off the last strip of tape and unfolds the flaps.

And then it's out.

"Oh... whats...?"

She opens the cover and catches her breath. Her as she was, 70 years ago. Karen and Natalie look in, too, and Rod cranes his head over the table. Natalie's eyes widen with delight. Karen just looks. Not a flicker.

"Is that you, gran? Gosh... weren't you beautiful."

She doesn't pick up on the comment. She lets out her breath at last.   "Where did you get these from?"

"I borrowed them from your box. I just scanned them into the computer. Some of them needed a bit of work. Creases and spots and that. They've mostly come up alright."

She turns through the pages, head rolling left and right as she does so - a new catch of breath each time.

"I don't know what to say."

She comes to the one of Michael - full page, bigger than she's ever seen it before. She puts her hand to her mouth.

And then the waitress is suddenly standing there holding two plates.

"Two beef roasts?" she says.

I know it as soon as she opens the album. I know it's a mistake. It catches her out. It's just too much. All those faces. All those memories - made larger, enhanced. The family ones. The wedding ones. The children ones. Me. Karen. Michael. Michael looking as he did, not long before he died. Michael as we'll always remember him - as he'll always be. Then the best ones of each of them, together and singly. And the final two. The polka-dot frock and the ceremonial uniform, juxtaposed, looking towards one another across the divide of the page. Both of them, as they were, in the flush of youth, with their lives ahead of them - yet to become completely enmeshed, but close to it. A time when they knew each other. When love was fresh and full of hope, and promises made. The beginning. The end and the beginning.

She's so overwhelmed she has to leave the table. Her dinner's there, but she has to go. Karen follows her out to the toilet, and Rod asks the waitress if they can hold the meals back for a bit. She says that's fine and takes them away again. Natalie picks up the album and starts to look through it. Rod's eyes follow Karen and she turns and gives him a look that says *'don't worry... it'll be okay.'*

We sit there in silence for a few moments. Rod takes a drink and I stare at mine.

"These are beautiful photographs," Natalie says.

"Yes," I say.

I get up.

"I'll just be a minute," I say.

I need to get out. Just out. I can't stay there. I walk past the bar as if it's not there. I don't look. I just see the door and head for it. The door. I know what I want. But I know what I need. And I need to get out.

It catches up with him in the end. The years of shelters and hostels and rooms and bedsits and tunnels and skips and sheds and benches and huts and boxes and boats and squats. The years of drinking and smoking. The years of self-abuse and roughing it, and being out in it all, and never getting straight and clean long enough to start all over again properly. It's just start all over again all over again, again and again, and each one a little further back from the last. Finally, one night in summer he's asleep on the beach, just his clothes and his carriers and his cans, and they set upon him. Four of them - young and high and out for a bit of fun. They rough him up, slap him about, kick him and punch him, break some teeth, black his eye, take his stuff and leave him bleeding and bruised and beaten. He's beaten. Totally beaten. Fucked. He can't do it any more. He just can't do it. He has to surrender. This is the end. He's had it now. Give in, Nat boy. You just can't take it any more. You can't beat it any more. It's beaten you instead. Give in.

He gives in. 69 and surrendered. They find him a home. Another room, three square meals, his own telly, medical attention, full-time care. He starts to recover, puts on weight, looks healthy for the first time in years. He smokes in his room, watches his films, keeps it together. On his 70th birthday they bake him a cake. The family comes. Tom. And Eve. She still comes, despite it all - all the years and the strife and the worry. She's still there. The first and only. For each of them, the first and only. All that history. So she comes.

They take him out for a drive. Down to Sussex, where he used to deliver with the lorry, back in the day, after the war, when they got together and settled down to start a family. There's the photo of him with the lorry, outside the house, looking young and fit and ready - ready to take it all on, ready to do it, ready for life and all it would bring. Up for the challenge. Young and fit, and strong as an ox. Surrender nowhere in sight. No sign of giving in. No one to beat him (let them try it!) All that life, just waiting there, ready to live. All that life. All those days and weeks and months and years and decades. The barrel full and the tap hardly turned yet. All that life, trickling out, a day at a time. All those days.

All those days.

Waiting...

70. How did it happen? Where have those days gone? What happened to it? What did he do? What did he do with all those days, handed there to him like wads of banknotes? Here it is, boy. It's all yours to spend as you will. All that life, all those days, wadded up, stacked up, all yours. How will you spend it? What will you spend it on? Where will you start? And where has it gone now? Where's it all gone? Hard to believe it's all gone. What's it been used for? Where's it all gone?

Outside, I find an empty picnic table, off to one side, and sit there alone. The people at the other tables are drinking and chatting, enjoying the sunshine. Starlings are hopping around between the tables, pecking at the grass. The sheen of their feathers makes them look waxed. I can see the Rolls parked up over there, dwarfing everything else - even the stupid great 4x4 monster a couple of spaces over. I can feel my heart, like a hammer-drill in my chest. I can feel the sweat in my hair - running down my back. My hands are shaking. I need something.

There's a plate on the table, left from someone's meal - a few cold jumbo chips spattered with ketchup. No one looking. I take a couple of the chips and slip them quickly into my mouth. Two chews. Straight down. I don't taste anything. I take another couple. I need something. Just enough to make it pass. Everyone's still drinking and chatting. No one notices. It begins to settle. There's heat in the sun, sitting here, sheltered by the hedge. I take another chip, but someone looks over suddenly and I throw it down, towards the starlings. They jump at the movement, but then they're straight down again and on it. Pecking and squabbling...

...like in the park that day. That day, way back down the tunnel of years. The birds there, pecking and squabbling. Karen in the pram. The river flowing under the bridge there. Walking along the railings - the river flicking between them like a slow-moving film. The sun sparkling on the surface. A million tiny glints, like fishes glimpsed in the grime.

'Shall we go home and get Daddy's dinner, then?'
'Da-ee!'
Her smile. The white of her teeth and the red of her lips.
Her hand reaching down.
'That's right. Tommy, Karen and mummy go home and see
Daddy. And get Michael from school.'
' 'ichael.'
'That's right. Get Michael. Then go home to dinner...'

The plate's empty now. Just dabs of sauce, like blood - the knife and fork to one side, holding down a used serviette. An ashtray with a couple of stubbed out cigarettes - one with lipstick on the end. Next to it, a couple of glasses. A tumbler, like the one I have for my drink, with a lemon rind in the bottom. Just the rind. The drinker's eaten the lemon, too. Maybe that was their lunch, as there's only one plate and the glasses are together. The other glass is a wine glass. One of the big ones that holds quarter of a bottle. There's almost an inch of wine left. A good mouthful. A thick, deep red. A Cabernet, maybe. Why leave it - a wine like that? Why would anyone leave that much? How much does a pub charge for a glass of wine like that? Almost as much as a bottle, probably. Why would anyone buy a glass of wine like that and then leave some behind? Who could be so fucking stupid? Who but a normal fucking drinker.

People drinking and chatting in the sunshine. The starlings, bubbling in the grass. No one looking at me. No one noticing. The sun glints on the chrome-work of the Rolls. The figure there, on the radiator grill. The Spirit of Ecstasy - her arms reaching out behind her, as if in flight. Leaping away from the ground and into the air. Flying. Ecstasy.

I edge my fingers across to the glass, without looking - watching the people, drinking and chatting, as normal people do at pubs. Drinking and chatting, enjoying the sunshine. Relaxing. All perfectly normal.

My fingers touch the base, work their way over it, find the stem, wrap around it, clutch it. Pull it. Slide the glass across the table. Over the weather-smoothed wood. Like moving a chess piece. There it is now. Right there in front of me. I look down at it. I move it around in circles, watching the wine swirl up the sides. A good wine. Full-bodied. Enough to do the job - for now. A good mouthful. Just enough. I lift the glass. It's halfway to my mouth. It's all there - the whole thing. All there. I can already taste it. Ecstasy. Normal chatter in the sunlight. Almost there...

"Tom."

Karen. Standing there. She sees. She sees. She thinks she knows what she sees. The glass. Almost empty.

The look on her face. It's all there. Everything.

"Karen, I..."

But she's already turning away. She's already going. She's already got her back to me. She's already decided.

Summer again and he's better again. Nice to feel good. Nice to be settled. Nice where he lives. All he needs now. Nice to go out for a walk. Needs a stick now, but still gets about. Out for a walk. Down to the town. Look in the shops. Sit on a bench and feed the pigeons. Have a cup of tea in the café. Read the paper. Have a flutter, maybe. Then back to the room. Family visits. Everything good again. On a level. Everything good...

A drink would be nice. Just one. Just a pint. A pint won't hurt. A nice day like this. A walk to the town, a nice quick pint, then back for lunch. Just the one. Can't hurt now. Past all that game now. Can't handle it now. Just the one. There's always the offie on the way back, too - just in case. A couple of cans to take back to the room. That'll be nice. No one will know. It can't hurt now. Just a couple of cans, after a nice pint, to set the seal on it. Just a couple. It's summer, anyway. A lovely day. One of those days. Just a day in your life. Do it while you can, son. Might be dead tomorrow. While you still can. Only a couple. Only the once. Just this once. Just today. This wonderful day. Seize the day! Make the best of it. You only live once, so enjoy it. Can't drink when you're dead. Can't take it with you. Only live once. Who's going to know, anyway?

Just today.
A day.
Just a day.

~

Monday

Fog enclosing. The windows are smoked. It's cold indoors, so I put on layers: t-shirt, sweat shirt, hoodie, jumper. A pair of track bottoms under my jeans. Two pairs of thick socks. Lots of mugs of hot chocolate, tea, coffee. I put the boiler on to take the chill off, but I can't run it for long. I'm scared to go down and look at the meter. It must be close to the end. It's not a good day today. Not good.

I'm supposed to go to the library, but I call in sick and go to group instead. I sit for an hour and listen to the others talk about their drinking. I talk about my drinking, and how long it had been since I'd picked up a drink, and how it had made me feel not drinking, and what I was doing to deal with the stuff that I used to be able to deal with only when I'd got some drink inside me, and how long it seemed to be taking me to learn that, and how hard it was, just how fucking hard it was, because all I'd ever done before was deal with those things with a drink, because that was all I knew and all I could do, and the only way I could cope. That's what they don't understand, these people like 'I used to be an alcoholic, until I got my act together' Rod, and Karen, and all those others I've met over the years, the ones who talk about 'piss-heads', and 'alkies', and 'people who can't control their drink', and who say that all you have to do is not drink, which *is* all you have to do, but which is like saying to a hydrophobic non-swimmer who falls in the river 'all you have to do is stay afloat, that's all you have to do, just stay afloat and you'll be okay', while they're thrashing around and swallowing water and panicking and sinking down further and further. Just stay afloat. Just don't drink. Just stay off the drink. Stay afloat. Don't sink. Don't drink.

Don't drink.

And I tell them about Sunday, about the dinner, about what happened, about how I was caught with a glass in my hand, about how it ended. About how I fucked it all up once again. In trying to do it right, I got it wrong.

If she hadn't appeared, would you have drunk it?

I don't know. I really don't know. I wanted to. But I didn't want to.

I think you would.

Probably. I just don't know. It was there. It wasn't pre-meditated. It was just there. In a glass. Waiting.

You know what would have happened if you had.

Yes. Probably. Light blue touch paper. Stand clear. And I had nothing to lose anyway. She'd seen me - an almost empty glass in my hand. She'd seen it enough before - with me, and with dad. What could I do? Ask for a breath test to prove I hadn't? I might as well have drunk it anyway. But I didn't.

That's the main thing. You didn't do it. You got through it.

But the fallout was the same as if I had...

I catch up with Karen at the bar, where she's asking if the meals can be served again. She doesn't look at me.

"It wasn't what you think."

"Think? I don't need to *think* about it."

"It was on the table and I just picked it up. I didn't touch it."

"Oh, it was on the table. Okay."

"I just went out for some air."

"Right. It doesn't take long, does it. Quick glass of air."

She turns back towards the table. Mum's seated there again, next to Natalie, chatting to Rod.

Karen looks back at me quickly.

"Let's not spoil this completely. It's her birthday."

And then she strides over there - the gallant rescuer of the day. The one who steps boldly in and sorts it all out and makes it right.

And all I can do is follow behind.

As always...

What was the fallout?

Huh! Just how it was. Literally like fallout. Like a mushroom cloud, opening up over the table, dropping its shit on us.

Arguments?

No. I apologised to mum, and she said don't be silly because it was her fault, and she gave me a kiss and thanked me and nothing more was said...

Nothing more is said. Not about that, anyway. We eat our meals and sip our drinks, chatting about trivial stuff - just chatting to keep the tone up, for mum's sake. Rod talks about some of the orders at work. Natalie mentions her coursework, and her hopes for university. They want her to study law or business. She wants to study sociology or literature. Play to her strengths. Karen does a lot of listening. So do I. We don't look at each other once. Mum looks at her brooch again, and her DVDs, and her CD. She has the album there, too. She says she looks forward to looking at them all later. All the presents, I guess she means. Maybe she means all the photos. She doesn't refer much to the past, which is unusual. TV, the health of her neighbours, stuff she's found on her laptop. When we've finished, I get up to go to the toilet, and while I'm up I go to the bar to pay the bill with my credit card. Rod's there by my side in seconds. She's sent him.

"You're not going to pay for all of this, Tom. You can't..."

I stop him before he can say it.

"I insist. It's my treat. It's the least I can do."

"No," he says, putting something in my back pocket. "We share this. She's Karen's mum, too."

I feel the twitch in my face, but I say nothing. Of course... I'm just trying to hog the limelight, aren't I. The barman offers me the handset and I type in my PIN.

"Listen... what Karen thinks she saw, she didn't see, okay?"

"What was that?"

"She'll tell you soon enough."

We gather everything together and go out to the car. The picnic table has been cleared. It sits there, in the shelter of the hedge, empty.

"That was lovely," says mum. "Thank you all so much."

"That's alright," says Karen.

We sit as we had before. We drive back. In silence this time. When we hit the seafront, I ask them to drop me. I tell mum I'll call her later, and she thanks me again. We say our goodbyes. Kissed cheeks. Handshakes. No eye contact from Karen. Then I get out of the car and stand watching them as they drive off to take her home. Natalie's hand appears through the top of her window, waving. I wave back. Along the seafront, Sunday afternoon walkers turn their heads to look at the car as it passes - a big silver cruise missile, flying towards the last of the sun.

I go indoors. I take off my jacket and shoes. I go in the bathroom. I see my face in the mirror - a face I recognise from somewhere else. Like a photograph. Then I kneel down on the floor, over the toilet, and bring everything up again. Everything. The whole day - forced out, ejected. Flushed away. I rinse out my mouth under the tap and dry my face. I get my earplugs from the bedroom and put them in. I put my headphones on top. I wrap my duvet around me and lie down on the sofa. I put a cushion over my head, leaving just a small hole to breath out of, and I shut the world down, and I shut my brain down, and I sleep. When I wake again, it's dark. I go to the toilet. I get a drink of water. I take an aspirin. I lie down again and wrap myself up again and sleep again. The phone rings at some point, but I ignore it. I don't get up. I sleep right through.

It's the only way.

Another home. Another time on the streets. Another home, and another. And then it happens. Out one day, a can in his hand. The zap in the head. The arm and leg going dead on him, him falling into the road, lying there, blood in his eyes and beer all over him, unable to move, left there for a paralytic drunk, ignored.

Then somebody there. People. Green overalls. Boots. A hand on his neck..

'Can you tell us your name, sir?'

He tries to speak, but it's not there. He gags.

'Alright, don't worry. We're going to put you in an ambulance now and get you to hospital.'

The lifting. The carrying. The lights overhead. The movement.

'It's alright now, mate. We're on our way. We'll soon be there.'

Not long now. Soon be there.

They all sat there, looking at me in the silent pause.

You did the right thing, Tom. You can't blame yourself for what happened.

But it happened because of me.

You weren't to know how she'd react to those photographs. Anyway, it was a lovely thing to do for her. She'll treasure them.

Maybe.

Have you spoken to her since?

I rang her this morning.

And how was she?

Fine. She said what a special day it had been. She thanked me for the photos. And she said sorry.

There you are, then.

Why did she have to say sorry? It wasn't her fault. I put her in a position where she felt she had to say sorry to me.

But there's no real harm done, is there?

I suppose not.

And what about your sister? Have you heard from her?

No.

Have you tried to contact her?

No.

Will you?

I don't know. I don't think it matters what I say to her.

Maybe give it some time.

Maybe.
Maybe I'll give it some time...

...or maybe I won't give it some time...

Group's over and I'm walking down the hill alone. Molly and Geoffrey offer to come with me - we do that for each other, just in case - but I say no, it's okay, I'm fine. You stay and have a smoke and a chat. I want to get going. There's something I need to do in town.

Just something I need to do.

It's turned out a nice day. Warm. My clothes are sticking to me. Talking about it always does that. It's a double-edged thing. Out it all comes. Fessing up. Confronting it head-on. Talking about it. How much, and what it did, and where it led. And why, despite all the damage and chaos it causes, we still go back to it. It's madness. Complete fucking madness. Why does someone with emphysema smoke? Why does an obese person keep stuffing it in? It's the illness. The fucking mad illness. And talking about it brings it up - up in your mind. Like getting an erection from talking about sex. It preps you up for it. Keeps you thinking about it. Makes you want it.

I've come on the bus. I could have cycled, or brought the bike, but I fancied the bus again. I brought a book, but I didn't read any. It was just nice to sit there looking out as we drove through the villages and countryside to the city. A good time to think about things. Put it together and see what it made. The thing at the pub - with mum and the album. What happened with Karen. I did the right thing, yes, I did. She wouldn't see that, though. She'd never believe it, either. The times we'd been through it. Sorted it. And still it always felt like I was the odd piece - the bit of puzzle that doesn't quite fit, that has to be trimmed with the scissors so it'll go into place... and then there's always a tiny piece more cut off than needed to be, so there's a gap. Yeah. The odd piece, trimmed up, with the gap. Wouldn't be her, of course. She always fitted in perfectly - always connected up right with the other bits. Blended in with the colours.

You need to drop your attachments, Tom.

That's what they'd tell me in the rooms. Drop my attachments. Have the serenity to accept the things I cannot change. Accept. A lot of it's about acceptance. Most of it.

But why do I have to do all the accepting? Why is it me who's always off track? Because I have a disorder, is that it? I have a *dis*order, whereas everyone else has order. So I'm the one who has to concede - who has to make himself fit. Succumb to the scissors.

Or the knife. Yes... I can cut myself - but not to make myself fit. Why would I want to fit in with them, anyway? What's wrong with my version of reality?

What's wrong with my 'order'?

I'm like I am because of them, anyway. All of them. Right the way through, from the start. Right from school. Everywhere I went. The threats. Giving them things to keep them away - and all it did was bring them back for more. The fights. The hiding. The running. The fear - like a beast inside, thrashing around. The nights at home, in my bedroom, dreading the next day. Stopping at the school gates and turning around. Walking away. Disappearing. Taking a geographical. That's what they call it, though I didn't know it then. That's what it would become. A geographical. Taking myself off somewhere else, away, alone, somewhere where no one knew me, where no one could find me. Where I could be with myself and escape from it, and do what I liked. Escape from the fear. Years later, the drink would do that. Take me away. Take me away from them. If you can't beat them - leave them. Leave them the fuck behind. You can't be like them. You don't want to be like them. Get away from them. Be you. Not them. Even the women. Lucy. You loved her as much as your own life. But you couldn't be with her. You couldn't. You just couldn't do it. You can't do it.

How can you love someone so much, and not want to be with them? How does that happen?

It makes no sense. None of it makes any fucking sense. None of it.

None of it.

Drop your attachments....

It's a lovely day. The sun up there. The sky. The light and colours. The birds flying. The movement. The traffic, coming and going. And none of it makes any sense at all. Just things happening, without reason. Past the pub there - *The Roman Centurion.* Boarded up now, fenced off, shut down. Ancient Rome. Dead. *Deficit omne quod nasciture.* Dandelions squeezing up through the tarmac. Weeds in the brickwork. Life pushing through - but the place dead. Empty and dead. Beyond it, the barracks. A soldier standing there - camos, beret and boots, standard issue slung across his front. Hardly old enough to drink. Still got spots on his face. Dad would take him to task if he could see it. *'Hold your fucking back up, boy. Chest out! Chin in! Call yourself a fucking soldier?'* I could charge across there now. Charge him. See what he would do. *Halt! Who goes there? Friend or foe?* Fucked if I know, son. Fucked if I fucking know...

...and yes... Michael standing there. It could be. He could be standing there. Just like his dad. Followed in his footsteps - as I did, but differently. Made him proud. He could be there now. *Friend,* I could say. *Brother. It's me, your brother. Remember? Remember the times? The holidays? The Christmases? The games? The fights? I blacked your eye once. A cricket bat. Remember that? And remember the fair? The goldfish? The man? The man at the fair? What man at the fair? What man? What did he do? Do you remember? I remember... remember remember...*

Down the hill now, quicker. Move through the day now. Get it going. Past the school, past the prison, across the car park, onto the city wall. A flag snapping on the roof of a department store. The cathedral rising up there like it's carved from a mountain. Buttresses. Peaks. Stone stalagmites pricking the sky. The sun catching on a jet, glinting like a star in the mid-afternoon. Shreds of cloud, like scuffs in the sky.

Stop on the walkway here, over the road. The heat and roar of traffic in the day, passing under. People passing. Faces. All buried in their own private worlds they are. Like me.

Moments like this… right in the heart of life, it feels. Movement and sound and light and heat. I can almost taste the day - on my tongue, at the back of my throat. My mouth feels dry. I lick my lips. Savour the flavour of it. Feel it go down.

Further along - beyond the shops and streams of traffic - the buses parked up at the station. Pulled in on both sides, herringbone fashion. One every fifteen minutes. No hurry - though I don't want to stay here, really, do I. What do I want here? What does this place have for me? Too many people. Too much noise. Too much traffic. A head-fuck. The whole thing, thundering in...

Step down from the walkway, head for the underpass. A *Big Issue* seller standing there. Shit! Don't have much cash on me. About seven quid. If I buy a copy, that leaves about four. I can't pass him without buying one. Look obvious if I turn around and go the other way. Four quid. Maybe if I just spend that on something else, then get on the bus and go home. What can I get for four quid? A coffee and a cake? Four quid for a coffee and a cake? Fuck that!

Could top up my gas card. That's what I'll do. Got it in my ruckie. Top up my gas card, then go home. That's what I'm going to do, isn't it. It's not what I planned - but it's what I'm going to do. It's the right thing to do.

Pay him, take it, put it in my ruckie to read on the bus.

"Thanks, mate. Have a good one."

"You too."

"I will."

I will.

Down through the underpass, dark and pissy smell, graffitied tiling (*FUCK THE WORLD SIDEWAYS*), echo of the traffic like a blast wave, out the other side. Take out my gas card. The Co-op does them. Bit out of my way. Could wait 'til I get home. But I'll do it now. Slide the card into my back pocket ready.

Uh... something in there.

Slip my fingers in and feel it. Paper. Not my bus ticket - that's in my jacket. Thick paper. My back pocket. Rod slipped something in my back pocket, at the pub. Forgotten it. Thick paper - a folded note. Can feel the thickness of it. Take it out.

A fifty.

WHAT?

The bastard.

The whole bill had only been £53. No starters, five main courses, three desserts. Pub food. Hadn't even paid for half of mine.

The *bastard.*

He could fucking well have it back. Every fucking penny. I don't need subsidising by a fucking knick-knack man, or anyone else come to that.

Fifty quid.

The *fucking* bastard...

Look at the note. One of the new ones. He got hold of that pretty quick. The green band on the front. Bolton and Watt on the back. Businessmen and inventors. Like our Rod - wayfinder in the wonderful world of mass-produced pound shop bollocks. Joke-meister extraordinaire. Rod with the Rolls. Rods Royce. Wanker. Karen's man - the standard to which she's risen. The standard against which all others are measured. Done so well. Done so well. She's done oh so fucking well *well.*

Fifty quid.

The *fucking bastard...*

Hm...

I'll need some for when the bill comes in. Won't have it otherwise.

A new fifty.

Should give him some of it back, anyway. Half. Give him half back. It's the principle. Okay... give him twenty. Then he's paid thirty and I've paid twenty-three (plus the tip I left). Seems fair, as there's two of them - even though she's not working. Seems fair to me. Give him twenty, which leaves me thirty.

He won't take it, of course.

I'll *make* him take it. I'll say it's only fair. I'll insist.

And so will he.

The cunt.

But hang on a minute...

I paid for the drinks, too. We only had one. Didn't mention drinks again after my glass of wine that I never had. An hour and a half there, and they had one drink each. An hour and a half to drink a pint of fucking bitter! Our so-called 'used to be an alcoholic' Rod! *Jesus!* Karen left a drop of hers, too... and mum struggled with the sherry, though at least she drank it. *Christ!* And I paid for them - as I was happy to, and wanted to, and meant to. But add that on and that's £65, plus the tip. Paid for my corner, then. Fuck it! The fifty's mine. Why not? He can afford it. I can't. So, fuck it. It's mine.

Mine.

Okay?

Okay.

Crowds milling around the station, but I want the Co-op. Just off down there, in the square down that side street by the coffee place.

Maybe do a bigger top-up now. Twenty quid on the gas. Keep me warm for a while. Couple of weeks. Just have it on for two hours a day. Leave it 'til the evening, when it's colder. Then I've still got thirty left. Something to tide me over. Still got to pay that bill, anyway. And Christmas coming. Won't worry about that. I won't. Won't worry about it.

First one without a drink, too. First one. First one for... *how* long? When has Christmas ever been without a drink? Part of the craic. Makes the whole fucking thing bearable. Forced together with everyone, having to be seasonal and merry with everyone. Fucking... *seasonal?*

Forget about it, anyway. A month away. No one's got any money (except Rod). We're all in the same boat. They'll have what they get. Tins of biscuits. Boxes of chocolates. If they don't like it...

Still a month off. Fuck it. Don't project. Keep it in the day. That's all you've got, all you need to worry about. Yesterday's history, tomorrow's a mystery... all that bollocks. What's the other one? What's the other one they like to wheel out?

When you've got one foot in yesterday, and the other in tomorrow, you can only piss on today.

And what the fuck does *that* mean? What's *that* supposed to be saying? Today's all you've got to piss on. And that's what I've got. A foot each side, with my old chap out, and the day to piss on. Keep it in the day. Just piss on today, and let tomorrow take care of itself...

Christ, all these people. Too many fucking people. This is a mistake. Should just get on the bus.

When you're home alone, you're behind enemy lines.

That's bollocks, too. These are enemy lines. All this lot. All these faces. Bodies with heads on top, rushing in. Playing with their phones. Everyone - playing with their phones. Keeping in touch, all the time. Always having to keep in touch. Why? To know they're real? Prove they exist? Who wants to know? Who gives a fucking toss?

Ought to get home. Safer there. Safer.

Can feel it again, building up. The sweat, the breathing, that thing down there, inside my drains, scrabbling around like a rat in the dark. It's going to get me. My legs. Just need to sit - get out of all this. Past Tourist Info and the jewellers, and... oh yes, this...

The Wayfarer's Rest.

Yes.

Just the right name, too. How about this?

Yes...

Quiet inside after the lunchtime crowds. Cosy. Like a parlour room, almost. Small tables. Landscapes in big gold frames.   Subdued lighting.   A middle-aged couple sitting together there, facing one another, leaning in, glasses of Coke or Something-and-Coke within reach.   Office workers, looks like. Work-day smart.   Both married... but not to each other.   The body language tells it.   The looks.   A little tryst.   Hands getting close across the table, but not touching.   Elderly chap there, propped up on the end of the bar.   Dralon blazer, cavalry twills, tan brogues, reading *The Telegraph*.   Low-lit corners.   Hushed conversation.   Even the fruit machine seems muted, blooping and beeping like it's underwater.

Yes, this is nice.

This is better.

This feels good.

Calming.

Still a faint tang of nicotine in the air after all this time. Settled to an essence now - like incense in a chapel.   Like in his rooms.   Makes me feel like a cigar.   A cigar might just be nice. Round it off.   Wouldn't hurt.

The taps on the bar.   Pedigree.   Abbot.   Landlord's. Carlsberg Export.   Orangeboom.   Stella.   Something called Winter Brew - some northern brewery.   Strong one.   5.8%.

Hm...

The barman appears from the shadows - like one of those old weather house things... coming out to tell you if it's warm or cold.

It's warm.

A big, warm smile.   The biggest, warmest smile I've seen for weeks.   Months.   All year, maybe.

"What can I get you, sir?"

Hm... choice...

I have a choice here.

Lots of things...

Soda water won't cost.   J2O.   Coke with ice and a slice - that'll perk me up.   Nice hot coffee.   Espresso, maybe.   *Double* espresso.   That'll hit the spot.   Coffee and a cigar, outside, in the sun.   Nice.   I have a choice.   Let me see...

"Have you got any single cigars, please?"

"Panatella?"

"That's fine... and.... and a pint of Winter Brew, please."

"Winter Brew?"

Is that what I said? Did I say that?

He puts the cigar on the bar mat.

You can stop him. You can still change your mind.

He takes a pint glass, holds it up to the light.

Still time. What are you going to do?

"Er..."

He glances at me. Stops.

What? What?

The coin has almost stopped spinning - still upright, though. Slowing... slowing... Will it stay on it's edge, or topple? Slowing...

I nod. It topples. He pulls the pint. I watch.

Dark colour, though not as dark as a stout. Thin head coming up. Nice. There it is, on the bar, a run of foam down the side. Like on her coffee mug that day. *'Part Girl'*. What's the other part? A part that's missing. The space on her desk. Looking out of my window, over the sea.

'What a wonderful view to wake up to.'

Gone now. Gone. Another wish unfulfilled. Like all of them.

"Anything else, sir?"

More choice. What else? Boat's out now.

"A large Bells, please."

"Large Bells?"

He turns to the optics. I look at the pint.

No sending this back. No getting a refund on this. Too late now. There it is. How long has it been? How long?

"Ice?"

"No, thanks."

"Seven sixty-five altogether please, sir."

"Change a fifty alright?"

"Should think so."

He takes the note, looks at it closely. First time he's seen one too, perhaps. He rings it up. He counts my change out to me. Five pence, ten pence, twenty pence, a two, two tens, a twenty.

"Thank you very much."

He goes back through to the other bar. Just disappears. Like he was never there.

Sit on this stool and look at the drinks. The old boy rattles his paper, sniffs, sips his pint, turns a page. Opening it out... like he's going to smother a fire, or origami a fighter plane. The finance pages. A buy-in. £500 million. Two suits beaming from a corporate backdrop, shaking hands.

£500 million. 10 million times the amount of money I just had. How big would your pockets have to be to hold that? How high would it go in a pile of pound coins? How many suitcases would you need if it was all in used 20s? 25 million £20 notes...

The Bells rings down my gullet without touching the sides…

And there it is.

Gone.

Feel that feeling. *Feel* it. Feel everything... changing... slowing down... settling down...

There it is.

Yes.

Why wouldn't you want to feel it?

Yes.

Pocket the cigar, pick up the pint, take the top off. Tangy. Malty. Strong. Chasing it down. Putting the lid on it.

The couple laugh over something, heads nodding closer together. Clerky types, definitely. Spectacles, glinting in the light. White blouse, white shirt. Grey suits. Pumps and Oxfords. Black nylon showing at her instep. A quiet lunch together. Something going on. Something beginning to happen. A secret thing. Bring the excitement back – make it interesting again. What else is there? What's it worth if you can't have something? Something to pep it up again. Bring it back. The feeling. Feeling it and knowing you're feeling it.

Hands touching now... fingertips, knuckles. Locking together now. Looking into one another. Two bespectacled heads. The symmetry of it.

Feel that feeling.

Why wouldn't you want it?

Life's too short.

Give it something.

Feel it.

The barman swings out from his house again. The old chap nods at him. He picks up a glass and turns to the optics. Out in the street, a siren whoops – a Banshee wail above the mumble of traffic. The day skips a heartbeat. Heads turn to the window. Stop. Turn back again – the trance broken. Take the pint and head for the garden.

Sheltered out here. A few smokers sitting around, enjoying a fix in the sun. An empty table, back in the corner. Bum a light in passing. First taste is fucking horrible. A good mouthful to wash it away. Starting to settle in now, calming it down. Sit back and puff the cigar. The precinct there, through the trellis – people bustling. Herds of sheep, all over the place, everywhere.

Another mouthful.

Don't know what to think about now. Don't want to think at all. Just let it flow. Go with the flow of it. Doesn't matter any more. None of it matters.

Woman coming out of a shop with a pink carrier bag. Big arse on her. Chap in a suit at a café table, smoking, checking his phone. Teen with a rucksack and iPod, shuffling along, jeans crotch to the knees, hems worn to shreds. Pigeons pecking at the cobble stones. Pecking and jabbing. Jabbing and pecking and jabbing...

"Hello, my pretty."
Her huge head and her eyes.
The pattern on her scarf. Like a face...

'Go home and see daddy, shall we?'
'Da-ee...'

Hospital. Rehab - for the stroke and the drink - and then the next place. No leaving this time. 76, and this is it. No leaving this one - except in a box. All you want here. Room, meals, staff to look after you, people to talk to. People your own age. People who've lived through the same years, seen the same things, done the same things, know the same things...

Except...

'They're all didlo, boy. Shot away. Senile. Nothing to say. What they do say is bollocks. Gobbledegook. Codswallop. Lost all their marbles. Gone as Christmas. Brain-fried. Dopey. Bonkers. Nuts. Completely fucking shot away.'

And there's the irony. There's the tragedy. All that boozing, all that abuse, all those years... and you're still as sharp as a tack. Still got it all there. And you can see it all, too. See what's happening. See what's going on. See it all. See how they're treated. Don't miss a trick. See it all.

No one believes it. You believe it, don't you, boy? You believe me? You believe your old man? No bugger else does. I see it, but no one believes me. No one does nothing. No one. I see it all and no one believes it, and nothing gets done.

Nothing...

Nothing.
Yes.
Calm here.
Good.
Relaxing.
The cigar. The drink working its way through the threads and fibres... doing its stuff. The day going by. Here in this nice, comfortable place. Sit here, away from it. Not have to take part. Not have to do anything. Not have to do a blind fucking thing. Not have to be a part. Never have been anyway. Never been a part.

Apart.

That's it.

Just sitting here watching. Right here, in this place. Here in the day. In the day. Right here.

In the day...

Glass half empty already. Not half full. Each mouthful takes it lower. The sadness of it... like a day off your life. The more you take, the less left. Savour each one. Milk it.

Live for today, boy. Sod tomorrow. Might be your last.

Spread it out across the table. A twenty, two tens, a two. Twenty pence, ten pence, five pence. A lot yet. The promise of it.

Fuck 'em.

Rake it together again, back in the pocket, puff the cigar, take a sup. The flavours mixing. The feeling of it. The day passing around from the fixed point of here. The table. The fence. The weeds sprouting from the cracks in the brickwork. The road out there. The traffic. The people. The granite and stone and dust and tarmac and earth and sun and sky. The colours. The noise.

The day...

One last puff. Finish the pint. Get up and go back inside.

The old chap at the fruit machine, paper folded on his stool, another pint waiting, another short. Waiting there for him. The clerks have gone – ice-melt in the bottoms of their glasses, lemon slices like marooned skiffs. Beached yellow smiles. The barman's in his house, waiting for the weather to change again. Warm and quiet and drowsy just now. Shards of light glinting on every surface. The optics. The smell of it. An essence. The drops on the bar. The pump handles. The beep and bloop of the machine. The music, only heard here, like this, at times like this, in a place like this. The soundtrack to the moment. The pump handles. The optics. What's next, then?

What's next?

The machine hammers out a chunk of cash. A tiny whoop from the old boy. Out it comes.

I can feel it. The whisky... the cigar... the beer... the thing they've created... stirring up now… coming…

Just make it in time. Out it comes. The monster - every last slop and membrane of it. Kneeling there, heaving it all into the bowl in the stink of piss and disinfectant. Shit-marks on the porcelain. Even when it's all gone, something still wants to come. An exorcism, is it. Ripping the fucking devil out, stink and all. Pull the handle, flush it away. Get thee gone. Cold water now. Rinse it out. Over my face and through my hair. The mirror. Is that me? Is that him? Me as he was?

Can't take much more of this. Treated like shit. No one will listen. Had enough of this. Time to show them, see who they're fucking dealing with. Treat me like shit and see what they get. Just see what they fucking get...

Out in the street... the world moving at strange speeds and different angles... like standing on a fairground waltzer...
Like at the fair, remember? The man? The crowds?
'Fuckin' 'it 'im.'
Lean into the crowds... body weight taking me forwards... no volition involved in this... a matter of gravity... something falling. People looming up, sliding at the edges. Like walking with my head in a bubble. Vacancy in there now. Just what I want. No thoughts, no feelings, no past or future. Not even the day any more. Now-moments connecting in the spaces ahead. A line on the pavement, shifting around... weaving through the mass of bodies. Take the corner, shift the bearing, follow your nose, keep going forwards... keep going 'til you're there... wherever it is... wherever it goes...

...crossing a road.. car blaring at me from somewhere, a voice shouting, traffic passing close... shops… another pub… a bike place… a chippie… an *offie*...

Now... here we go. Good choices here. Need something inside now. Space to fill. Empty space...

The chippie. Warm in here... lights, shiny surfaces, hot smells, radio playing. REM. *Losing my Religion*. Ha! No! *Finding* it, mate! Born again...

"Sir."

"Cod and chips, please."

"Open?"

"Yes, please."

Shovelling it in the paper parcel... piling it up... vinegar, tomato sauce, decent frosting of salt, falling down the gaps. Tastes so good... sitting on the wall here, breaking it up... steaming white chunks of it... feeling it go down, filling the space... best thing for ages, even if it's crap. Crap food, polluting the system, filling it up, clogging it up. Who gives a shit, anyway? Who gives a fuck? Does it matter? Who's going to care? Who's it hurting? Just tastes so fucking good. Fills the space... lines the stomach... preps it up. Ready for the next bit...

The offie... *yes*, the offie. The choice in here now. All the choice. All yours now, whatever you want. Take your pick, mate. Primed up now, ready for it. Fours cans of Special, half a bottle of vodka. Do the trick for now... keep it going... fill up the space...

Back along to the bus station. Bus waiting there, just right... straight up the top, down the back, in the corner... best place to be... warm and cosy and snug and secluded... just a couple of others up here, sitting forwards, looking out the windows, heads plugged into music and phones. This is the place. The long way around... through the villages, along the coast. A good hour. A good session. The best place to be, looking out on the world, passing through it. Passing through the day... right here in the middle of it... right here in the day...

in the day

idling along now... traffic lights... roundabouts... lines of shops with filthy windows.... stopping to pick up at Aldi's... people with carrier bags, looking up... nice and warm up here... the first can open and on the way, the bottle open, a good swig chasing it... this is it... this is the feeling... why would you ever want anything different... can't beat this... fucking wonderful...

the music beating out from that student's phones like a heartbeat, a background blood-rush of static... down that can goes, getting right in there, working its stuff, mixing the juices, numbing it down...

the scrap yard there... the cars piled up like dominoes... rusty dominoes... down it goes... the sewage works... the council flats... kids playing football over there, out in the street... a girl on a scooter... give her a wave, now, give her a wave... another stop...

along a bit further, over the crossing... out on the open roads... doing its thing... a pocketful of loose change and a carrier bag of sunshine, and nothing else... nothing else... that would be good... the idea of it... nothing else... just here with my stuff on this nice warm bus, riding out through the day, the world losing its edges, nothing solid or definite any more... the eye of the vortex... everything spinning dog-mad around, me in the centre...

detached

apart

still

happy

all focussed down on here right here in this spot in the warm and safe and aloneness of it... swig this can back now... no one watching... all in their own little worlds, me in mine... another nice swig from the bottle to chase it... wash it down... don't want the slow burn now... speed it up... get there... get there...

up over the brow of a hill now... the in-between spaces... the fields and woods and hedgerows rolling off to the distance... the lake down there... an angler's tent pitched up... cosy-looking... nice place to be... a few cans and a fish for dinner... pull the tab... no one listening... who gives a fuck... rooftops poking up in the folds... a tractor moving on the ridge of the hill... birds tumbling behind like tiny kites in the wind out there... the play of the light... the day brighter now, the story-book colours and textures, the sun and the sky and the earth and the day...

this day... right here in it... these forces working in just this moment, just for me... a rare sense of privilege in it... this world of mine... this day of mine...

the copses there... the huts... that caravan, like a lonely boat in an empty ocean of nothing... i could do it... just get off now and start walking, across those fields, going where it takes me, disappearing, not being anywhere, ceasing to exist... why not... do it... what's life for, anyway... places out there to be... hide... places to sleep, be away from it all, be free of it all... the complications, the shit, the people... free of all of it... free of it all... having nothing, so nothing to lose...

nothing

another good pull on the bottle, sun hot and bright through the glass... the sea over there now, coming up now, the ships way out, white in the sunlight, the turbines waving, welcoming me, winding me in... close my eyes now... the day orange through my eyelids... shut it all out now... comfortable... gentle rocking, like a cradle, a hammock on a breezy day... a pram...

'Hello, my pretty... Who are you, my pretty darling?'

The fingers on the straps, on the buckles. The pram rocking on its springs. The strap giving...

...the birds in the park. By the river. The bridge there. The cars going over. The bus going over, the people inside. The river flowing under. The sun flashing on it. Flicking between the railings... flick - flick - flick...

'See the gulls, Tommy.'

'Goes...'

...the sparks, ripping across the velvet of night. The fire there. The flames. The faces in the flames, like phantoms...

...the spikes of light... the wailing... the weight of the man... the smell of the man... the thing...

' If you tell anyone, I'll come and get you. I'll rip your guts out. Do you hear me? I'll kill you...'

'PUT IT IN!'

' 'it the cunt.'

jesus

the slip road on the bypass...

where's it gone... the space between gone... just this bit of road... off at the roundabout, cross the flyover, past the park, into town... four stops... still two cans left and half the bottle... four stops... swig it back, feel it go down...

what's the options... what's to do, rest of the day...

find somewhere.... anywhere... somewhere to hitch up, shut down, finish it off... finish it... finish the day... shut it all down...

the footbridge coming up there... someone standing on it, this side... looking down at the traffic passing... a toy figure... stupid bastard, breathing all that shit... better places to be... up here, like this... a nice good swig...

getting closer now... standing up there, looking down... arms stretched out along the railings... a *woman*, looks like... hood up, hair blowing out at the sides... shining in the day...

who is she... what's she doing up there... what's she looking at... what's she looking for... looking for *me*... not so far apart eh... another detached soul... another one apart...

those among us who are not among us

let her know... let her know she's not alone... communicate... acknowledge it... the understanding... complicity... alone together... apart together... a good swig... getting closer... two lanes of traffic ahead... the rush of it... through the trees over there, the sun sparkling on the sea over there... the sun in her hair... speeding down the hill now... almost there... passing right under... few more seconds... waving at her... waving... her eyes in there, under there... seeing something... not moving... frozen there... the dead stare... dead eyes in there... dead eyes... nothing there...

past now... down to the roundabout... around... turning back to her... the footbridge stretching out there over the road...

empty

no one there

no one

no one there

Out they put him. Out he goes again, with nowhere else to go. Nowhere. Too ill to go it alone now. Too ill to be out there. Can't do it now. So the final place. The end of the line. A tiny room. A bed. A table. A chest of drawers. A wardrobe. Photographs. That's all there is. The photographs. Done by the boy. Everyone there in them, all the way through, right from the start. The faces. The young faces. The memories. All there is left. The memories.

'Terrible here, boy. Can't stay here. Nowhere else to go.'

Food in the drawers. Sandwiches uneaten. Can't eat it. Just want the cans. All there is left. Nothing else. Just the cans. It's all I need.

Everything caving in, running down, collapsing. The face caving in. Skin like orange peel. Livid. Pocked. The machine running down now. Nothing left.

The fit in the night. The hospital. The final place. The final days. No food now. Everything shutting down. The tubes. The mask. The faces coming in, looking in, going out, fading. The family there. The boy. The lad. The last one left. All yours now. Over to you.

'I'm wishing my life away, son. Don't want it anymore. Had enough of it. Wishing it away.'

The final night. Everything stopped. The flame gone out now. The machine giving out. Still. Finished.

The final drop touched to his lips. Taking it with him. Passing it on.

Finished.
The journey over.
Finished.

the final stop, the station
"All change here."

back on the street... holding it up... feeling okay, feeling good... two cans left, swig of vodka... need some more now... the offie... nip in here for four more... keep it going... keep the change... along past Jimmy's now, down the alley, onto the seafront...

Who was she? Where did she go? The look in her eyes... seeing, but not seeing. Dead eyes. Nothing there. Her hair blowing out in the wind, the sun on it, glinting. But the face in there blank. Seeing, not seeing. Dead.

Where did she go?

Who was she?

the jetty there... the arm, curving out to the sea... and the pier head... alone out there... detached... apart...

nobody on the arm... like a path out, above the sea... out to sea... the bench at the end, and no one there... empty in the late afternoon... the sun on the surface, bright in the day... ships out there, on the horizon... the turbines turning... working it forwards... working the day to its end... waving... beckoning...

the sea all around... gulls, diving and crying... mournful... the waves rushing against the sides... the light and the sound of it... all of the day...

out to the end, now... the bench... finish the bottle, get it down... pop another one...

the shoreline behind, like a row of smashed teeth... the clock tower... the arcades... people walking along... the bandstand... the café there... blackjack... the sky up behind it... clouds scudding by, like boats up there... flags snapping... gulls crying... diving... the sea rippling through... the sound of it, fresh...

my flat there... my little rooms, up there, next to the pub... steam from the café... everything... my windows... the things I can see from my windows... the fragments of the day... the pier head out there...

there it is, out there... out on its own... empty... nothing there... a place to be, maybe... place to be... apart... away from it...

a good swig from the can... the others there... plenty yet... enough to do it...

seeing it all from here, all of it... the buildings... the people... the things going on... the whole wide fucking world going on... and out here alone, detached from it, watching it... there, but not... as always... all the way through...

always

and the pier head out there... always there... always seeing... a place to be... alone out there and away from it...

i could be out there

that's where i could be

want to be

standing there at the railings... the can in my hand... the carrier... ruckie on my back... all I need... nothing else... i see it out there...

see it

should be out there... where it is...

the end of the arm... the sea all around me... the sea and the sky and the world and the day... the turbines turning, pulling it in... pulling it in... winding it up... finishing it...

the end of the day

i could be there... the distance between... not far... could make it that far... could be there...

over the railings now... the sea there, all around me... the world behind me... apart from it... behind me now, and the sea there, all around me... the beautiful sea...

the distance... not far... i could make it...

could make it that far...

i could...

BORDERLINE PERSONALITY DISORDER

Borderline Personality Disorder (BPD) can affect both men and women, though it is more commonly recognised and diagnosed in women. As with many mental health conditions, its causes are unclear - though they are most likely a combination of both hereditary and environmental factors. A particular contributing factor is trauma experienced during childhood: neglect, disruption, abuse, etc. Major symptoms are emotional instability, disturbed thinking patterns, impulsive (including self-harming) behaviour, and unstable or dysfunctional relationships with other people. Mood swings can be severe and unpredictable, and can occur over a short space of time. They are usually underpinned by pervasive feelings of emptiness and isolation, and people with the condition will often act out in desperation to be heard and understood. Suicidal thoughts are common, and a large proportion of people with the condition will have attempted suicide at some point in their lives.

Once correctly diagnosed, BPD is treatable with psychotherapeutic and other interventions. Many people with the condition respond favourably to treatment and go on to function well in life.

ACKNOWLEDGMENTS

The Wrestler; Wild Bunch Productions and others; 2008 (title quoted)

Blue Highways: A Journey Into America; William Least Heat-Moon; Houghton Mifflin Company, Boston; 1991 (one line quoted)

November; Gustave Flaubert; Hesperus Press edition; 2005 (two lines quoted)

We Need To Talk About Kevin; BBC Films, UK Film Council and others; 2011; based on the novel by Lionel Shriver; HarperCollins; 2003 (title quoted)

Losing My Religion; REM (Berry, Buck, Mills, Stipe); Warner Bros; 1991 (title quoted)

Jim Jarmusch, for an inspiring line from *The Limits of Control*; Focus Features and others; 2009 (you said steal... so I did!)

I'd also like to acknowledge all my friends on the *ABCTales.com* writers' website. Many of the chapters from *In The Day* were originally posted there, and the responses I received were a tremendous source of encouragement and inspiration for me. Thank you, everyone.

Last but not least... thanks, Bob, for having faith and giving me a chance.